Nationally Bestselling Author
KATE ANGELL
"Kate Angell is to baseball as Susan
Elizabeth Phillips is to football. Wonderful!"
—*USA Today* Bestselling author Sandra Hill

New York Times **Bestselling Author**
SANDRA HILL
"Some like it hot and hilarious,
and Hill delivers both."
—*Publishers Weekly*

USA Today **Bestselling Author**
JOY NASH
"Nash creates a suspenseful, haunting and
high-tension romance."
—*RT Book Reviews*

SANTA, Honey

KATE ANGELL
SANDRA HILL
JOY NASH

LOVE SPELL NEW YORK CITY

LOVE SPELL®

October 2009

Published by

Dorchester Publishing Co., Inc.
200 Madison Avenue
New York, NY 10016

ISBN 10: 0-505-52753-7
ISBN 13: 978-0-505-52753-0
E-ISBN: 978-1-4285-0753-1

The name "Love Spell" and its logo are trademarks of Dorchester Publishing Co., Inc.

Printed in the United States of America.

10 9 8 7 6 5 4 3 2 1

Visit us online at www.dorchesterpub.com.

SANTA, Honey

CONTENTS

Ho, Humbug, Ho

KATE ANGELL

Chapter One

Santa wore a smirk that could set Christmas back eleven months.

He had the shoulders of a linebacker.

Black hair that curled at his collar.

Ice blue eyes.

A Rogues tattoo on his left biceps.

And abs that would never shake in laughter like a bowl full of jelly.

Confined to a dressing room at the back of the Jingle Bell Shop, Holly McIntyre faced off with Alex Boxer. He was six feet of aggravation. His testosterone set her teeth on edge.

"Here's your Santa suit." She draped the outfit over a straw reindeer statue, soon to be displayed at the front of the store. "You dress and I'll—"

The man had no modesty. He'd tugged off his navy T-shirt and shucked his jeans before she finished her sentence. He stood in front of her now, wearing black boxer briefs and a naughty grin.

He'd tried to shock her. And he had. They stood so close, his body heat pressed her breasts, nestled into her cleavage. She blushed.

Unable to avert her gaze, Holly took in the sight of him. His chest was deep and well-defined. His chest hair arrowed low and a Batter Up tat was visible at his groin. His legs stretched long and muscled, the swell of his package fully loaded. She forced herself to blink, to swallow, to breathe as he stepped into the red velvet Santa pants, trimmed at the hem with fake white fur.

Alex was six inches taller and twenty pounds heavier than the previous year's Santa. The pants fit snugly. The red jacket set off his six pack. There was no room to stuff a pillow. Santa looked tall, fit, and North Pole hot.

Any woman would love to have him drop down her chimney, with or without presents.

"I'm going to bust a seam." His expression was dark as he bent in an attempt to pull on a pair of black boots. His feet were big and brawny, and his heel crushed the patent leather. "Too damn small." He kicked them aside, went back to his Nikes.

Santa in sneakers—they'd moved beyond the traditional image. There was nothing apple cheeked, warm, or caring about this man. He was anti-Christmas spirit.

She held up a wig and eyebrow set, complete with wired mustache and full, fluffy beard. "Elastic straps go over your head."

Alex frowned. "That's got to itch."

Holly was prepared; she'd brought baby powder. She tapped talcum onto her palm, then proceeded to pat the powder onto his face. His cheeks were angular, his nose ran blade straight, his mouth set full, yet masculine.

His skin warmed, and his lips parted beneath her touch. Talcum soon whitened the afternoon shadow on his chin.

A hint of powder collected at one corner of his mouth.

Holly tapped the excess with the tip of her finger, and his breath broke against her palm, hot, moist, and triggering shivers.

She pulled back, annoyed that such an irritating man could raise goose bumps. Visible bumps, which turned his gaze a wicked blue. He knew he'd affected her. And took pleasure in her discomfort.

She dusted off her hands, her voice stern. "Put on the wig set."

Alex took his sweet time. He fit the short white curls over his head, sneezed into the mustache, and adjusted the beard along the rigid set of his jaw.

"Glasses, stocking cap, and gloves." She handed him each item.

He squinted behind the round, wire-rimmed glasses. "My vision's blurred."

"The previous Santa was near sighted," she explained. "I had prescription lenses put in the glasses."

"Where's the old Santa now?" he asked.

"He's, um, dead."

His sharp exhale bristled every fake hair on the Santa beard. "I'm wearing a dead Santa's suit?"

"The man didn't die wearing the suit," she assured him. "It has been dry cleaned."

Alex shoved his hands in the white gloves. Gloves that didn't stretch to his wrists. "Damn, I'm squeezed into red velvet, have fake mustache hair in my mouth, and can't see beyond my nose. An unfair punishment for driving fifteen miles over the speed limit."

"You were in a school zone," she reminded him.

"It was *Sunday*."

Judge Hathaway protected his own, Holly knew. Hathaway hadn't cared that it was Sunday and the entire town sat in church. Alex Boxer had been busted for speeding. His good cheer had been left on the outskirts of Holiday, Florida.

The judge had ordered Alex to pay a substantial fine, then tacked on forty hours of community service during Christmas week.

The service would be playing Santa Claus at Wilmington Mall. Alex had growled his objection. The hotshot baseball player had called his attorney, who'd argued with the judge.

In the end, Hathaway's ruling stood.

Alex's Saleen S7 had been impounded. The lowslung silver sports car with the gull-wing doors had quickly become a local attraction. Law enforcement opened the compound twice daily. The Salvation Army set up a stand and rang the bell for donations. Money rolled in at Alex's expense.

The one hotel in Holiday had been booked for the season, which forced Alex into the loft above the Jingle Bell Shop. The one bedroom was small, cramped, and jammed with Christmas decorations. He'd complained his feet hung over the end of the bed. And that the pillow was sized for an elf.

The small Florida town faced Christmas with a scowling Santa. There was no ho-ho-ho in this man.

Holly watched as Alex fought with the stocking cap. It was too tight. The pom-pom swung, bopped him on the nose.

Alex ripped it off. "Not going to happen." He looked around the shop, found a long red bandanna, which he wrapped as a skull cap. There was no cuddly softness to this Santa; he looked street-corner tough.

"A couple of rules," Holly went on to tell Alex. "Be

gentle when you hoist the children on your lap. Keep smiling even if they pee, whine, tug on your beard, or burst into tears."

"Pee on me?" That caught his attention.

"Children get scared," she explained. "Peeing is a natural reaction to fear. Not every child loves Santa on his first visit."

His mouth thinned beneath the mustache. "Can the kids sit beside me and not on my lap?"

"Not an option."

"This job sucks."

"Volunteer Santas are jovial," she stated. "They embrace Christmas and bring hope and joy to children."

"I'm not a volunteer, I'm court ordered," he ground out. "I should be in Miami by now. I was supposed to meet up with my teammates to celebrate winning the World Series. Warm weather, cold beer, and a pair of hot twins. Time to cut loose."

"Instead of your buddies, you'll spend your week with a moose, an elf, a gingerbread man, and a nutcracker."

"Lucky me."

"I have to write up a daily report for the judge on your cooperative efforts," she told him. "So give it your all."

His jaw shifted left, then right, and his stare turned cold. Santa had gone all silent and wintry.

She returned to the rules. "You must be as nice to the last child as you are to the first. You ask each one what he or she wants for Christmas, but never promise the delivery of the gift. Many parents can't afford what their child requests. Afterward, the elves from the photo booth will snap the holiday picture."

Alex looked down at her. His ice blue eyes were magnified behind the prescription lenses. "What part do you play in this insanity?"

"I'm the nutcracker."

"Perfect typecasting."

She ignored him. "Your Santa bag is filled with candy canes."

"I hate the scent of peppermint."

"Get used to it," she said flatly. "Each child gets a cane. There will be a decorative gift box by your chair with discount coupons from the local merchants. You'll need to give an envelope to each parent."

"You're asking me to remember a lot."

"Try to extend your mind beyond bat and ball."

He cut her a sharp look. "Stop cracking my nuts."

"Speaking of which, I need to change into my costume." She motioned toward the door. "Step outside, please."

"I dressed in front of you. Feel free to strip before me."

"Not in this lifetime, Santa. Hit the door. I'll be with you in fifteen," she instructed.

Alex Boxer sauntered out. He'd have liked to watch Holly undress; it would've turned him on. He'd always had a thing for blondes with gold hoop earrings in flirty yellow sundresses. She touched on pretty with her big brown eyes and sexy mouth. Unfortunately, she was too thin for his liking. He preferred a woman with a nice rack and curvy booty. He enjoyed the wiggle and jiggle of the female body.

He'd been looking forward to a lot of jiggle in Miami. Skimpy shorts and thong bikinis flashed a lot of skin. Spandex hugged a lot of curves. Alex and six other single guys on the Rogues baseball team had booked condos on South Beach. They'd planned to raise hell between Christmas and New Year's.

Instead of suntanned and oiled twins, he now faced children sitting on his lap. Any one of them could pee on him. He'd be handing out candy canes and store coupons. Not close to the wild time he'd originally planned for the holidays.

"I'm ready." The crack of the door revealed Holly to him.

Costumed as a nutcracker soldier, she could barely fit her big wooden head through the frame. Painted in the Old World style, the face had severely arched eyebrows and wide black eyes. A tall black hat topped her head. A moveable lever below her left ear opened and closed her jaw.

A red jacket with gold epaulettes hung large on her small shoulders. Baggy black pants and boots with gold glitter rounded out her outfit.

Rifle in hand, she poked him with the bayonet. "Down the hall and to your right, the door will open into Santa's Workshop. There will be hammering elves, a dancing moose, and a gingerbread man decorating his freshly baked house."

Alex backed against the wall. "Honest to God, I can't go through with this. I feel stupid."

"Stupid is as stupid does. Playing Santa is the price you pay for a speeding ticket." She jabbed him a second time. "The kids are waiting for you. Move your red velvet butt."

"Careful where you poke," he cast over his shoulder. "No need to ream me a second."

He made it down the hall, even with the glasses

distorting his vision. There was a clamor beyond the door, loud with pounding, laughing, and what he swore sounded like an animal's bellow.

He cracked the door, squinted. He didn't like what he saw. "There's a live reindeer tied to a post beside my Santa chair."

"His name is Randolph." He heard Holly expel her breath within the hollow head of her costume. "He wasn't supposed to be here this year. He offends people."

"Offends people *how?*" Alex asked. "Does he bite? Kick? Spit like a camel?"

"None of the above."

"Then *what?*" he pressed.

"He passes gas."

"Son of a bitch," Alex snarled. "Kids peeing on my lap and now reindeer farts. Could it get any worse?"

The day went downhill fast.

Holly suggested that he give a robust "ho-ho-ho" on his entrance. His greeting was far from jovial—it sounded low, guttural, and grumpy.

His appearance silenced the crowd.

He felt captured in a freeze frame. Everyone stared at him.

The fathers looked skeptical.

The mothers were oddly appreciative.

The children shifted nervously.

One little girl started to cry.

Alex didn't mind crowds. He was used to them. The Richmond Rogues drew tens of thousands of fans to James River Stadium. He'd been cheered and booed by the best of them.

A line of holiday shoppers didn't faze him in the

least. Let the people stare. It gave him time to check out Santa's Workshop.

The day topped ninety degrees, yet the mall had been transformed into a winter wonderland. Muzak blasted "A Holly Jolly Christmas" above air-conditioning units cranked to the max. Frost hung on the air, and Alex swore he could see his breath.

Mock snow crunched beneath his Nikes as he walked the short path to Santa's Workshop. Garlands and tiny white lights wrapped a red corduroy high-back chair. He swung the bag filled with candy canes off his shoulder, settling it between himself and Randolph the Reindeer.

Randolph didn't give him the time of day. The reindeer kept to his business of munching hay. His white tail twitched.

The scent of cinnamon wafted from the gingerbread house.

The evergreen decorated with enormous red and green balls cast the rich fragrance of forest pine.

"Back to work." Holly the Nutcracker clapped her hands, and the elves returned to their workshop tasks.

The commotion grew as Santa's little helpers put together bikes and wrapped toys for the mall customers.

Alex watched as the costumed moose danced down the line of children patiently waiting to relay their wish lists. The moose was tall, thick, but light on his feet. He played a triangle to the holiday tunes.

Alex sucked air. The sights, sounds, and scents of Christmas smothered him. He'd grown up in a wealthy household where holidays meant international travel. He'd never done small town, never sat on Santa's lap. The experience cramped his style.

"A Chippendale Santa," he heard one woman at the front of the line say.

"He's so hot he could melt the North Pole," her friend agreed.

Alex felt hot, all right. Not sexy hot, but sweaty armpit-and-groin hot. The Santa suit now stuck to his body in places he'd rather have a loose fit. He discreetly tried to pry the plush fabric off his abs and thighs as he took a seat on the padded chair. He was certain to have a wedgie when it came time to leave.

A female elf materialized at his side, short, plump, and dressed in a green jumper and red tights with black patent-leather mary janes. "I'll call each child forward, and you can ask what he wants for Christmas." She squeezed his shoulder encouragingly. "Maybe you could smile a little."

Smiling proved difficult. Each time he moved his lips, he got a mouth full of mustache.

The first boy to step forward came with a list a mile long. Alex heard a moan rise from those in line. Impatience could turn a crowd ugly. He'd have to hustle the kid along.

"I'm Tommy, and I'm four," the boy in the denim jacket and jeans told Santa as he climbed onto Alex's lap. He held up his list, written in crayon. "Bring me these, please."

Alex scanned the list, which consisted of a jumble of letters. The kid favored the color red and the letter *B*.

Alex patted the boy's shoulder, punted. "Books . . . do you like books?" He damn sure hoped so.

Tommy scrunched his nose. "No books on my list."

Crap. Alex went with, "A bicycle?"

The boy shook his head. "I already have one."

"Baseball." The nutcracker soldier jabbed Alex from behind, again with the bayonet. "Bat, ball, bases. Tommy's printing is perfectly clear."

Clear his ass. "You have a favorite team?"

Tommy puffed up proud. "Tampa Bay Rays."

Alex snorted. "They weren't even in contention this year."

"Win or lose, Tommy's still a fan." Again from the nutcracker.

So be it. "I'll see what I can do," Alex said, then handed the kid a candy cane.

Tommy ran back to his mother, and the nutcracker returned to handing out small bags of whole walnuts to those in line. Holly proved a personable nutcracker. She worked the lever on her jaw, spoke to every single person.

The moose danced toward Holly, gave her a quick ballroom spin. The people applauded. The moose next produced a sprig of mistletoe, which he held over Holly's head. The animal dropped a light kiss on the nutcracker's wooden cheek. The crowd ooed and awed.

Alex wondered if moose man and cracks nuts were a couple. The thought irritated him. They were flirting and having fun, and he was stuck coddling a drooling baby.

Definitely not fair.

Two hours passed, and Alex needed to stretch. He had butt prints on the red velvet pants from all those who had sat on his lap. His left thigh had gone numb. He'd yet to be peed on, which he considered a blessing. He did, however, doubt he'd recover from the blinding camera flashes. All he now saw were spots.

"Break time," he said to the elf who controlled the steady stream of children. "I'm taking ten."

The elf looked shocked, as if Alex had declared there'd be no Christmas this year.

"There are no breaks," the elf hurriedly informed him. "We work six-hour shifts."

"Not this Santa," Alex said as he pushed to his feet. The costume was tight and had cut off all circulation to his groin. He limped his way to the side door.

"Problem?" The nutcracker blocked his escape, bayonet drawn.

Holly had lowered the lever on her wooden mouth, and Alex could see her entire face. Her blond hair plastered her skull and sweat sheened her forehead. The collar on her gray T-shirt showed a wet ring.

She was as hot in her costume as he was in his.

He felt a flash of sympathy—but only a flash. "I'm tired of sitting," he told her.

"Sitting is part of your job," she hissed. "Santa doesn't stand or walk around, he *sits*. The chair is well padded."

He leaned toward her, his beard brushing her wooden nose. "I need to adjust my junk." His tone was confidential.

She stepped back so fast, she bumped into the fake fireplace. The red plastic flames licked her ass. "Fine, fix it."

"Fix *them*, sweetheart. It's the full package."

Holly McIntyre couldn't breathe. She'd seen the bulge in his boxer briefs and knew any awkward shift would make him uncomfortable. He'd had kids wiggling on his lap for two hours. No doubt parts of him did need rearranging.

That he would discuss it with her made her cheeks

heat. She closed the jaw on her nutcracker head, motioned him to take care of business.

He took thirty minutes to make his adjustments. Holly timed him. No man needed a full half hour to "fix his junk." When he came back through the door, he had pizza on his breath.

"You ate lunch," she accused.

He shrugged one broad shoulder. "Got to keep up my strength."

She followed Alex back to the Santa chair. He was all slowness and swagger. Once he was seated, she unwrapped a candy cane and jabbed it in his mouth. "Fresh breath."

He gagged. "I hate peppermint."

"Then don't throw yourself a pizza party when the line's a mile long."

Damn, the line to see Santa had doubled while he'd bolted three slices of pepperoni with the mall custodian. The man had been on his lunch break and welcomed Alex to join him.

It didn't help to have a full stomach when the kids now bounced on his lap. The really young ones jerked around like Mexican jumping beans. The bigger kids seemed to weigh twice as much as they had earlier that morning. He needed an Alka-Seltzer.

"Hey, dude, can I have your autograph?" the question came from a long-haired teenage boy, wearing a Rogues baseball jersey.

Alex took the offered pen signed *Santa Claus, North Pole* on the paper. "How's that?" he asked, handing it back.

"Get real, man." The boy flipped the paper, slipped it back to Alex. "Rumor has it you're Alex Boxer"

Not good. He'd expected word to leak out that he was in town. His sports car had become a novelty, but he'd hoped his stint as Santa would slide under the town's radar. Apparently it hadn't.

The Rogues' publicist would cringe to see his name linked to a speeding ticket should the story hit syndication. He was the man of the hour, having caught the final out in the World Series that October. He'd become a household name. He was Alex-friggin'-Boxer.

Sports Illustrated and *GQ* had cornered him for photo shoots and interviews. The last thing he needed was his picture plastered in the newspaper in the ill-fitting Santa suit. Tight red velvet was not an image he wanted to promote.

"What are you doing in line, Jerry Petree?" The nutcracker came to stand beside the teen seeking Alex's autograph. Holly lowered her jaw. "You're over ten—that's the cutoff age for visiting Santa."

Jerry dipped his head, looked sheepish. "I wanted Boxer's autograph," he confessed.

"Alex Boxer is Santa for the next three hours," she said, laying down the law. "He turns back into a jock at three o'clock."

"Catch you on the sidewalk." And Jerry turned away.

She leveled her gaze on Alex. "Small smile? Little cheer? The kids believe you're real."

He looked down his body, from the pizza sauce stain on the tip of his beard to his too-tight suit. "Yeah, I'm definitely the real deal."

She nodded toward the line that swelled with children anxious to sit on his lap. "Fake it, Boxer. Impress me, and I'll put in a good word on your behalf with the judge."

"Think Hathaway would cut my community-service hours by two days?" He could be in Miami by Christmas Eve, knocking back Jack and celebrating his ass off.

"I've seen the judge show leniency."

Not an outright promise, but it gave him hope.

"Ho-ho-ho!" His voice echoed off the walls, loud and jovial. Everyone stared, surprised by his merriment.

His enthusiasm scared the next two girls in line. The sisters broke into tears.

Holly took both their hands and led them forward.

Alex hauled them up on his lap, stiff and sniffling. He could barely get their bodies to bend.

With Holly's nudging, he learned that Amy was three and Allison five. When the girls finally started talking, they went on and on. Alex got the rundown on their four older and very evil brothers.

Typical boys, he thought, they teased and played pranks on their sisters. They'd grow out of it.

He knew he'd zoned-out when Allison tugged on his beard. "Do we have a deal?"

"I'll do my Santa best."

The girls bounced off his lap, all bright-eyed and giggling. "I can't wait to have sisters," Allison sighed. "You can give our brothers to any parents you like."

Holly shuffled to his side. She'd released the lever on her jaw, her face visible, her expression pained. "Not smart, Santa. Did you hear a word those girls said? You just agreed to switch out family members."

"I'll pay more attention," he said to pacify her.

"And you didn't give them any store coupons," she accused. "The mall merchants need the holiday business."

Damn. "I forgot."

"Try to do better."

His lip curled. "I need to shine in your report to the judge."

"Sarcasm is beneath Santa." She stepped back, motioned the next child forward.

"I'm Louie," the boy announced as he stepped on Alex's tennis shoe in his attempt to climb on his lap. He looked six, stick thin, and quite serious. "I want ten pounds for Christmas."

Alex lifted a white brow, asked, "Ten pounds of what?"

"Weight." Embarrassment pressed Louie's chin to his chest. "I'm skinny and get picked on a lot."

Bullies. Santa could fix this. "I have a friend, Alex Boxer, who's a Major League baseball player. He'll be in town later this week. Maybe I could introduce you to him."

Louie looked up. "Never heard of him."

Major punch to his ego. "He's famous," Alex assured Louie. "I could send him by your school. He'd impress a lot of kids, especially those who like sports."

"It's the kickball kids who never let me play."

"If Alex was team captain, I'm sure he'd pick you first," Santa said.

"You think?" Hope shone in his deep-set eyes.

"Get with the nutcracker." Alex pointed toward Holly. "She'll set up a day for Alex to visit."

"What's the guy's last name again?"

Kid had a short memory. "Boxer, Alex Boxer."

Louie nodded. "A baseball player for show and tell. Can he wear his uniform?"

"Good possibility." He'd have one FedExed. "Alex might even autograph a few baseballs."

"Alex will be better than Mary Murphy's rabbit." Louie was excited now. "It hopped and pooped all over the classroom."

"We can only hope so."

Louie threw himself against Santa, hugged him with his skinny arms. "You look different from last year's Santa," he said against Alex's red velvet chest. "Mommy said Santa Claus has a good heart. You're not scary up close."

Alex surprised himself by patting Louie on the back. He didn't do kids or comfort. Louie slid off his lap, all bouncy and happy.

The boy's smile faded with his first step, and the air turned foul. Louie pinched his nose with clothespin fingers. "Stinks," he choked out.

"Not me, dude," Alex was quick to say.

Then who? A snort and the swish of a white tail clued them into the culprit. Randolph the Reindeer had cut the cheese.

Chapter Two

All the elves scattered and the people in line backed up several steps. Alex could barely catch his breath.

It was Holly who sprayed the area with Crystal Frost air freshener. She then took Randolph by the halter and led him from Santa's Workshop. Alex watched the crowd part like the Red Sea for the nutcracker and her reindeer. No one seemed sad to see Randolph leave the building.

Holly returned in a matter of minutes. "The custodian has the reindeer until his owner can pick him up. Apparently Henry Hanson figured he could earn extra money by renting Randolph to the mall. I'd told him twice we weren't interested. Especially after the reindeer tried to hump our moose last year."

Alex couldn't help smiling. "The dancing moose playing the triangle?"

"His name is Hank, and he wears dark musk cologne," said Holly. "Randolph got off on Hank's scent. The reindeer knocked him down and, well, you get the picture."

Alex grinned. "Nailed by a reindeer in the mall."

"It wasn't pretty." She turned then, motioning for the next child to meet Santa. "This is Gracie," she said, introducing a Tinker Bell blonde to Alex.

Light green eyes evaluated Santa before she let him

lift her onto his knee. Gracie was tiny, fragile, and very tired. She sighed, settling deeply against his chest.

"What do you want for Christmas?" Alex asked her.

"A Barbie bake set. I like cookies," said Gracie. She yawned widely, her right cheek fully buried in his beard.

"What kind of cookies do you like best?"

"Peanut butter for me." Her words were no more than a whisper. "Sugar cookies for Santa."

"Put out cookies and milk," Alex agreed. "I'll be hungry by the time I reach your house."

Her head bobbed, her eyes closed, and her body went soft against him. Tinker Bell Gracie had fallen asleep on his lap.

Her mother rushed forward. "It's her nap time," she explained. "Gracie's had a long, busy day, but she didn't want to miss Santa."

An elf took a quick photo for the holiday picture, after which Alex gently lifted the little girl into her mother's waiting arms. Neither the noise from the workshop nor from those still standing in line woke Gracie as her mother carried her to the nearest exit.

"Sweet moment," murmured Holly the Nutcracker, who now stood by his chair.

"Maybe you should get a copy of that picture and show it to the judge," Alex suggested.

"Perhaps I will." It was not a definite promise.

Stiff from sitting, Alex stretched out his legs and rubbed his thighs. "How much longer?" he asked.

She looked at her holiday watch, its face showing a Christmas tree. Twelve red ornaments made up the numbers. "Under an hour," she said. "We'll close off the line shortly. Those coming in late will have to return tomorrow."

"Four more days. I'm dying here."

"You'll be making an early-morning appearance at the local elementary school," she reminded him. "You promised Louie Kessler to be his show and tell."

Alex needed to make a phone call. He'd told the kid he'd wear his Rogues uniform. He had twelve hours to make it happen.

"Hurry the line along," he said to Holly. "I don't have many ho-ho-hos left in me."

Holly McIntyre motioned to the elf to send the next two children forward. Three-year-old twins, a boy and a girl, they were more interested in playing with Santa's beard and glasses than in relaying their Christmas list.

To Holly's surprise, Alex was quite patient. He eventually captured their hands in his own and forced them to smile for their picture. A toothy, squirmy picture where the boy's eyes were closed and the girl stuck out her tongue. Alex then wished them a happy holiday and told them to mail their Christmas list to the North Pole.

"Next," he called out.

Holly and the elf kept the line moving quickly. The last little girl to sit on his lap hugged Alex as she recited her toy requests. She then cried her eyes out when it was time to leave. She loved Santa and wanted to take him home with her.

To calm her down, Alex gave her six candy canes and three envelopes of coupons for her parents. The girl's sniffles became a small smile as she rushed back to her father.

Alex pushed to his feet. "The end."

"Back to your street clothes, Santa." Holly returned Alex to the storeroom in the Jingle Bell Shop.

He helped her remove her wooden nutcracker head, then proceeded to draw off his skull cap, along with his wig and beard set. He scratched his cheeks, ran a hand through his hair. "I'm hot and sweaty and in need of a shower."

"I need to freshen up too."

"There's a shower in my loft," he suggested with a slow grin. "Together we could conserve water."

"I've used that shower, and it's small. Very, very small," she said.

"It's all in the positioning," he replied with a suggestive lift of his eyebrow. "There's always a way to fit."

Holly was certain the man could fit blond twins in the stall if he so desired. He looked capable of twisting, bending, and locking all the right parts.

"If I hadn't gotten busted for speeding, I'd be in Miami, sipping Jack and getting laid." He tugged his Santa coat over his head, and Holly came face-to-pecs with his magnificent chest. Her breath cut off, and her knees gave way. She shifted to keep her balance.

"I can buy whiskey at any liquor store." His light blue eyes studied her closely. "It's a woman I'm after."

He stroked her cheek, gently slipped the damp tendrils behind her ear. "I'm looking for someone who cracks nuts for a living, but doesn't bring her work to bed."

Sex with Alex Boxer. A man so hot women would line up to heat his sheets. He'd be good in bed, she guessed. He was built to bang the headboard and make the box springs squeak.

However tempting, it wasn't going to happen. They were polar opposites. Holly embraced Christmas. Alex was the antithesis of the Jolly Old Soul who uplifted the world with peace, hope, and cheer. He was total humbug.

After his week of community service, he would drive slowly out of town, cautious of the speed limit. He'd celebrate New Year's Eve in Miami with breasty twins.

"Knickerbocher's Liquor Locker is two blocks down on your right," she directed him. "As far as you, me, and sex, use soap and enjoy your solo flight."

Alex chuckled, a deep, sinful sound that made her tingle. "Dinner then," he offered. "Join me?"

She shook her head. "Sorry, I have to work."

"Nutcracking's not your full-time job?"

"It's only for the holidays," she said. "I own A Midsummer's Ice Cream on Main Street. I usually work days, but during Christmas I switch shifts."

Alex heel-toed off his Nikes. He then loosened the drawstring on his Santa pants and let them drop. Damp with sweat, his boxer briefs stuck to his body, showcasing him fully. He patted his stomach, shrugged. "A banana split or sundae for dinner—not my usual, but I'm game."

"A purchase over ten dollars lets you ride the carousel on the boardwalk for free."

"Hot time in a small town," he grunted. "Will the excitement never end?"

Showered and shaved, Alex strolled into A Midsummer's Ice Cream as sunset washed the sidewalk in orange and gold. His shoulders filled out a white knit shirt, and his creased khakis ended in brown leather loafers without socks.

He was the sexiest man ever to enter Holly McIntyre's shop. She hoped his heat wouldn't melt her ice cream.

He looked around, took it all in. "You work in an ice cream cone."

That she did. Holly loved the architecture. The exterior was cone-shaped, and the roof swirled with two scoops of strawberry. The design drew dessert lovers off the street and into a whimsical blend of pink brick walls and mint-and-yellow polka-dotted booths.

All the flavors had silly, fun names. Customers got a charge ordering Tutti Frutti Butti, Cotton Candy Circus, or Banana Fana Fo.

The Ex-Boyfriend was a daily request, comfort food for the broken hearted. Young girls healed fast over six scoops of ice cream.

Near the ceiling, a raised track and operational choo-choo train ran the rails. Suspended from sturdy light fixtures, model airplanes, miniature hot-air balloons, and tiny rocket ships twirled in the breeze whenever the door opened. It was a kid's paradise.

Along with Holly, two employees worked the shop. Their uniforms consisted of hot pink T-shirts and white shorts. Both the women checked out Alex as if he was the flavor of the month.

"Dipstick." Celine likened Alex to a frozen banana, dipped in chocolate and sprinkled with nuts.

"He's Smoochy Goochy." Marissa tagged him a rich blend of peanut butter and toffee drizzled with two sticky toppings.

Lewd Licorice, Holly thought, and had it confirmed

when Alex lowered his voice and said, "Sixty-nine flavors—lots to lick."

The man was a piece of work.

"Can I help you?" Teenaged Celine smiled the smile of a twenty year old.

Fortunately, Alex saw her as jailbait. "What do you suggest?" he asked Holly.

"Eat Dirt."

The ballplayer blinked. "I came for ice cream."

"Eat Dirt is a flavor," she informed him. "A chocolate sundae served over crumbled-up Oreo 'soil' in a plastic flowerpot."

"We'll scoop and fling for you," Celine offered.

"I'll catch," said Marissa.

"Kinky," from Alex.

Holly snorted. The man put a sex twist on scooping ice cream.

Celine moved to the far end of the counter, grabbed a scoop, dug into the chocolate tub. Marissa stood at the opposite end, holding a decorative flowerpot half filled with Oreo crumbs.

With a flick of her wrist, Celine flung one scoop of chocolate in a high, perfectly launched arc.

Marissa caught the ice cream in the pot.

Alex applauded. "You girls are good."

"You have no idea how good." Marissa winked at him. "Holly can catch flying scoops in a cup balanced on her forehead or chin. A real God-given talent."

Alex Boxer caught Holly's blush. The hot spots on her cheeks were sexy as hell. The lady had entertainment value, he mused. She was someone to play with while he was marooned in Holiday, if she'd hang out with him. Her outright aversion stuck in his craw.

It didn't matter much either way. In four short days he'd blow this popcorn stand. The bells of freedom would ring, and he'd soon be lying by the pool with topless twins slathering oil all over his body. He could feel their hands on him now, touching, rubbing . . .

The image made his dick twitch.

Holly noticed his stir and cast him the evil eye.

He immediately went limp.

Alex hoped it wasn't a permanent affliction.

"Here you go." She passed him his sundae. "Enjoy."

He nodded toward a secluded polka-dotted booth where he hoped to capture her attention. "Grab an extra spoon and Eat Dirt with me," he requested.

"We're busy, and I'm working," she begged off.

"Busy" his ass. There were three women behind the counter and only one other customer seated, munching a vanilla waffle cone. It was obvious she didn't want to join him.

He shrugged, took over the booth himself. He could do alone. He just wasn't good at it. He liked people, loved notoriety, and lived to be the center of attention. Holly had snubbed him. Her loss.

He'd taken two bites when a group of teenage boys walked in. Jerry Petree from the mall led the pack. "Told you Boxer would be here." The kid had the nose of a bloodhound.

"Have a seat." Alex motioned them over.

Christmas came early for the teens. They tripped over themselves to reach him.

The booth was meant for four, yet all six squeezed in. Surprisingly, they left him enough space to eat his sundae.

He cut a look at Holly, caught her deepening frown.

He understood her concern. Seven people now occupied a booth and only he was eating ice cream. There were no profits in sitters talking baseball.

He slid his hand into his side pocket, drew out a money clip. He passed Jerry a hundred-dollar bill. "Go order." He nudged the boy toward the counter.

Within minutes, cups of every imaginable flavor were spread across the table. The kid handed him twelve cents in change.

He glanced again at Holly, caught the slow curve of her smile. Business was good, and the lady was happy.

That pleased Alex as well.

An hour passed, and his entourage multiplied.

Two hours later, Alex felt mobbed.

He was compressed in a booth with fans pushing closer and closer, making him claustrophobic. This was a laidback beach community, yet the crowd still wanted a piece of him. He'd signed autographs, posed for pictures, kissed a baby, and talked baseball until his voice was hoarse.

He needed five minutes to breathe.

He glanced over his shoulder, found fans packed ten deep behind him. He had no easy means of escape . . .

Until Holly McIntrye elbowed through the crowd, her voice raised, polite but forceful. "Excuse me," she repeated over and over again as she struggled to his table.

Once she got within arm's reach, she flashed two yellow tickets and said, "You purchased over ten dollars' worth of ice cream—it's time to ride the carousel."

Alex had never been so glad to ride a merry-go-round in his life. Amid disappointed groans, he bumped Jerry and his friends from the booth, then followed Holly out, relieved to be free.

At the door, she turned, facing all those gathered. "Alex Boxer is in town for a few more days. Everyone will get a chance to see him again."

"Same time, same place tomorrow?" Jerry Petree asked.

"Only if Alex has a taste for more ice cream," was as far as Holly would commit.

Back on the sidewalk, he rubbed his stomach. "I tried every flavor. My gut's about to burst."

"You're a crowd pleaser and great for business."

He wanted her to see him as more than free advertising. "I've never dropped a hundred on ice cream."

"Profits rose tonight."

"I'm a bankable commodity."

"Mind if we walk?" she asked. "Otherwise I'll locate a golf cart."

Alex couldn't remember the last time he'd taken a walk, nor could he recall spending an evening with a woman when they weren't headed for bed. Relaxed and casual had gotten lost in his tailspin life.

"Walking works." He decided to give it a try.

A Midsummer's Ice Cream fronted on the Holiday Boardwalk on the south end of town. The twenty-block, wooden-planked promenade ran north, the perfect setting for visitors to catch their first view of the seashore.

Holly pointed out sites along the way. "The Morrow House is the oldest beach cottage still standing in Holiday. The Victorian is now a bed and breakfast. It has twenty-two rooms, a basement, an attic, and twelve-inch brick walls."

The Atlantic Beach Library was located next door. The Bohemian Café stood two lots down. A small verandah charmed passersby with rose paint and deep purple shutters. Lime green wrought-iron tables and chairs offered dining al fresco.

"The Bohemian's known for its Corn Flake french toast. Stop in one morning," she suggested. "Order a big glass of fresh tangelo juice."

All future breakfasts depended on the judge's mercy. Alex hoped Holly would present the official with a good progress report, and he would soon be driving cautiously out of town. If not tomorrow, hopefully the next day.

He blew out a breath, kept right on walking. The souvenir shop windows reflected their progress. The scent of vendor hotdogs and nachos hung on the air.

Few people strolled the planks, leaving the sounds of the ocean to fill the night. In the distance, strains of seasonal music and enormous neon signs drew residents and tourists to the arcade and amusement park. That was the heart of the action.

"The boardwalk lays claim to its fair share of proposals and honeymoon moonlight strolls," Holly commented. "There's something about the night air, the firefly stars—"

"The smell of dead fish." Alex coughed.

"Be glad it's not Randolph."

He smiled. "The reindeer's a charmer."

Athletic games from the basket toss and balloon darts, to the baseball throw caught Alex's eye the moment he entered the arcade. He wanted to play. He was good at winning stuffed animals for women. He'd show off for Holly. Just a little.

He laid down a buck, and the worker passed him a basketball. "Take three shots," the man behind the counter said. "Sink one for a kewpie doll, two for a rubber duck, three for a teddy bear."

Alex went for the bear, only to miss all three baskets. Son of a bitch. Heat climbed his neck, and his face went hot. "Again." He smacked down another dollar.

An Andrew Jackson later, he had yet to win a prize.

The worker turned to Holly, asking, "Would the lady like a turn?"

"The lady would," she agreed.

Agitated, Alex slid the man two dollars. He figured two tries were plenty for Holly. Then they'd move on.

He watched as she centered herself, then tossed the ball using some backspin. Her aim hit true, bounced off the tilt of the upper lip and dropped through the hoop.

Double damn. Two turns and she'd scored both the duck and the teddy. She passed Alex the duck, which quacked when he squeezed it.

"Later, Wally." She waved to the worker.

The man nodded, grinned at her.

"You know the guy?"

"I grew up in Holiday," she reminded him. "The arcade was a second home."

His competitive nature kicked in. "Balloon darts next."

She followed him to the booth, where she kicked his ass a second time. Holly walked away with a cuddly Mickey Mouse.

Lady was racking up prizes.

"Ring toss." He felt his luck shift.

He dropped fifty dollars before Holly hauled him

over to the baseball throw, his saving grace. Ten groups of bottles offered the challenge, each group positioned with three bottles at the base and two stacked on top.

He was a professional athlete. This would be an easy win.

He received four baseballs for five dollars.

"Knock over three of the four bottle groups and take home Lola the stuffed leopard," the worker said.

Alex took aim and Holly moved behind him. "Lola's been at the arcade for five years," she whispered. "She's impossible to win."

Alex set his back teeth.

He was taking Lola home tonight.

A Ben Franklin later and Holly stepped between him and the counter. "You've spent more at the arcade than you did on ice cream. Let's ride the carousel, call it a night."

A crowd had gathered. Fifty people now watched him make a fool of himself. He was a ballplayer with an accurate arm. He should be able to knock over those damn bottles.

He wasn't a good loser.

Holly pressed into his side, her voice low. "The bottles have lead bases. Throw low, split the bottom two."

He turned on her. "You tell me this after I've blown a hundred bucks?"

"You're good for our economy, Alex Boxer."

He shoved up his sleeves, untucked his shirt, and got down to business. His next three balls bowled down the bottles.

Those gathered cheered him on, then applauded wildly with his win. Alex victory-pumped his arm— Lola was his.

In the end, he decided to give Holly the leopard. "All yours." He presented her with the stuffed animal.

She looked surprised. "Maybe you should hold on to Lola, give her to your girlfriend."

"I've no one special in my life." Blond twins awaited him in Miami. Somehow it didn't seem fair to give one a life-size leopard and the other a bathtub ducky.

Lola belonged to Holly.

He'd worked up a sweat, and it was time for a cold one.

He swept his gaze down the arcade. "Any chance of a beer?"

"Root beer." Her reply was a downer.

They walked to Frosty's. "Hank Conrad, the moose from the mall, owns the beverage stand. I'll buy," Holly told him. She left him holding Lola, Teddy, Mickey, and the rubber ducky. "You'd make a great poster boy for Animal Planet," she threw over her shoulder.

Alex shifted, waiting impatiently for his soda.

"You won Lola!"

Alex watched as a mother and her three daughters approached. The little girls were bouncing excitedly, their eyes on his prizes.

The kids were stair steps, Alex noticed as they raced toward him. He figured them at four, five, and six. The mother could barely keep up.

"Girls' night out," the woman said as they stopped in front of him.

"Daddy's taking a college class so he can get a better job," the oldest of the girls blurted out. "He was studying, and since we couldn't keep quiet, Mom brought us to the arcade."

"We're burning off energy," the mother said.

Mom looked burned out herself.

Alex stood stiffly as the girls patted Lola, Teddy, Mickey, and eyeballed the rubber duck. Their clothes were clean, although slightly faded. All three needed a new pair of tennis shoes. The youngest had knotted laces.

Where the hell was Holly? Alex looked toward Frosty's, where he caught her chatting up Hank. The man threw back his head and laughed heartily over something she said. Holly didn't strike Alex as being funny, so the moose had to be flirting with her.

"Do you have daughters?" the middle girl asked as she stared wide eyed at the stuffed animals.

"No wife, no kids," Alex was quick to say.

"All those animals are for you?" the littlest asked.

He suddenly realized how silly he must look, standing on the boardwalk, clutching four prizes, believing himself a hero for winning Lola for Holly.

Alex hunkered down and looked the smallest in the eye. She was as exhausted as she was restless. It wouldn't take long for her to fall asleep. A part of him wanted her to have sweet dreams.

"Which one do you like the best?" He gestured toward his winnings.

"Duck." She chose, then clutched it so tightly it quacked. She giggled.

"Jenny loves bubble baths," her mother explained. "She'd sit in the tub all day if I'd let her."

"How about you?" he asked the middle girl.

The second in line looked at her older sister before making her decision. "Mickey for me, Lola for Sis."

The eldest was so excited, she hugged herself, spun in a circle, then did a happy dance.

The mother's smile came slowly, sincerely, and on a sigh. "I don't know what to say," she managed.

Alex looked at the girls. "I want you to go to your bedrooms when you get home and play with your prizes. Give your dad some space."

They all promised to be good.

"Thank you, Mister . . ." The mother hesitated, not knowing his name.

"Alex Boxer." He handed Mom the teddy bear.

Her eyes narrowed as she recognized his name. "I'm glad you were caught speeding." Her words were honest. "My girls won't forget your kindness. May Santa be as good to you as you were to them. Merry Christmas."

"Back at you." Alex refused to go too deep into the holiday spirit.

The girls each gave him a hug, then, clutching their prizes close, walked with their mother toward the arcade exit. The sound of the quacking duck echoed from the parking lot.

Alex turned and nearly bumped into Holly. Her expression was soft, disbelieving, as she passed him a root beer. "I left you with four animals and return to only you."

"I'm the best of them all."

"I imagine you could be cuddly."

"Try me."

"Drink your soda."

They stood amid the blinking lights and arcade noises, sipping root beer and watching people pass by. The crowd had thinned, and there were no riders on the carousel when Holly produced their tickets.

Alex looked at the ride curiously. He'd never ridden a

merry-go-round. His parents had always been too busy to take him to a fair or carnival. His old man banked big money in real estate, and his mother involved herself in every charity imaginable. Alex grew up with nannies, butlers, and little parental supervision.

He now took in the carousel's pressed metal ceiling strung with blinking Christmas lights, the mirrored middle cylinder, the multicolored horses with their jeweled bridles and shiny black saddles. Sets of leather-bound booths were dispersed throughout for those who preferred to sit instead of ride.

"This horse looks fast," Alex said as he swung atop a black steed with a purple jeweled bridle.

"Mine's quicker out the gate," Holly challenged, now astride a tan horse with a ruby-encrusted harness.

"Jingle Bell Rock" set the merry-go-round in motion. The horses rose up and down, and Holly's mount always seemed a nose ahead of Alex's.

"Having fun?" she asked.

He nodded, surprised at how much he was enjoying the simple circular motion of the carousel. It was soothing. The Christmas lights winked at him. He noticed the brass ring on the second go round.

"If I catch it?" he asked Holly.

"You make a wish."

Alex stretched, snagged the ring with his next pass. He suddenly felt lucky.

The carousel slowed, and they both dismounted.

Alex caught Holly between the horses. He touched the ring to her cheek, then suggestively brushed his thumb over her mouth.

"My wish is to kiss you," he said.

"Wish for something that could come true."

He wanted her and claimed his kiss.

She went wide eyed and pucker faced.

He did everything in his power to loosen her up. He nipped at her mouth, coaxed with his tongue, took his sweet time with her. The kiss went nowhere.

She had the passion of a metal pole.

Awkwardness set him back.

He felt like an absolute idiot.

Holly McIntyre just wasn't into him.

Chapter Three

Same Santa, different day.

A request from the mall manager to keep business booming drew an additional morning shift for Old Saint Nick. Alex had protested he'd wanted to sleep, and it had taken Holly's promise of coffee and a box of chocolate-covered doughnuts to rally him.

He'd shown up in the Jingle Bell Shop with wet hair and razor stubble. His white beard stuck to his face, forcing Holly to stand very, very close to adjust the mustache.

The scent of pine soap lingered on his skin, subtle, masculine, and Christmas-y. He smelled nice, vital, more lumberjack than ballplayer.

She glanced at him now, as he sat on the big red corduroy chair. He shifted right, left, couldn't sit still. Although he welcomed each child with a ho-ho-ho, he didn't have the warm, fuzzy manner that put children at ease. Many still looked leery, others outright fearful.

Alex frightened her most.

The man had kissed her on the carousel. His kiss had teased and tempted. A flame had lit in her belly, warming her from the inside out. She'd barely kept her balance. Had she given in, she would have been a goner. He could have kissed her naked in a very short time.

It had been the look in his eye that struck fear in her heart. He knew he could arouse her and was now out to prove it. The man was as competitive in seduction as he was in sports and arcade games. He saw her as a prize, much like Lola.

Her time with the famed ballplayer would come to an end Christmas Day. Unless she could persuade the judge to release him sooner. She'd yet to speak to Hathaway on Alex's behalf; maybe she'd do so today.

His continued mumblings about Miami and blond twins set her teeth on edge. Apparently, threesomes appealed to him.

Holly needed only one man to be happy.

The Rogue was out of her league.

"Cracks Nuts," Santa called to her.

What could he possibly want? There was a break in the line, and she cautiously approached him. "Yes, Santa?" She remained outwardly calm, although her stomach had knotted.

He motioned her closer. His too-small white gloves barely covered his knuckles. She bent, nearly knocking his temple with her big wooden head. He pulled down the lever on her jaw, spoke face-to-face. "What time do we leave for the elementary school? Velvet makes my ass sweaty, and I'll need another shower."

Holly looked at her watch. "Thirty minutes, and I'll close off the line. Louie's teacher wanted you to arrive for show and tell, then take recess with the kids. Mrs. Rome hoped you'd captain a team for kickball. If time allows, there's lunch in the cafeteria—"

"Slow down, Nutcracker," Alex interrupted. "You've got my whole damn day planned."

"You agreed to show and tell," she reminded him.

"You've added on kickball and lunch. Maybe I should stay for nap time to make up for the sleep I lost this morning."

"Third-graders don't nap."

"Shit." His expletive hissed between his teeth, fluttered his mustache. Fortunately, there were no kids close by, but the workshop helpers had heard him. They tapped their fingers to their lips.

"Shushed by elves." Alex shook his head. "The day's headed downhill fast."

A half hour later, Holly handed Alex a package that had recently arrived from James River Stadium in Richmond, Virginia. It turned out to be his baseball uniform, two dozen baseballs, and a set of his personal photographs.

Once he'd showered and returned as a Rogue, he was ready for show and tell. She stared, couldn't take her eyes off him—he was that rugged, that handsome.

The man was a star athlete, tall, muscled, primed. He looked hot in his uniform. He was a man other men would envy and women would deeply desire.

He returned her stare, in that tangible way that visually stroked her. She felt his touch, a hot trail of fingertips over her breasts and down her belly, followed by a slow slide beneath the waistband of her green capris.

She went wet for him.

His smile curved knowingly.

She nervously tugged on the hem of her pink flamingo top, ran her sweaty palms down her thighs. She'd never been more embarrassed.

Air, she needed air. "Let's go."

Once out on the sidewalk, she pointed to her yellow Volkswagen. "It's not your Saleen S7, but it will get us to school."

Alex settled his big body in the passenger seat. Holly was certain he purposely stretched out when he could have hugged the door. His shoulder bumped hers, and his thigh rubbed her own. He rested his hand between the seats, the tips of his fingers a mere inch from her hip.

She started the engine, shifted into first. Her knuckles accidentally brushed low on his side, and Boxer grinned.

Distracted, she ran onto the curb as she was pulling into traffic. The bump and jar rocked Alex sideways. He leaned against her a little too long.

She pushed him back, said, "Don't crowd me."

"Don't have an accident." He jabbed a finger at the car ahead of them, which had stopped short for a yellow light. "I'd have run it."

Holly hit the brake. "You would have gotten a ticket."

"Only in Holiday," Alex grunted. "Big cities are more lenient."

She was certain no Richmond cop would write Alex a ticket, no matter his violation. He was a professional athlete and would slide by on an autograph and the promise of game tickets.

They soon arrived at the school and youthful memories made her smile. "I attended Holiday Elementary," she told Alex as she pulled her VW into visitors' parking. "Classrooms were small and teachers taught until retirement. A few of my favorites still remain."

"They must be old," said Alex.

"The kids keep them young."

"I wouldn't have the patience to teach."

"It takes dedication," she noted. "My dad used to say 'if a person loves his job, he'll never work a day in his life.'"

"That's why I play baseball."

"So the boy never has to become a man?"

"You're cracking my nuts again." He scowled. "Trust me, sweetheart, I'm all grown up. There's nothing little about this man."

Holly had seen him stripped down to boxer briefs. He was definitely full grown.

Anticipation ran high in Mrs. Rome's class. The room was decorated with student artwork and an enormous chart that marked good behavior. Gold and silver stars abounded.

Holly stood back as Alex talked baseball. He was by turns serious and funny, told a dozen stories. He captivated every ten-year-old in the room.

He drew Louie Kessler to the front of the class, had the boy try on his big league glove. The glove with which he'd caught the final out in the World Series.

Afterward, Alex autographed baseballs and pictures and stood for a class photo. Mrs. Rome next suggested that Louie give Holly and Alex a tour of the classroom. Louie introduced them to the class guinea pig, Cute as a Button or Button for short.

"Clown fish aren't funny," Louie whispered to Holly when they stopped before a large aquarium near the teacher's desk. "They just have pretty colors."

Holly admired the fish with the orange and white

stripes. She was also quite taken by three small turtles in a separate tank.

"Huey, Dewey, and Louie." The boy smiled. "Louie always sits on the center island under the sun lamp. He's the warmest."

Mrs. Rome clapped her hands and gained everyone's attention. "We have time for a quick game of kickball before lunch," she announced. "Team captains will be Alex Boxer and Sarah Hanover. The boys will play the girls."

The girls' team proved one player short and Holly was nominated to play. Growing streaks had left the girls several inches taller than most of the boys. Louie was the shortest kid in the class.

"We'll take the outfield first." Alex positioned his players, then looked indecisive about Louie.

"He'd make a great pitcher," Holly called to Alex.

She could see by the pull of his mouth, Alex didn't quite agree. Louie, however, thought her idea brilliant. The kid grabbed the rubber ball and trotted out to pitch.

Alex's jaw shifted as he took over as catcher.

The girls cheered Holly, who was up first to kick. She was glad she'd worn a pair of navy Keds. Louie's first roll of the ball stopped well before it crossed the plate. His second and third tries also fell short.

Alex jogged to Louie, gave the boy a quick lesson in pitching. Alex demonstrated by rolling a ball to Holly.

"We're not bowling," she reminded Alex as he aimed the ball hard and fast at her ankles, attempting to knock down pins. "It's third-grade kickball."

"Nothing wrong with friendly competition," he returned.

Alex was far from friendly. He played to win.

Holly had once been good at kickball. When Louie finally got the ball over the plate, she skimmed it with the side of her foot, a kick that sent the ball straight back to the pitcher.

Louie fell all over himself, but finally scooped up the ball. He then ran after Holly in an attempt to throw and tag her out.

Today was Louie's day, and Holly wanted the kid to perform well. She gave him a chance to put her out. Louie's toss at her hip was a foot ahead of her stride. She had to pick up speed to get hit. She feigned frustration at not reaching first.

The boys all jumped, pumped their arms, praised Louie. Holly walked back to the girls' bench. A few of them patted her arm, consoled her.

Alex Boxer's eyes narrowed on her. He had the look of a man who wanted to win, but he didn't want success handed to him.

Two additional outs and the boys went on to kick. Holly watched as Alex set himself up to kick third. If the first two boys could get on base, Alex would then boot the ball across the street. His team would be ahead by three runs.

Very unsportsmanlike in Holly's eyes.

The girls insisted she pitch, and Holly picked up the ball. The first boy kicked hard, and the ball shot between second and third base. The boys now had a runner on first.

Louie was up next and missed the first two pitches

by a mile. Alex pulled the boy aside and gave him a pep talk. Louie promised to do better.

With the third pitch, he connected, a soft roller back to Holly. She scooped up the ball, threw to second, got the lead runner out. Louie held at first.

Alex sauntered to home plate. He stood before Holly in his Rogues uniform, looking big and badass and ready to kick the ball down her throat.

She didn't like him much at that moment.

Alex knew Holly expected him to run up the score. He planned to do the opposite. He wanted to confuse this woman who'd rejected his kisses on the carousel. She'd shut him down when he'd felt lucky.

No one stole his luck.

He had every intention of kissing her again. Most women found him irresistible. Next time, she'd kiss him back.

Holly rolled the ball, and Alex let it pass.

"Strike one," from Mrs. Rome.

Alex swore the teacher was blind.

Alex caught the second roller with his toe. He popped the ball up, a double-bouncer to the girl at third. He'd provided just enough time to get Louie to second, if the kid ran all out.

Louie made it, but just barely. The girl at third had a wicked arm. She threw like a boy.

Runners were now on first and second. The next kicker punted a fly ball to Holly. She caught it easily. Two down.

From the corner of his eye, Alex caught Louie take off for third. The kid was trying to steal a base, looking to be a hero. Alex understood the boy's need to succeed.

A diversion, Alex thought, and he started for second. He needed to pull Holly's attention off Louie and onto him.

Holly took the bait; she wanted Alex out.

She came at him with quickness and grace. The boys went wild as Alex danced about, attempted to dodge her throw. The girls screamed just as loudly for Holly to nail him.

She had a good eye and decent aim, Alex was soon to find out. A double-arm toss caught his hip. But though he was out, Louie had snuck home. The kid scored the only run of the game.

Louie may have been small, but he was definitely mighty. His team cheered him loudly.

Mrs. Rome soon called her class to lunch. Alex snagged his glove off the bench and followed Holly into the cafeteria. He stuffed himself on macaroni and weenie winks.

Louie hugged him good-bye and Alex patted his shoulder. The kid would grow. He'd no doubt shoot up several inches over the next year.

Returning to the parking lot, Holly glanced at her watch, scrunched her nose. "It's time to return to the mall. Try to conjure a little holiday spirit."

Alex glared at her from across the hood of her car. "I've run out of cheer," he said. "I want to go to the beach, catch some rays."

"You need to serve your community hours," she said as she ducked into her VW. "The judge ordered you into a Santa suit—there's no beach break."

"I'm chafed from red velvet and have a rash under my chin from the beard," he complained.

"Use more talcum powder," she suggested.

"I'm not a baby."

"You sure whine like one."

Alex was done arguing. He climbed in, levered back the passenger seat, and placed his glove over his face. He'd nap on the ride back.

But it seemed Holly was out to get him. She popped the clutch, swerved unnecessarily, and stopped suddenly for no apparent reason.

He'd get back at her later. He planned to steal a kiss when she least expected it. He'd twist her inside out.

Back at the Jingle Bell Shop, he shot upstairs to shower. Again. His skin was starting to feel scaly.

Toweled dry, he came down the curving iron staircase in nothing but his boxer briefs. Near the bottom, he slowed, stopped.

From his vantage point, he viewed a tall holiday screen decorated with a vintage sleigh. Behind the center panel, Holly McIntyre stood in her bra and panties.

Alex went hard in a heartbeat.

He clutched the railing, tried to catch his breath but failed. Lady was hot in her lavender satin and lace. She had slender curves and long legs. And a really nice ass.

He knew he should make his presence known. She'd kill him for checking her out. But it was tit for tat in his mind. He was in his briefs, and she'd gone hanky-panky.

"I'm not a peep show, Alex Boxer."

Busted! Holly had eyes in the back of her head. He'd never seen a woman dress so fast. She'd transitioned to the nutcracker in under a minute, though she hadn't yet donned the big wooden head.

He took the remaining stairs, crossed to her. "I imagined you more cotton than lace."

"I pegged you a Peeping Tom from the first."

"A man likes to look."

"Get dressed." She produced his Santa suit. "Ten minutes, and I expect merry."

Jolly wasn't on his agenda. He went through the motions, but his heart wasn't in it. He didn't feel Christmas like the rest of the town. Holiday had an abundance of cheer. Alex felt lost to the spirit.

The afternoon moved forward, closing in on the dinner hour. His stomach growled at six-thirty.

"Only thirty minutes more." Holly pacified him with a free sample of a raspberry smoothie from the health food store.

He sucked it down in one sip, certain most of the drink now colored his mustache red. At least the color matched the season. He'd never seen so much red, green, and white in his life. It was as if no other hue existed.

"You're done for the day," Holly announced when she finally came to relieve him of his duties.

Alex stood, stretched, and felt red velvet creasing his ass. After the holidays, velvet would be dead to him.

He was halfway out of his Santa suit by the time he reached the Jingle Bell Shop. "You shouldn't undress in the hallway," Holly chided.

"When you're as hot and sticky as I am, you let the clothes fall where they may." He kicked off his Nikes at the doorway.

He caught Holly's look as she took him in. His hair was plastered to his head, his chest damp, his briefs clingy. Red lint dusted his calves. The talcum powder on his thighs and beneath his chin had turned to paste. He smelled. Still, she stared. And he grew uneasy. He shifted his stance twice.

"You've put in a long day," she finally said. "Take it easy tonight."

"What are your plans?" he surprised himself by asking.

She blinked, equally taken back. "I'm headed to Edna Murdock's house," she told him. "The senior citizens are baking and decorating Christmas cookies for less fortunate families. I'm going to help out."

Alex spent so little time in his own kitchen, he needed no more than a refrigerator for beer. "I can bake," he was quick to say. "I'm an artist when it comes to frosting and sprinkles."

Holly didn't believe him for a second—he could see it in her eyes. "What's your favorite Christmas cookie?" she asked.

"Sugar cookies. They're Santa's favorite too."

"Frosting?"

"Butterfat."

"You mean buttercream?"

"Yeah, right, easy mistake."

She debated, finally decided in his favor. "You screw up one recipe," she threatened, "and I'll shove you in the oven."

Hansel and Gretel came to mind. The crazy witch too.

He wondered if Holly would try to fatten him up first on spun sugar and cake.

Maybe he should drop breadcrumbs on his way to Edna Murdock's house, just to be on the safe side.

Chapter Four

Baking cookies with the over-sixty crowd was one thing; having Alex Boxer in Edna Murdock's kitchen was quite another. The man charmed every woman wearing granny panties. Holly had never seen him so friendly, so flirty, so polite. So not-Alex.

She stood back and watched him work the room. He'd taken a turn at every cook's station except hers. She knew which cookies were Alex's and which belonged to the ladies. Especially when it came to the apricot and raspberry thumbprints. There was a big difference between Alma Mason's delicate thumb and jock boy's. His print required an extra dollop of preserves.

He'd encouraged Greta Taylor to double the Bacardi in her rum ball recipe. He'd sugar-dusted the crescent moon cookies twice over. Two of his gingerbread men were anatomically correct. He'd made the older women blush.

At that very moment, Alex was eating chocolate chip shortbread off the cookie sheets faster than Emily Ison could bake them. He'd poured his third glass of milk.

He was relaxed, smiling, and very much at home.

Holly, on the other hand, was a nervous wreck.

The man gave her goose bumps. From the moment

he'd arrived, she'd gone all tingly and jumpy. Alex hadn't paid her the least bit of attention. Yet his occasional glance stole her breath and made her heart race.

She instinctively knew he'd try to kiss her again. She watched, anticipated, yet kept her distance. She was afraid if he caught her unaware, she'd respond. She didn't want to give him the satisfaction of another conquest.

Three days and he'd be leaving town. Unless he got off early for good behavior.

There were twins in Miami.

She didn't want to be his Holiday lay.

"Where are you from, Alex?" Edna Murdock of the white hair, kind brown eyes, and arthritic hands asked as she passed him a plate of warm snickerdoodles.

"Minneapolis," he replied.

"Tell us about your family," said Greta Taylor, who had lived all her eighty-five years in the small beach town.

"My father's in real estate, and my mother does charity work," he replied. "I have five older sisters, all married but no babies."

"You're a handsome guy." Edna winked at him as she added coconut to the macaroon batter. "Why haven't you settled down?"

"I haven't met the right Mrs. Claus."

The grandmas all giggled like girls.

Edna offered everyone tea, and once the pot boiled, the older women grabbed their cups and moved to the living room to put up their feet. They were tired from standing.

One last bite of snickerdoodle and Alex crossed to Holly at the kitchen counter. She was decorating sugar cookies in all the holiday shapes and sizes.

She hated the fact they were now alone. She had no buffer against this man. His closeness made her fidgety.

He nudged her with his elbow. "Can I help?"

She pointed toward three bowls of frosting and an assortment of sprinkles, gumdrops, dried fruit, nuts, and colored sugars.

"Frost, then decorate," she instructed.

Alex selected a star-shaped sugar cookie. He spread buttercream icing with a narrow rubber spatula, then shook on yellow-colored sugar. The star glistened.

"Good job," Holly begrudgingly praised.

She went on to decorate her own cookies, only to set them aside when she caught Alex fashioning a bikini on Mrs. Claus. The cookie had a peppermint frosting top with red gumdrop breasts and a slivered almond thong. X-rated.

"What?" he asked when she glared daggers.

"These aren't *adult* sugar cookies," she hissed. "They'll be eaten by children."

"Guess Rudolph won't fly either then."

Off to the left, a perfectly good chocolate reindeer with caramel sprinkles now had raisins for balls.

Holly picked off the raisins. "Go have a cup of tea."

"I drink strong black Columbian, not Earl Grey." He broke off the top of a Christmas tree, one recently decorated with green and red icing. He moved closer, their faces almost touching. He tapped her lips with the cookie. "Bite?"

She turned slightly, parted her lips. She hoped he'd leave after she'd taken his sample.

Alex moved on her so quickly, she never saw him coming. He caught her mouth, slipped her his tongue, and mated with slow, sensuous thrusts. He tasted of sugar and spice and all that was naughty.

He wrapped her in his arms, drew her into him. She settled her hands on his shoulders, absorbed his scent and heat. He was one delicious man.

They struck immediate sparks. There was curiosity and intensity between them, a warmth and rightness to their kiss. Her hormones went wild, and her insides totally melted. She was all sensitive skin and wobbly knees.

His erection thickened and rose against her belly.

Her center warmed and went liquid.

He was turned on, and he told her so. "I want you," he nuzzled near her ear.

She desired him too. The realization hit swift and jarring. Their intimacy had been as electric as it was fleeting. He'd kissed her with a lot of tongue and experience. It took her a moment to breathe properly.

Nothing about Alex spoke of promise, destiny, forever. His interests lay with blond twins in Miami, not with a nutcracker from Holiday.

She was his Christmas distraction, nothing more. They stood in Edna Murdock's kitchen where the older women could return at any second. She didn't want them catching her lip locked with the ballplayer, even if he had caught her by surprise.

She eased back, kept her voice light, "Sugar cookies certainly turn you on."

His blue gaze narrowed. "It's not the cookies."

"Baking with the grannies always warms my heart," she said. "Maybe it's rubbed off on you too."

"I'm still more humbug than ho."

"I'm all about the Christmas spirit."

"I'd let you jingle my bells."

"I don't do horny for the holidays."

"When do you do horny?" he asked.

"Not on the first date and only with the right man."

"I've known you two damn days, and we've spent a lot of time together." One corner of his mouth tipped, slow and sexy. "I've a fetish for nutcrackers. You could wear that big wooden head to bed."

His teasing made her blush, and her whole body went hot. Alex was too handsome, too rich, too experienced. She had no business playing in his league.

"Back to the kitchen. We have ten dozen cookies left to bake." Holly heard Edna Murdock moving their way.

She was grateful for the grannies' return. Flattening her hands on Alex's chest, she felt his heartbeat against one palm—strong, vital, and faster than normal. She gave him a push, and he reluctantly stepped back.

"It's time to make reindeer dust," Emily Ison said as she entered the kitchen. "All holiday baskets must contain a big jar."

"What's with the dust?" Alex asked.

"It's a mixture of oatmeal and glitter," Holly told him. "The reindeer feed on the oatmeal. The glitter is like a landing strip for airplanes. Kids spread it across their front yards so Santa knows where to land his sleigh."

Alex nodded. "Pretty cool. I'll help mix."

He stood by Holly's side, adding his glitter to her oatmeal, then shaking the jar until it blended together.

Alex pressed close, his breath warm near her ear. "If you sprinkled reindeer dust on your yard, I'd bring you a present."

"You have no idea what's on my Christmas list."

"You could sit on my lap and tell me," he said, his voice deep and suggestive. "I'd promise to deliver."

"I want peace on earth and good will toward men."

"That's a tall order, even for Santa." He scratched his jaw. "My thoughts were on gifts we could both enjoy. I'd wear a pair of Rudolph the Red Nose Reindeer boxers, the ones with the blinking nose on the fly, and you could slip into a green teddy with tiny gold bells at the nipples and a satin bow—"

She jammed her elbow into him so hard he sucked air. He immediately moved down the counter. Holly sent him a glare. The man didn't give up. He had Christmas sex on his brain, and she refused to let him unwrap her.

"Save the teddies for your Miami twins." She kept her voice low. "Bare Essence has a two-for-one sale through the end of the week, a big bang for your buck."

Alex Boxer rubbed his side. Holly's elbow could've broken a rib. Damn, she was difficult.

He'd never worked so hard to get a woman into his bed. He wanted more than one evening—he'd planned three all-nighters. That would give him plenty of time to enjoy and pleasure her.

He cut her a glance. She looked pretty tonight with her blond hair styled in a French braid. Her brown eyes shone warmly; her lips were glossed a soft pink.

A red tunic slanted off her shoulder, the strap of a green tank top visible beneath. Clusters of holly berries backed the pockets of her white jeans. Strappy sandals showed off her artful pedicure: tiny Christmas trees decorated her toes. The lady was a walking, talking advertisement for the season.

He kept one eye on Holly as he assisted Edna Murdock with a batch of angel-pink divinity. He sampled several pieces of the fancy candy, which melted in his mouth.

A knock on the kitchen door drew his attention to a new arrival. Hank Conrad, the moose from the mall. He also owned Frosty's on the boardwalk, Alex recalled. He hadn't officially met the man, who now shouldered a large cardboard box and greeted the grannies with high spirits and holiday hugs.

He advertized his good cheer by wearing a Santa hat and a T-shirt scripted with "Dreaming of a White Christmas."

It was doubtful that Hank would get his wish, Alex mused. They were in Florida, where sunburns trumped snowflakes.

Holly smiled up at the sandy-haired man with the lanky build. She seemed genuinely glad to see him. There was a cozy familiarity between them.

Alex's gut tightened when Hank set down the box and draped his arm about Holly's shoulders. She leaned into his side. There were long looks and intimate whispers. They acted like a couple.

Alex drummed his fingers on the kitchen counter, waited for an introduction. It was damn long in coming.

"Alex Boxer, Hank Conrad," she finally managed.

Hank nodded to Alex. "Hello, Santa."

"Moose," Alex acknowledged.

"I came to decorate the mistletoe arch," Hank explained. "Tomorrow we set the arch by Santa's Workshop. It's time for holiday kisses."

"It's tradition," said Edna Murdock. "The town gets in the spirit."

"It costs a dollar to stand under the arch." Greta Taylor slid the last batch of mocha-cinnamon meltaways off a cookie sheet. "The money goes to charity."

"Everyone has hot lips," Edna added. "Friends, lovers, married couples. No one resists."

"No one?" Alex looked at Holly.

"Mistletoe legitimizes holiday kissing," Edna chuckled.

Alex liked Holiday's way of thinking. He'd lay down a few singles to kiss the nutcracker. Hell, he'd drop a hundred if necessary, knowing she couldn't refuse.

Shortly thereafter, Greta Taylor started packing the Christmas baskets with cookies and containers of reindeer dust. Edna's turn came next; she took over and wrapped the handles with big red satin bows.

"The line for the arch will be as long as the one to see Santa." Greta grinned.

"There's a lot of teasing and blushing," Edna added.

"And most donate more than a dollar," said Hank.

Everyone's thoughts ran to kissing until Holly went to the sink to wash her hands. She'd bottled the last of the reindeer dust, and the glass containers sparkled with glitter. Santa would have the perfect landing strips for his sleigh.

Her hands now dried, she lightly touched Hank's arm. "I'll help with the arch," she offered.

"So will I," Alex surprised himself by saying. "I'm good with arches." He knew nothing about arches.

Holly's raised eyebrow doubted his capabilities.

Hank gave an offhanded shrug and led Alex to the

garage where twelve feet of wire twisted like a pretzel. "Edna backed her car over the arch last week," Moose Man said as he set the cardboard box filled with mistletoe on the cement floor. "It needs to be restructured before we can attach the sprigs."

Hank shoved his hands into work gloves, then held out pairs for Holly and Alex. "Be careful with the wire—it's sharp in places."

Holly accepted a flowered pair of gardening gloves. Alex, however, worked best bare-handed. He didn't need sissy gloves. His hands were strong, rough, callused.

Holly and Hank tackled one end of the arch and Alex began untangling the other. Small cuts caused his thumb to bleed, but he hated to ask for a Band-Aid. He'd refused the gloves and wasn't about to complain.

They worked in silence until Hank asked, "Has Libby Baker had her baby?"

Holly nodded, smiling. "A boy, Raymond Jay, born late yesterday afternoon. He weighed six pounds, seven ounces. Her husband stood on the corner of Main and Third and handed out cigars. I'm sure he stopped traffic."

"I saw Jane Palmer at the bank this morning. Her golden retriever had six puppies," Hank said. "You've been offered the pick of the litter."

Holly looked thoughtful. "Might be the perfect Christmas gift to myself."

"I'd buy the pup if you'd let me," offered Hank.

Alex watched Holly's face soften. "Save your money. The T-shirt shop beside Frosty's on the Boardwalk is going out of business next month. You could use the money to expand."

Alex listened as the two of them hashed over square footage, and the idea of adding a short list of sandwiches to Hank's menu. Holly made sound suggestions; she had a good head for business. Alex liked the way she looked at the expansion from all angles. She listed both pros and cons and commented on the best local contractors. She was damn smart.

Most of the women of Alex's acquaintance partied and passed out. Two-syllable words were the extent of their vocabulary. The sex and gratification were immediate. Dates were out the door before dawn.

He eavesdropped as Holly and Hank discussed other store owners, the refurbishment of the Boardwalk, and close friends they had in common. It was small-town talk, centered on grandmothers and their knitting, the weather, as well as the new stock of beach-and-boardwalk postcards being sold at the Holiday Tourist Center.

Alex felt excluded. The hometown chatter rode his last nerve. He had an unsettling urge to bump Hank aside, so Holly would focus on him again.

"How's the ice cream shop?" Hank asked her.

Holly cut Alex a look. "I've added a new flavor called Swing and a Miss. It's vanilla ice cream with chunks of red licorice and chips of peppermint."

Alex pulled a face. "I hate peppermint."

"I know."

She looked smug, Alex mused, as if she'd struck him out. He didn't take to scoreless innings. Home Run would have been a more appropriate flavor for her ice cream.

Hank straightened another foot of wire before he turned to Holly. "Will you be caroling at the community center tomorrow night?"

Holly drew up a step stool, needing extra height as she curved the wire near the top of the arch. "I'll be there once the cookie baskets are delivered," she said.

"Need help?" Hank offered. "Driving and dropping off could take hours."

"We've got it covered." Alex had found a way into their conversation. "Holly requested my assistance when we were making reindeer dust." An outright lie and damn pathetic for a grown man to go to such lengths to date a woman.

Holly's gaze narrowed on him. She could have busted him, but she was bred and born polite. Alex was known to hit low.

She cleared her throat, kept her cool. "You never fully committed," she managed.

"I agreed after our kiss."

Holly's fingers froze on the twisted wire. Alex, on the other hand, kept right on working. He winked at her. "You were quite convincing, sweetheart."

Hank shifted, looked uncomfortable.

Holly snapped off a piece of wire, shaped it like a noose. She looked ready to strangle him. "The kiss meant nothing," she defended. "There was—"

"Tongue," Alex interrupted. "You jingled my bells, babe."

Hank swallowed hard, paled.

Holly inhaled sharply, blushed torch red.

Alex knew he was being a prick. He deserved Holly's glare. Somehow she'd gotten to him, in a most unwelcome way. He could feel her around his heart and under his skin. He refused to analyze her indefinable effect.

He'd never done deep or serious, yet he hated being

the odd man out as she discussed small-town news with the moose. Alex had been excluded and wanted to re- claim ground.

He needed to regain her attention and hold it.

Even if he had to play dirty.

Hank was too much of a gentleman to cause a scene. The man cleared his throat and went on to ask, "How about Sue Schaffer's Christmas party? Need a date?"

"Holly invited me this morning." Alex was knee deep in lies. "She's buying a new red dress, one that shows Christmas cleavage."

Hank's eyes popped, and Holly's jaw dropped.

"*I* invited *you?*" She was slow to recover.

"You don't remember?" Alex feigned hurt. "We were at the Jingle Bell Shop, putting on our costumes. I was standing in my boxer briefs, and you wore lavender panties. You mentioned the party as we were checking each other out."

The corners of her mouth pulled tight. "We had just returned from show and tell at the elementary school," she quickly explained to Hank. "Alex took a shower in the loft and I was downstairs, changing behind the screen. It was all perfectly innocent."

"I found it intimate," Alex reflected. "I'm a fan of demi-cups and bikinis. How about you, Hank?"

Moose Man's jaw shifted, but he didn't share his pref- erence in women's underwear. Alex caught the man's hands shaking as he continued with the wire.

Hank was a decent man, Alex had to admit. The moose didn't discuss undies in mixed company, and he no doubt believed sex belonged behind closed doors. Alex was certain Hank slept in pajamas and socks and stuck with missionary.

Alex believed Holly needed a little naughty with her nice. Experimentation raised the temperature in the bedroom. He liked his sex hot.

In fairness to the man, Alex knew that Hank would never break the law or the speed limit. He wouldn't fantasize about blond twins in Miami. He'd be happy with Holly.

Holly. Masculine jealousy shot bone deep, irritating in its intensity. Alex hated the feeling. It was new and sharp and stuck him in the heart. He wasn't used to coming in second when he compared himself to another man.

His breath hitched, and his palms dampened. Hell, he'd only known the woman two days, yet the sensation of losing someone he'd never truly had bent him low.

He shouldn't give a rat's ass whom Holly liked or whom she dated. For some strange reason, it mattered. Too damn much. She was about to complicate his life. Big time.

The way Holly now looked at Hank irked Alex. She didn't want Hank to think poorly of her. Alex decided she must like Hank a lot.

Alex sucked it up, made repairs. "Our kiss was one between friends," he retracted. "The three-paneled screen protected Holly when she changed clothes."

Hank stopped working, stared at Alex. "Stop pawing the ground, dude. We don't have to lock horns over Holly. There's no need to explain your actions. You're her business, not mine."

Alex was lost. "I thought you were a couple."

Hank had the nerve to grin. "We're cousins. We look out for each other, so stop being such an ass, Santa."

Cousins? A fact Holly could have easily mentioned when they'd first been introduced, yet she'd skipped that part. He'd made a fool of himself over her. Alex didn't like being played.

Holly couldn't look at him. Her face was flushed, and her hands were all thumbs as she threw her energy into untwisting the wire at the top of the arch.

He'd get even with her, Alex silently swore. He'd donate a pile of one-dollar bills to kiss the nutcracker. He'd make love to her mouth until their lips went numb.

Another twenty minutes, and the twelve-foot arch curved perfectly. Hanging the sprigs of mistletoe came next. Alex tied bright red-and-green striped bows around the sprigs, then attached them to the wire. He felt like a floral designer.

The arch was soon transformed into a sweet, festive bower of leathery evergreen and waxy white berries. Several longer sprigs of mistletoe hung along the top; the leaves provided the kissing couples a bit of privacy.

Project completed, Hank pulled off his gloves, picked up the empty cardboard box, and moved toward the garage door. "You two should initiate the arch," he cast over his shoulder, then was gone.

Holly went red at his suggestion.

Alex rather liked Hank's idea.

She resisted when he took her hand, scuffing her feet and leaning backward. He was stronger and got his way. The urge to kiss her proved as undeniable as breathing. A final tug and she was his.

He circled her waist, noted how nicely she fit within the circle of his arms. He wanted her to feel every inch of him. Their bellies brushed, and he snuck a knee between her thighs. Their jeans created a friction that shot straight to his groin. He stirred, a significant twitch against her stomach.

She shivered, all raw nerves and expectancy. She pressed her garden-gloved hands to his chest, held him off by an inch. "The mistletoe arch is for charity. You have to pay to kiss me," she stalled.

A one-handed dip into his side pocket, and Alex pulled out a money clip. He thumbed off a fifty, slipped the cash into the back pocket of her white jeans. His hand lingered over her left butt cheek. He had big hands and she a small ass. He squeezed and eased her so close they were breathing the same air.

He stroked his palms over her hips, along her waist, worked up her spine. Time slowed, seduced them both, in the silent, dimly lit garage.

Gently, persuasively, he brushed his lips along her cheek, then her nose. The sugary-soft scent of cookies mixed with her own sweet essence.

He let Holly come to him. All she needed to do was angle her head ever so slightly and let him take her mouth.

She was slow in doing so. When she finally looked at him, open and trusting, he framed her face with his hands, and stared deeply into her eyes. He felt her tremble and knew she feared as much as wanted him.

Anticipation quickened their heartbeats, thrummed in their blood. Their attraction was undeniable. He knew one kiss wouldn't be enough. Once their tongues tangled, their bodies would heat, grow restless, and he'd want to take her against the garage wall.

Something inside him wouldn't allow a zipper-down quickie with this woman. She deserved more. Holly needed a man to take his time with her, to make her feel desirable, cherished, a man who'd be faithful. Alex didn't qualify on any level.

Every time he looked at her, touched her, her warmth and Christmas spirit rubbed off on him. The people of Holiday were merry and embraced the season. They'd welcomed him, even as he counted down the hours, eager to leave.

Miami called. Blond twins awaited him at a cabana by the pool. He and his fellow Rogues would go wild; it would be the blowout of the decade.

Baseball, body shots, and booty made up his life.

Not a nutcracker, ice cream, and Christmas cookies.

His conscience spoke louder than his need for sex. Kissing Holly would mean more to her than it did to him. She deserved promises and commitment. Alex had a phobia for both.

Reason and respect warred with the desire to kiss her senseless, and, in the end, Alex was honorable. His lips touched hers in a kiss that lasted less than a second. Holly didn't have time to close her eyes.

Her gaze widened now as she stared at him; her lips were parted, her cheeks a flustered pink. The moment stretched, turned awkward.

"You deserve a refund," she eventually managed, her voice soft, unsure, as she reached into the back pocket of her jeans and returned his fifty.

He refused the money. "Give it to charity."

A heartbeat of silence passed before she licked her lips and asked, "Is that how you see me, Alex, as a charity case?"

"I wanted to kiss you." He owed her that much.

"But you stopped."

She looked hurt, Alex saw, and her pain made his chest ache. "You're decent, kind, and deserve better."

"Better than what?" Confusion darkened her brown eyes.

"Better than me." The words were tough to say.

"I damn sure do." Her agreement set him back. "A kiss under the mistletoe is holiday fun. No one takes it too seriously. You, however, look like you're standing before a judge."

"You look nothing like Judge Hathaway." The judge had a receding hairline, a sun-weathered face, and a hostile disposition.

"Look closer." She gave him her profile. "Some say I have his nose."

She had his nose? "You're related?"

"He's my uncle."

Chapter Five

Holly's admission punched Alex in the gut. He was so startled he forgot to breathe. He choked, coughed, studied her closely. She'd claimed Hank as her cousin—they both had blondish hair and brown eyes—yet the judge was another matter. Hathaway had authority: he'd stuffed Alex in a loft above the Jingle Bell Shop and court ordered community hours.

Had Holly spoken in his defense, Alex was certain the judge would have shortened his time. He'd have burned the itchy velvet Santa suit and never bellowed another ho-ho-ho.

He could be in Miami right now. The thought made him a little crazy. Instead of partying with bikinied babes, he presently stood beneath a hand-crafted mistletoe arch, bone hard yet bowing out, being honorable.

He raked one hand through his hair. "The judge is your uncle?" It was damn hard to believe. "You never reported my good behavior?"

"*Good behavior?*" She rolled her eyes. "You've been difficult, arrogant, ornery, and horny."

"I'm always horny." That was nothing new.

"You've been a halfhearted Santa at best," she said. "You have no holiday spirit."

"I baked Christmas cookies."

"You *ate* the cookies faster than the grannies could bake them. Your decorating efforts were X-rated."

Alex crossed his arms over his chest, shifted his weight from one leg to the other. "We could walk into the courthouse tomorrow and you could tell the judge I've been a good boy. He'd then release me on the spot. You wouldn't have to deal with me ever again."

"I could never lie to my uncle."

"Not even a little white lie?"

"A lie is a lie, Alex."

Damn. "You're cracking my nuts."

"That's my seasonal job."

"Look." He went for charming and persuasive. "If I don't complain for an entire day, will you get me released so I can be in Miami on Christmas Eve?"

"You sound like you're serving a jail sentence."

That was what it felt like to him. "Do we have a deal?"

Holly McIntyre released a slow, soft breath. She had the power to terminate his community hours right that second if she so chose, yet a part of her hated to see him go.

Alex was too handsome, too rich, too egotistical for her liking. She did, however, believe a good man hid behind his humbug and horniness. She had one day to draw it out.

She held out her garden-gloved hand. "Not one complaint, Alex, and we have a deal."

He took her hand, tugged her close, and dropped a light kiss on her forehead. He was all smiles now, his eagerness to behave almost comical.

Holly pulled off her gloves and glanced at her watch. "It's late, time for bed," she said.

"I can't wait to return to the loft and curl up in bed."

She knew the bed was too small for his big body. She'd seen him working the kinks from his neck and shoulders each day. She'd watched him stretch, caught his muscles ripple. He had a killer body.

"Get in my car and I'll drive you home," she offered.

"The Volkswagen's about the size of my bedroom."

Twelve hours later, Alex was again dressed as Santa and Holly wore the painted wooden head of the nutcracker. Alex had wakened cheerful for a change. He'd grinned through two cups of black coffee and four donuts.

Holly was surprised his red velvet outfit still fit. The man liked his sweets.

He blew her away with his boisterous ho-ho-ho. While he still looked more Chippendale than North Pole, he welcomed the kids with open arms. A few even got hugs.

The man could behave, she noted, when he wanted to. He just needed the proper incentive. If leaving town early meant so much to him, she'd keep her word and talk to her uncle.

Judge Hathaway would be lenient. Despite what Alex thought, her uncle was a fair man. He'd sat on the bench for forty years, admired and respected by the community.

The excited mood in the mall turned giddy when her cousin Hank delivered the mistletoe arch. People started giggling, gossiping, and going in for kisses. A lot of money would be raised for charity.

At the end of Alex's shift, a third line had formed near the arch, all single women. "What's going on?" he asked as he pushed off his chair.

Holly lowered the jaw on her wooden head and explained, "The ladies are waiting to kiss Santa."

Alex's surprise was almost comical. The man's concentration had been on the kids and not on the females dying to kiss him. There was even a set of triplets.

He looked at Holly. "Can I take off my beard?"

"Not in front of the children."

"I'll get lipstick on my mustache."

Her heart clenched. "Santa's known for pecks on the cheek. You don't have to French them."

"Do I get extra Brownie points for no tongue?"

"Behave, Alex." Her tone was stern.

"Got a breath mint?"

She held up a candy cane. "Peppermint?"

"Gag me with a spoon." He broke off a tiny bite, freshened his mouth. "Let the kissing begin."

Holly's day was done, yet instead of changing into her street clothes, she stood off to the side and watched as Alex Boxer satisfied sixty women. He'd jacked the price to five dollars a kiss, all in the name of charity. No one seemed to mind.

The line moved snail slow as he flattered and teased every female. Most of the ladies were blushing as they rose on tiptoe for their Santa smooch.

Alex had been right, Holly noted, the longer he kissed, the more lipstick rubbed off on his mustache and beard. A few ladies tugged his whiskers aside to take his mouth more deeply. Holly wondered about the best way to remove shades of hot pink and climax red from the fake white curls.

A sigh escaped, and her heart turned suddenly sad. An unexpected emptiness expanded within her chest.

She felt half, not whole. The sensation made her body ache.

She was witnessing what Alex Boxer did best: he charmed women and made them want him. Dozens had kissed him, then gotten back in line, anticipating a second time. The five dollars appeared money well spent.

Twenty minutes into the kissing and Holly'd had enough. The nutcracker costume was hot; the wooden head weighed heavy on her shoulders. The time had come to deliver the holiday baskets that Hank had stacked and packed in her car after he'd set up the arch. She would make the rounds without Alex.

Even if the deliveries took longer than expected, Christmas carols would be sung late into the night at the community center. Agnes Smith would play the piano until her carpal tunnel acted up.

Back in the Jingle Bell Shop, Holly took in the silence. The storage room was quiet without Alex. She missed his growling, grumpiness, and sex appeal. He was easy on the eyes, and his suggestive humor turned her on. She liked the way he kissed.

He'd soon be leaving. She already missed him. Holiday wouldn't be the same without him.

She struggled with the wooden head and set it on a corner table. She unbuttoned her red jacket and let it hang open. She'd just kicked off her gold-glitter boots and dropped her baggy black pants when the side door flew open and Santa charged in.

His gaze swept her, and his grin turned naughty. "I'm suddenly jolly."

She clutched the lapels of the jacket together but

had nothing to cover her legs. His once-over skimmed from her peach bikini to her painted toes.

After gazing his fill, he jerked off his beard, dragging air into his lungs. "Between the closed-mouth kisses and mustache hair up my nose, I damn near suffocated."

He looked pale, miserable, and sweaty.

Holly had never felt happier in her life. "How much money did you raise?" she asked.

Alex did a mental count. "Hank closed the arch at forty kisses. We made two hundred dollars."

"There must have been some disappointed women."

"My lips got tired." He rubbed the back of his hand over his mouth. "The ladies kissed, then whispered their Christmas list. They wanted me to come down their chimney."

He peeled off his skull cap, ran a hand through his hair. "No more kissing for today. We have holiday baskets to deliver—that takes precedence."

His words surprised her. "You remembered?"

"I would never forget what's important to you."

The man was being considerate. His expression revealed the depth of his sincerity. Gone was the cockiness, the arrogance, the swagger. For the moment, he appeared conscientious and helpful.

Her heart skipped two beats, and she softened to him. Alex being nice was new to her. She wasn't quite certain how to take him at his best.

"Go shower. We need to hit the road in twenty minutes," she told him.

He turned, took the stairs to the loft two at a time. A quarter of an hour later, a damp-haired Alex joined her once again. A brown button-down shirt stretched

over his wide shoulders; a pair of khakis ran his long
legs. Sperry Top-siders fit his feet.

He looked cool, desirable, and all male.

His gaze narrowed as he took her in. "You look like
Mrs. Claus."

She patted her white wig, adjusted her granny glasses.
Her dress was red and long sleeved and fashioned with
a white apron. She'd slipped on red tights and black ballet slippers.

"This time of year, Santa needs all the help he can
get," she said.

"Christmas is a real ball-buster," he agreed.

"You should enjoy and embrace the season, Alex.
It's special."

He didn't look convinced.

She pulled her car keys from the pocket of her
apron, dropped them on his palm. "You drive, I'll deliver. I'll give you directions as we go."

"I can turn left or right."

Alex Boxer had never driven a Volkswagen Bug, and
it took him a few adjustments to settle his big body in
the seat. The VW had the chug-chug of the Little Engine that Could, not the silky smooth ride of his Saleen
S7. If all went well with the judge, he'd soon be back
behind the wheel of his sports car. Zoom, zoom, zoom.

He'd be leaving any day now, and the realization
that he'd miss Holly twisted his testicles as only a nutcracker could do.

She had a way of making people smile, he noticed, as
she slid from the VW to deliver the sixth basket of the
afternoon. The door to the small, boxy house swung
wide, and the nursery rhyme "The Old Woman Who
Lived in a Shoe" came to mind.

Eight children poured out, followed by one tired-looking mother. Holly gave the family three big baskets of cookies and reindeer dust. The youngest child immediately spread a runway for Santa, and the lawn soon glittered brightly.

"What's their story?" Alex asked once Mrs. Claus returned to the vehicle.

"Mary Lambert has three children of her own and went on to adopt the remaining five when her sister and brother-in-law were killed in a car accident," she explained. "Her husband, Jake, works construction and goes where the pay is highest. Right now he's building condominiums sixty miles north on Vero Beach. He drives home every night to be with his family."

Alex's hands tightened on the steering wheel. "That's a tough way to survive."

"People do what they have to do," she said softly. "Jake's a good man. He took on the responsibility of two families when he was twenty-five."

Alex was older than Jake, yet his deepest thoughts ran to twin blondes and a case of beer. The freedom of the road beckoned him. He took care of himself, but no one else.

He shifted uncomfortably on the seat, felt the need to do something nice for someone other than himself. He looked at Holly and asked, "Is there anything I can do for the Lamberts?"

"It's nice of you to ask, but Jake would never accept charity. He's too proud." Holly slipped off her granny glasses, looked him in the eye. "Holiday takes care of its own. When the kids come into my ice cream shop, I give them each an extra scoop with sprinkles. At the grocery store, the owner slips Mary an envelope of coupons. The doctor always has pharmaceutical samples of medication to give out when the kids are sick. Should their car break down, the mechanic charges for parts, not labor. We all look out for one another."

He was suddenly at a loss. "I'd still like to do something."

"Why, Alex?"

Because I have a million dollars in the bank and this family is living hand-to-mouth. "Seems the right thing to do, Holly."

He heard her swallow, saw her eyes well up. She was looking at him differently now, as if seeing him for the first time. He didn't want her seeing more in him than was actually there, so he shrugged. "I can be a good guy sometimes."

"It's called Christmas spirit," she told him. "It's far better to give than to receive."

She surprised him then by leaning across the seat and kissing him full on the mouth. He'd expected the cheek, but he'd gotten lips, and he took advantage of her gratitude.

He kept the kiss soft, light, easy, one between friends, until she sighed and a sense of belonging warmed his heart.

Alex liked kissing her. There was nothing wild or demanding in their exchange, no straining to tear off their clothes. There was a sweet innocence about Holly. She cared and shared, and allowed him into her life.

It felt right to take his time, to learn what she liked and to give what she needed. The experience was new, exciting, seductive. Holly McIntyre was a natural high.

There was honesty in her kiss. She saw beyond his

status as the Most Valuable Player of the World Series. She didn't want to bask in his fame or count the zeroes in his bank account. She was into him, into Alex Boxer, the man. Her kiss told him so.

He wished they'd met under different circumstances. He'd served his community hours with a royal chip on his shoulder, giving her nothing but grief. He had a few regrets . . .

A sudden knock on the car window made them both jump. Alex hit his head on the ceiling of the Bug, and Holly scrambled to find her granny glasses.

He could barely contain his smile when he met the wide-eyed stare of a little girl, no older than six, whose freckled nose now pressed the driver-side glass.

"Mommy, some man's kissing Mrs. Claus!" The girl's shout echoed through the entire neighborhood.

Alex gave Holly time to straighten her wig before he rolled down the window and white-lied, "Mrs. Claus and I shared a sugar cookie. I was wiping crumbs from the corner of her mouth."

"With your tongue?" The kid had a set of lungs on her. She needed to learn how to whisper.

He looked toward the house. "Where's your mother?"

"Making dinner."

"Maybe you should offer to help," suggested Holly.

The girl produced a five-dollar bill. "Mommy sent me to the store for milk."

"Can we give you a ride?" Holly offered.

The girl shook her head. "I like to walk. I count cracks in the sidewalk, and halfway down the block, Peach Corbett's drawn hopscotch in orange chalk."

Holly gave the girl a wave. "Take care, sweetie."

The girl sent Alex a meaningful look. "Only Santa should be kissing Mrs. Claus." And she took off.

"Guess she told me." Alex chuckled.

They continued with their deliveries. As they drove through the neighborhood, he took note of the holiday yard decorations. There were no Frosty the Snowmen, no ice sculptures.

Instead, people strung Christmas lights on their palm trees, hung Santa caps on their pink flamingo lawn ornaments. One house showcased elf statues in swim suits beside a kiddie pool, while another had straw reindeer with red bows tied to their antlers lining the driveway. Florida had its own sense of Christmas.

Alex watched as each family greeted Holly as if she were an angel. Everyone hugged and clung to her and thanked her profusely.

A sense of purpose warmed him from the inside out. Today was all about sharing, connecting, and making a difference. He got into the groove, hummed "Joy to the World."

Following their last delivery, Holly leaned back against the seat and sighed. Her shoulders sagged and tiredness showed in her eyes. Silence settled like an old friend between them. Alex had never felt so comfortable with a woman, so compatible.

Stifling a yawn, she slid off her white wig and granny glasses. "Thanks for your help."

"I make a great chauffeur."

"You're a good man, Alex Boxer."

Her words surprised him. Women had called him arrogant, cocky, sexy, and desirable, but never decent. He liked the fact that Holly thought well of him. He wasn't, however, certain he deserved her praise.

"I'm prone to be bad," he warned. "I can be selfish as hell, and I don't believe in monogamy."

"Then you've yet to sleep with the right woman."

Maybe, maybe not. He'd bed-hopped since he was sixteen. Relationships came and went. He liked one-nighters. Two weekends in a row gave him the willies. Dating someone for an entire month felt as suffocating as an engagement.

"Ready to sing some Christmas carols?" she asked.

"I'm not known for carrying a tune outside the shower," he admitted as he followed her directions to the community center.

The entire town had turned out to sing "Jingle Bells," Alex noted, as he scanned the meeting hall. A pianist pounded out the jolly rendition. Everyone from grandparents to babies shook bells in time to the music.

The song was loud and a little off-key, but no one seemed to care. It was all about smiles and spirit and being together.

Holly was immediately drawn into the crowd, while Alex edged back. He found a space against the far wall. He had no desire to be the center of attention, he only wanted to observe.

Someone handed him a paper cup with holiday fruit punch along with a frosted oatmeal-raisin cookie. He figured this was dinner.

During "O Christmas Tree," he spotted Holly surrounded by her friends and family. One of those relatives was her uncle. During a break in the music, Holly whispered in Judge Hathaway's ear. Alex instinctively knew she spoke on his behalf. She was asking her uncle to shorten his community hours by two days.

Hathaway rubbed the back of his neck and frowned. He turned to pin Alex with his darkest judicial stare.

A tall man passed in front of Holly and the judge, blocking Alex's view of Hathaway's reply. Alex had no idea whether her uncle nodded or shook his head. He'd have to wait for Holly to join him to get Hathaway's answer.

She came to him during "Silent Night." The room had grown still, the mood solemn, holy. The voices blended, and people reached out, held hands. Holly laced her fingers with his, her palm soft and warm. A sweet gesture, Alex thought, as he gently squeezed her hand.

Once the song ended, the crowd slowly dispersed, and Alex followed Holly back to her Volkswagen. He tossed her the keys, let her drive. Once inside the vehicle, she turned to him. A hint of sadness darkened her eyes before she straightened her shoulders and put on a stiff upper lip.

"The judge has pardoned you," she told him, "on the condition you play Santa for one more day. Afterward, you can pick up your sports car. You can be in Miami by early evening."

Freedom. Alex's heart beat with a sense of relief. He would soon be gone. No more sweaty, sticky red velvet Santa suit, no more peppermint, no more sleeping in a tiny loft meant for elves.

No more Holly.

His chest heaved and his stomach suddenly hurt; he felt a little nauseous. He should be shouting, pumping his arms, yet an unidentifiable loss settled in his chest, compelling him to breathe deeply.

He'd been in Holiday too long, he decided. He'd allowed the Christmas spirit to sink bone deep. He locked his jaw, forced his life back on track. Small town was not his style; he liked the restless pulse of bright lights and big cities. South Beach was calling his name.

"Thanks for pleading my case," he finally said.

It was the end of the road. Neither spoke until they reached the Jingle Bell Shop. It was Holly who broke the silence. "See you in the morning," she said as he got out of the VW. "Tomorrow will go fast, Alex. You'll be on your way in no time."

Alex's run as Santa ended with two kids peeing on his left leg, one right after the other. Holly had warned him it could happen, and it finally had, just as he was wrapping up the day. He couldn't wait to shed his Santa suit.

He stripped before her in the storeroom, down to his gray boxer briefs. He was hot, sweaty, and in desperate need of a shower. He wanted to talk to Holly before he left. She'd put up with him during Christmas week, even when he'd been an ass, which was all too often.

"You sticking around?" he asked.

She stood in her nutcracker outfit, minus the big wooden head. "I'll give you a ride to impound so you can pick up your car."

"Give me ten minutes." He took off for the loft.

Holly McIntyre felt her chest tighten. Her body suddenly ached, and she didn't have the energy to change into her street clothes. She'd drive Alex to the lot, then clean up afterward. Her cousin Hank had agreed to switch from Moose to Santa following Alex's departure.

She needed to stop off at the dry cleaners and have the costume cleaned; a trip to the grocery store was also necessary. She made a mental list of all she needed to accomplish. If she didn't stay busy, she'd crumble.

He came downstairs, handsome in a blue polo and jeans, an athletic bag in hand. She tried to smile but failed. She bit her bottom lip to keep it from trembling.

He looked down at her, his expression serious. "Thanks for tolerating me—you have the patience of a saint."

"It wasn't all bad," she said lightly. "Remember to slow for school zones."

His blue eyes darkened. "Had I not been stopped and sentenced, I'd never have known your town existed. I'd never have met you, Holly."

Community service hours had thrown them together. In a few short days, she'd come to understand his recklessness and vulnerabilities. She'd grown fond of the Richmond Rogue. He'd leave her with many holiday memories. He'd made an imprint on her soul.

"Maybe you could stop for ice cream on your return trip." She could only hope. "I'll have created new flavors—"

He shook his head. "I won't be back."

Her throat constricted, but somehow she managed to nod. Alex Boxer was going to drive out of her life for good. Their time had come to an end.

Silence traveled with them to impound, oppressive and suffocating. Holly could barely breathe by the time the cop on duty tossed Alex his car keys. The Saleen S7 looked like the kind of vehicle he would drive. It was sleek, hot, and seemed to exude the same restlessness she sensed in Alex.

The policeman slid the gate open, and Alex was free to go. He tossed his athletic bag onto the passenger seat, then looked at her questioningly. "Hug?" His voice was deep, low, hopeful.

She couldn't resist the lure of having his arms around her one final time. She stepped to his body, and he held her tight. His warm breath fanned her forehead, and the rise and fall of his chest seemed erratic for an athlete.

She wanted to climb into his shirt pocket, hear his heart beat, stay with him a little longer. For a few seconds, she allowed herself to believe he wouldn't let her go.

In the end, he was the first to break their embrace.

He kissed her cheek. "Merry Christmas, Holly."

"To you as well, Alex."

He swung up the gull-wing door, slid behind the wheel, then closed himself inside. He revved the engine, and she stepped back, out of his way.

His gaze remained on her as he drove the car out into the sunshine. She managed a small wave. How pathetic she must look, standing in her nutcracker outfit, watching the taillights on his sports car disappear down the road.

Look back, turn around, she silently prayed.

He kept right on driving.

She'd seen the last of Alex Boxer.

Her heart splintered into a thousand pieces.

Holly survived the next two days on autopilot. Hank made a great Santa Claus. He was born to ho-ho-ho. The mood was festive and cheerful as shoppers scrambled for last-minute gifts.

She was grateful for the nutcracker's big wooden head. Publicly, she didn't have to smile. No one had to know that Alex's departure had flattened her.

"Are you attending the Schaffers' party?" her cousin asked after the last child in line had told Hank his Christmas list. The mall lights dimmed, and the shops would soon be closing.

She lowered the lever on her wooden head. "I don't think so. It's been a long week."

"Alex Boxer could tire the Energizer Bunny."

"I fell in love with him." She and her cousin had grown up close. She'd always trusted him with her secrets.

"I was certain he cared for you, too." Hank was sympathetic. "Alex got jealous the night we built the mistletoe arch when he saw me as a rival."

"I wasn't special, just the challenge of the moment."

"Alex is a professional ballplayer," Hank said. "He's surrounded by women, but not every woman's you, Holly. Holiday rubs off on a person."

"Alex told me that he wouldn't be back."

"Never say never." Hank took off to change clothes.

Holly struggled with her wooden head and set it on the floor. She then crossed to the high-back Santa chair, decorated in corduroy and wrapped with garlands and tiny white lights. She sat down slowly. Even after Hank had spent the day in it as Santa, she still sensed Alex's presence. He remained larger than life.

It was Christmas Eve, and the maintenance crew was quick to dismantle Santa's Workshop. The men wanted to get home to their families.

The mock snow was swept away and the floor

mopped. The air-conditioning and Muzak were cut off. Only the red emergency lights lent life to the mall.

"I'd like to sit a few minutes," Holly said to the head custodian. "I have a key, so I can lock up when I leave through the Jingle Bell Shop."

"Need an ear?" the man asked.

"Thanks, but no." Words couldn't describe a broken heart. The ache was dull, numbing, exhausting. It hurt to breathe, to swallow, to lift a finger.

Her only ambition was to sit in the chair, close her eyes, and forget. Time passed, and she didn't care.

"What have you done to me, woman?"

She jerked so abruptly, she nearly fell off the chair. She blinked, believing Alex Boxer no more than a dream. Peering into the shadows, she found him very real. He stood just inside the door, looking disheveled and wild-eyed.

"I couldn't get you out of my head." His voice was deep, dark, agitated. "Everywhere I looked, I kept seeing you in my rear view mirror, standing on the sidewalk in that nutcracker outfit, looking so damn sad."

Irritation poured off him. "I arrived in South Beach to busty blondes and body shots. I hit clubs, went skinny dipping, and tried to drink you out of my mind." He raked his hand through his hair, glared at her. "You wouldn't leave."

"Why did you come back?" She was afraid to ask.

"I forgot my damn toothbrush."

She'd been to the loft, had seen it on the bathroom counter beside the damp towel left from his shower. "They don't sell toothbrushes in Miami?"

"Not the kind I like."

His toothbrush was a Colgate, hard-bristled with a flexible head. It could have been purchased in any drug store or grocery for less than three dollars.

She eased off the chair, locked her knees so they wouldn't buckle. "A man can't live without his favorite toothbrush."

"Nor can he live without the woman he loves."

He loved her. "Are you sure?"

"I need you the same way I need baseball," he confessed. "You're both my life."

Still, she hesitated. "We've just met, Alex."

"Time can't dictate how the heart feels." Quite poetic for a ballplayer. "Give us a chance, Holly. We'll make it work."

"I believe in you, in us."

He crossed to her then, took her hand and led her down the hallway to the storeroom. Once inside, they climbed the staircase together. The loft was small, the single window a tiny triangle.

Twilight faded to black.

A crescent moon claimed the night.

Alex smiled at her, and she grew warm inside. He had the experience. She let him lead.

Their shadows merged against the wall as he caught her to him, and two became one. They took pleasure in their closeness.

Her fingers gently stroked his face.

His thumb grazed her lower lip.

He watched her with a wanting that stole the breath from her lungs. He held her transfixed.

One side of his mouth lifted. "I've envisioned you in a satin teddy, yet that damn nutcracker costume does it for me tonight."

He massaged her from shoulder to spine, banishing her tension. Her body turned liquid.

"I want to do everything for you, do everything to you," he whispered near her ear.

She pulled herself tighter against him.

His stubble abraded her cheek, and the slow scrape of his teeth along her jaw raised goose bumps. He kissed her chin, her throat, then finally her lips.

It was a kiss to remember, one where tender turned fierce with a slant of his lips. Alex drew her outside of herself and into him. There was neither awkwardness nor indecision. He made her thoughts turn sinful. She wanted him more than she'd ever wanted anything else in her life.

She clutched his shoulders, scored her nails through his knit shirt. His muscles bunched, and his breathing deepened. His mouth burned against hers, the play of his tongue primal, masterful.

She felt his desire all the way to her soul.

Anticipation filled her. Their affection was as open and magnetic as their attraction. The air snapped, sparked, sizzled with life.

Long before he undressed her, he toyed with the gold buttons on her jacket. The simulated twist and tug sensitized and tightened her nipples. Her breasts ached for his attention.

He took his sweet time, drawing out each moment until the air grew thin and their breathing became labored. Folding back the lapels, he stared fully at her breasts.

"Beautiful," he admired.

The heat in his eyes made her pulse skip. Warmth worked up her spine the same instant shivers shot down.

Her skin tingled with awareness so intense her body pulsed from it. She craved this man.

He parted the front clasp on her white lacy bra and the straps slipped off her shoulders. He palmed her breasts until her heart pounded in her ears. She could no longer think, let alone breathe.

His fingers skimmed down her ribs, past the silken dip of her navel, and curved over her hip. Locating the side zipper on her baggy black pants, he slid the metal tab down. Her pants pooled at her feet. Her white bikini panties quickly followed.

His hand moved within the shadows of her thighs, and he parted her legs. He found her wet and ready for him.

He whipped off his clothes with equal speed. He was even faster at snagging a condom from the pocket of his pants and sheathing himself. He took her to his mattress, was all over her. They became a tangle of limbs.

She touched, stroked, clawed at his back. His shoulders were wide, his chest powerful. His abdomen rippled with muscle. His legs stretched long, and his feet were large. His sex, totally impressive.

He covered her body, and she savored his weight.

Her knees parted, and she lifted her hips against him.

He thrust, streamlined into her.

Skin against skin, they mated.

Slow was not an option. Their desire demanded release. The moment was upon them.

His rhythm soon built, and her hips moved furiously.

The mad thump of her heart matched his own.

Heightening pleasure arced through her body.

And Alex pushed her over the edge.

A bolt of white heat ricocheted off him and into her. Their bodies twisted and shook with release. Blissful aftershocks left them sated. Nothing had ever felt so good.

Alex rolled to his side and pulled her close. She rested her head on his chest, just above his heart. He traced her shoulder with his fingertips.

She closed her eyes and smiled when she heard him sigh. "Ho-fuckin'-ho."

Naughty or Nice

SANDRA HILL

When my son Rob was a little boy, he asked, "Mommy, are Santa Claus and God the same person?"

"I like to think they are," I said.

So, this book's dedicated to Rob—my rebel—who tries so hard to be a "bad boy," but will always be a Santa at heart.

Chapter One

Only winos and weirdos shopped at the Piggly Jiggly Supermarket after midnight. But tonight there was also a thirty-year-old desperate woman dressed as Santa Claus.

Correction. A thirty-year-old desperate woman dressed as Santa Claus, *packing a forty-five in her pocket.*

As she waited her turn at the service desk, Jessica Jones grimaced at the ludicrous situation she found herself in. It was the "Christmas Curse," of course. For as long as she could remember, something really awful happened to her during the Christmas season.

She'd thought she was over the bad luck for this year when her fiance, Burton Richards, dumped her two weeks ago, but uh-uh, the fix she found herself in now was even worse. A definite ten on the Christmas Curse Richter scale.

Jessica hitched up the wide belt beneath her sagging Santa stomach with determination. *Like the old song goes, I'm not gonna take it anymore.*

A very tall, broad-shouldered woman walked by, swishing her hips in a red nylon mini-dress—not a good choice for a cold Philadelphia winter. Clearly a male, the cross-dresser was probably a prostitute. She . . . he . . . smiled at Jessica and made a kissy sound through thickly painted lips. *Criminey, Santa was be-ing propositioned.*

Jessica shook her head vehemently.

The hooker shrugged as if to say it was Santa's loss, and walked over to the cigarette rack.

Good grief!

An old man standing in front of her, waiting to have his welfare check cashed, turned and slurred out, "Wha'dja say?"

His boozy breath almost knocked Jessica over. Her knees were knocking together as it was, and her hands, were shaking so badly she had to stuff them in her wide pockets. She shifted the pillow higher and felt with her right hand for the pistol nestled against her thigh. *Help! This is not happening.* "Nothing. Just get moving, okay?"

"Some grumpy Santa you are," he muttered.

Her eyes darted about the area, casing the automatic exit doors a few feet away. She was the last person in line. The only other person nearby was a gorgeous guy with a light brown ponytail, leaning lazily against the wall, scratching off a lottery ticket. Amazingly, he wore a Santa Claus outfit, too, but his hat, beard, and wig were stuffed in his belt.

He resembled Brad Pitt, but older . . . and better.

The Brad-Santa glanced up, gave her a quick once-over, and winked.

Darn! Caught smack dab in the middle of a leer! Her heated face probably matched her suit. Jessica lifted her chin haughtily and pretended she'd been looking at something else, like the bare wall behind him. *Hah! Who am I fooling? And, Lordy, haven't I had enough of womanizing egomaniacs in my life? I can't believe I'm about to perform a criminal act, and I'm ogling some lech in costume.*

The lech laughed.

She was about to snarl, but it was her turn at the service desk.

Taking a deep breath, she stepped forward. "Put up your hands. This is a stick-out," she yelled in a too-shrill voice to the gum-chewing guy behind the counter whose name badge read "Frank Brown, Assistant Manager." He gulped and swallowed his gum with a squeak.

Brad peered up at her with faint interest through eyelashes that could double for brown feather dusters. "Stick-up, baby. You mean stick-up," he offered helpfully, his lips twitching with amusement.

"This is a stick-up, Frank," she amended, brandishing her gun. *Thank heavens the thing isn't loaded or I'd be in big trouble.* Pointing the weapon at the smiling Santa, she ordered, "And don't give me any of your lip, buster, or I'll wipe you up, too."

"Wipe out, not wipe up," the long, tall Santa laughed.

His ridicule made her so mad she clenched her fingers over the gun, which, to her amazement, went off accidentally. And, holy cow, it shot a big hole in the Pepsi machine about three feet to the right of the jerk's ear.

Her heart slam-dunked to her throat. *Oh, no! Julio told me it wasn't loaded. I even shot it once in the woods and nothing happened. It can't have real bullets in it. It can't.*

She took another peek at the Pepsi machine. There was an opening the size of a basketball in the glass front. The bullets were real, all right. *Oh, geez!*

Frank screamed.

The hooker called out, "Way to go, big boy! Ho, ho, ho!"

And the Brad-Santa ducked.

Through her peripheral vision she saw a young girl at a cash register, a bag boy, and two customers throw themselves to the floor.

One man cried out, "Oh, God! This is probably one of those maniac postal workers taking us hostage. I'll miss Christmas with my kids." Then as an afterthought he added, "Hallelujah!"

"Do you think we'll make CBS News?" the female clerk asked. "Wouldn't ya just know this would happen on a bad hair day?"

"Shit!" Brad exclaimed, his lottery ticket fluttering to the floor. "Are you nuts?"

Her heart was slowing down to a gallop. *Okay, that was a close call, but I'm okay now. No serious damage. I can mail a check next week. Calm down.* Pretending that her shot had been deliberate, she threw her shoulders back and aimed directly at the shivering assistant manager, being careful not to touch the trigger again. "You're next, Frank, *if* you don't give me my money."

"An . . . anyth . . . anything you want," Frank sputtered. He started to stuff bills in a cloth bag.

"No!" Jessica interrupted sharply. "Just thirty-nine ninety-five."

"Wh-what?" Frank choked out.

Everyone was gawking at her like she was a psycho. She was, of course. "You heard me. Give me thirty-nine dollars and ninety-five cents. And make it quick. I've got an itchy thumb here."

"Trigger finger, sweetheart," the smirking Santa

corrected again, snickering. "You gotta get the lingo right if you're gonna follow a life of crime."

She frowned in confusion.

"It's an itchy *trigger finger*, not thumb," he explained patiently.

"Thumb, trigger finger, big difference!" she said, waving her gun dismissively at him. "And stop interrupting me."

"Hey, be careful where you aim that thing," he growled, edging toward her. He probably planned to tackle her. Not a good idea when the curse was in motion.

"Stay where you are," she warned, raising the revolver higher.

He stopped, eyeing her warily.

"Thirty-nine ninety-five!" Frank squealed. "Hey, I know who you are. You're that whacko nun who came in here last week demanding her money back for a defective Buzzy Burp Bear."

"I am *not* a nun," Jessica said weakly.

"Piggly Jiggly has a two-week refund policy," Frank explained to the wino and Brad, "and the damn nun . . . I mean, the nun . . . had it for a month before she brought it back. Said it wouldn't burp. Hah! She'd probably been playing it nonstop all that time and wore out its burp battery."

"A nun?" the wino whimpered, backing away from her as if she had something contagious.

"I am *not* a nun."

"Hot damn!" the Santa-with-an-attitude whistled. "A holy bandit!"

"I am *not* a nun."

"Clara . . . that's your name, Sister Clara," Frank

chortled. "Boy, you are in *big* trouble, lady. I'm gonna report you to the police . . . and the Pope."

"I'm not Clara, I tell you. I'm . . . I'm Clara's hit guy." She realized her mistake at once, and before Santa could pipe in, she corrected herself, "Hit man." Then she added, "And I'm not in big trouble, because you owe me . . . I mean, Clara . . . the money for the stupid bear, and that's not stealing. And I'm going to pay for the damage to the Pepsi machine. So there!"

"And here I thought I was gonna have a dull Saturday night. This is more fun than playing the lottery, or doing laundry."

Jessica gave the crud-that-would-be-a-heartthrob a withering appraisal. As if he had any difficulty filling his nights! He probably had women lined up with numbers. He probably drove a Porsche. He probably had a penthouse. He probably posed for centerfolds.

Unfortunately, she knew a few guys just like him; in fact, one of them had been her Christmas Curse six years ago. Except he'd looked like Mel Gibson with a paunch.

The guy's arms were folded casually across his chest and he grinned from ear to ear. Even with the padded Santa suit, she just knew he didn't have a paunch.

"Give me my money," she demanded, turning back to Frank as she felt the situation deteriorating around her. "I'm not leaving without my thirty-nine ninety-five, dammit."

"Tsk-tsk, nuns aren't supposed to swear," Santa chided.

"Tell it to your reindeer, bozo."

She had no choice then, she had to show she was in control. She aimed for the Little Debbie cupcake stand over to the left. Although she fired two shots, the second one came up blank. That must mean the gun was empty.

But, more important, instead of hitting Little Debbie, she winged the pyramid display of Buzzy Burp Bears. Immediately brown fur flew everywhere as stuffed animals careened to the floor and a chorus of bears began burping to the tune of "Jingle Bells." It was a scene out of the Three Stooges, or her worst nightmare.

Jessica groaned.

Everyone's mouth dropped open in surprise, including the jerk Santa's.

"Now . . . give . . . me . . . my . . . thirty-nine ninety-five," she spat out evenly in her best Clint Eastwood voice, and tacked on in a gravelly rumble, just for effect, "or make my day."

Frank didn't hesitate. With quivering fingers he counted out the bills and coins and shoved them across the counter.

She put the money in her pocket and was about to leave when she saw a flash of dark blue race through the exit door. *A security guard.* Immediately a loud alarm began to ring throughout the store. *Oh, great! What should I do? What should I do?*

Jessica tried to think what a genuine robber might do. *A hostage. I need a hostage.* Quickly Jessica scanned her possibilities: Frank, the wino, the cross-dresser, the sales clerk, the two customers, or Brad Pitt.

"You're coming with me," she yelled at good ol' Brad.

"No, I'm not," he said, backing up.

"Yes, you are. You're my hostage." She leveled her

now-empty gun at him—first, at his chest, then lower. Yep, a guy like him would care more about protecting those assets than his heart. Her upper lip curled with disdain. "Listen, Mr. Legend-of-the-Fall, I'm in the middle of my Christmas Curse, and I'd hate to see your dead body be my bad luck this year."

"Curse?" Brad barked with disbelief. "You're pulling a heist because of PMS?"

She blinked at him with confusion. "Oh, you idiot! Not that kind of curse. My Christmas Curse is the real kind—black magic, evil eyes, that sort of thing."

"Give me a break!"

"Really. My parents died in an automobile accident on December twentieth when I was ten. The following yule season, I was in the foster home from hell. I broke my leg on Christmas Eve when I was twenty."

"Coincidences."

"Oh, yeah? Then how about the time my dog Fred impregnated a pedigree poodle at that fancy private kennel five years ago, even though he was fixed? That curse cost me a thousand dollars in legal fines."

"Apparently Fred's fix-job leaked." His hazel eyes twinkled with humor.

She sliced him a sneer of disgust. "I will never forget my Christmas-party blind date last year with the guy who arrived wearing a plaid hunting cap with ear flaps. The wheels of his pickup truck were so high I had a nosebleed for a week."

"I once had a blind date with a girl who had tattoos on three-fourths of her body," he contributed irrelevantly. "Does that qualify as a curse?"

"Quit stalling," she ordered, realizing that he was trying to keep her talking until the police arrived.

Even though she knew her bullets were gone, her hand still shook when she raised the gun in a threatening manner.

He said a foul word under his breath as his eyes darted to her trembling fingers. She could practically see the gears grinding in his chauvinistic brain. He was probably worrying about her panicking, or her fingers slipping.

Raising his arms above his head, Brad surrendered. "All right, all right, take it easy, babe. I'm all yours." It was a real Kodak moment.

Actually, there was probably a security camera filming it for posterity. But she couldn't think about that now. With the barrel of her pistol pressed into the back of the guy's neck, she pushed him forward through the doors, yelling over her shoulder, "If anyone follows me, this creep is dead. Do you hear me?"

At first, Luke Carter had been amused by Dirty Harriet. But not anymore. He walked compliantly out of the grocery store, his arms upraised, a gun crammed into his nape, but he was really, *really* pissed. It was humiliating for a man of his background to be kidnapped by a dingbat Santa.

And he just knew that the six o'clock news tomorrow was going to have a stillframe from the security tape of Santa being taken hostage by Santa. The news media would make him the laughing stock of the country.

Luke could have taken the woman down in a flash . . . in the beginning . . . before she'd started ripping out bullets. Hell, he was a bodyguard. And he was wearing a bulletproof vest, having just come off of an assignment. It was his job to disarm potential political assassins or crazy celebrity fans. He'd been trained in the CIA, and had done very well these past five years, thank you very much, operating his own private bodyguard business, "Watchdogs, Inc."

But the worst danger in the security business was a looney-bird. And if a woman—who might, indeed, be a nun—dressed as Santa Claus, wielding a forty-five, ranting about Christmas Curses, and robbing a supermarket for thirty-nine dollars and ninety-five cents wasn't a looney-bird, he didn't know what was.

It was all his sister's fault, and he was going to tell her so, too . . . *if* he was alive after tonight. Since he'd already rented the Santa outfit for his gig protecting Janet Jackson at her concert today at the Spectrum in South Philly, Ellie had talked him into playing the jolly ol' fellow for her third graders' Christmas party afterward. It had seemed reasonable to zip on over to the elementary school where Ellie taught, and it had been fun, too.

Later they'd gone out for pizza and she'd berated him ad nauseam about the dismal state of his personal life. Too many women—"bimbos" was her exact word; no commitments—"How long are you going to mourn Ginny? She's been dead five years"; his biological clock ticking away with no children in sight—"Men don't have biological clocks," he'd pointed out; dirty laundry up the kazoo—okay, she had a point about the laundry piled up in the back of his car; and on, and on, and on. So Ellie was responsible for his present predicament. If not for her nagging, he never would have come out at midnight to do his laundry and met Ms. Psycho Santa.

"Where to, babe?" he asked with a sigh of resignation. "Where'd you park the sled?"

Ms. Santa hesitated, glancing toward a van hidden around the side of the mall behind a dumpster. Emblazoned across its sides was the logo "Clara's House." *Hell, she must be a for-real nun, like that Frank character said.*

He immediately made a mental revision in his strategy. Taking the perp down at the first opportunity had been his original plan. He'd been unconcerned about whether the weird woman got hurt in the process.

But he couldn't in good conscience risk taking out a nun. His sister would never forgive him. The news media would have a field day. His business would be shot to hell.

Besides, she was kinda cute.

"Where's your car?" she asked, biting her full bottom lip—a nervous habit he'd noticed right from the start, which only called attention to her puffy, very kissable mouth. "The van's too easy to follow. And stop jerking around so much. I don't want to shoot you accidentally."

"How about not-so-accidentally?"

"Don't tempt me."

Man, oh, man, she reminded him of one of those "Magic Eye" pictures. Once you saw the hidden image, you couldn't stop looking at it. Her lips were like that. Now that his splintering brain registered how sensual her lips were, they drew his eyes like a magnet. *Maybe I inhaled too many bleach fumes tonight.*

"My car's over here," he said, chastising himself silently for his wandering mind as he indicated a metallic gray Bronco across the empty parking lot, "but, listen, I left all my clothes in the dryer over at the Suds 'n Duds." He pointed to the laundromat down a little ways in the strip mall. "That's why I was in the supermarket. I needed quarters for the machine, and that slimeball assistant manager at the supermarket wouldn't give me any change unless I bought something. So I got a lottery ticket. Hey, I left my ticket back on the floor. Maybe I'm a millionaire. We should go back and check." He was deliberately babbling away in hopes of diverting her attention so he could grab for the piece.

"Forget the clothes and the lottery ticket, buddy. This is more important." She walked him over to the car with the forty-five still imbedded in his neck, too high for his lead corset to protect him.

"I hope you've got the safety clip on that gun," he said.

"What's a safety clip?"

He moaned.

"Don't worry, I'm being careful."

"Yeah, like you were careful with those farting bears."

"Oh, you are so crude. They were *burping* bears."

"Well, that's better, of course. Did anyone ever tell you that you have incredible lips?"

She blinked at him as a current of electricity seemed to ricochet between them. "Oooh, you are smooth. And the answer is yes. My Christmas Curse eleven years ago."

"Huh?"

"Larry the Lizard told me I had a sexy mouth. That was just before he slept with my best friend, Alice."

"I wouldn't sleep with your best friend," he vowed. "I'd rather—"

"Get serious." They were on the driver's side of the car. "Now, slowly, I want you to take out your keys and open the front and back doors." When he did as ordered, she told him to get in the driver's seat. "I'll sit behind you where I can aim my gun right at your head."

"Puh-leeze!" Luke frowned. *This is not good.* He'd been hoping she would sit in the passenger seat where he could more easily grab for the weapon . . . or his own rod on the floor under the driver's seat.

"What's that thing?"

Oh, damn! Her eyes had homed in on the tip of his revolver peeking out like a beacon.

"Move back," she demanded, training her firearm on his face while she leaned down and picked up his gun gingerly between a thumb and forefinger. For a moment, he saw fear flash in her eyes. "Are you a crook or something?"

He couldn't help grinning. "You mean like you?"

"No, not like me, you jerk. I mean a real crook. A bank robber, or a rapist, or a murderer."

He shook his head. "I'm not a bad guy. Well . . . uh . . . I'm not all that good, either, but—"

"Shut up," she snapped, motioning him into the car.

"Testy, are we?"

She slipped into the back seat, immediately positioning her gun with a bead on his unprotected skull, the whole time muttering about Jeffrey Dahmer and Freddie Kruger.

"How 'bout lowering the gun, darlin'? I'd hate to get my hair mussed."

She started to comply.

That's it, honey. Put my metal undershirt in your cross-hairs.

She changed her mind when she realized his back was pressed against the seat. "Just drive."

He was easing the Bronco out of the parking lot when he saw in the rear view mirror a police car, bubblegum light flashing, pull in front of the Piggly Jiggly. The two officers who got out didn't seem in any big hurry. They probably thought it was a routine shoplifting.

"Where to?" he asked, slanting the woman a glimpse over his shoulder. She was biting her bottom lip in concentration.

Those lips again.

"Just head down the highway. I have to think."

That would be a refreshing change. "You could probably take off your disguise now," he advised. He'd like to get a better look at her. All he'd been able to see thus far were high cheekbones, a light sprinkling of freckles over a slightly upturned nose, and big, big brown eyes. She was probably a redhead, if her eyebrows were any indication. He hoped she was ugly, so his wandering lust would come to a halt. Even so, he wondered what kind of body she hid under that Santa costume.

But then he immediately brought himself back to reality. *Why the hell should I care? I know my personal life is going down the toilet lately, but this is the pits. I'm having impure thoughts about a nun with PMS?*

"Geez, watch the road," she shrieked as he almost drove onto the berm. Luckily there wasn't much traffic. "And I'm not taking off my disguise . . . yet."

Yet? "Why not?" he asked suspiciously.

"Pay attention and drive faster," she commanded, ignoring his question. When they'd traveled a few miles, she told him to turn right onto a rural road. After a prolonged silence, she added, "So if you're not a crook, how come you have a gun?"

"I'm a bodyguard."

"A bodyguard!" she exclaimed. "Like Kevin Costner?"

"Yep! Except that women say I favor Brad Pitt." He cast a sidelong glance at her over his shoulder and jiggled his eyebrows. Women loved it when he did that.

"You're too old to look like Brad Pitt."

"Hey, I'm not *that* old. I'm only thirty-five. How old are you?" *Boy, see if I waste my eyebrow jiggle on you again!*

"Thirty, and believe me, I feel pretty darn old sometimes."

"Thirty? Old? No way! Back to me—" he said.

She made a rude sound of disgust and mimicked, "Back to me . . ."

"What's that snort supposed to mean?"

"Men. Everything always comes back to them. And I don't snort."

"Are you trying to say I'm vain?" She snorted again, and it was a snort, no matter what she claimed. "Just because I'm in my prime?"

"And because you think you look like Brad Pitt. An *older* Brad Pitt."

"You've got a real attitude problem, lady. Anyhow, you *really* don't think I look like Brad Pitt? You called me Mr. Legend-of-the-Fall," he reminded her.

"A slip of the tongue," she asserted. "With all that hair, you could be Michael Bolton."

"Michael Bolton? Are you blind? He's blond, and

has a big nose and a receding hairline. And he doesn't even have good hair." Affronted, he gritted his teeth and stared straight ahead. Now that he thought about it, he *had* noticed a few extra hairs in his brush lately. It took iron willpower not to touch his brow, just to check for a receding hairline.

He tilted the rear view mirror so he could see her face, and noticed her smiling . . . at his expense. Was he that transparent? Or narcissistic? Probably.

"If you're really a bodyguard, show me some proof. Do you even have a license for this firearm?" She pointed to his revolver which lay, outside his reach, on the far side of the back seat.

"Yeah, in the glove compartment." He reached over slowly, making sure he didn't make any abrupt moves that would surprise her "itchy thumb." Pushing aside a set of handcuffs and a box of condoms, he picked up his wallet, tossing it back to her. He was hoping she'd drop the weapon when she reached to catch his wallet, but no such luck. She let it fall into her lap while her eyes focused on the glove compartment.

"Oh, God, are you a pervert?"

He grinned.

"A gun and handcuffs and a box of condoms! Boy, oh, boy, this is the worst Christmas Curse ever. The Midnight Ride with Paul the Pervert?"

"Call me crazy, but I can't for the life of me see the connection between a gun, handcuffs, condoms, and perversion. Do you know many perverts who use condoms?"

"I don't know any perverts at all." She riffled through his wallet, checking his driver's license, muttering, "Lucas Carter," then studied his gun registration and his business card for Watchdogs, Inc. "So you really are a bodyguard, huh?" she commented with curiosity.

"Damn straight."

"For how long?"

"Five years."

"What'd you do before that? CIA? Ha-ha-ha!" she mocked, leaning forward and picking up his hand-cuffs, examining them idly, even clipping one on her left wrist.

When he didn't answer, she gasped. "Oh, great! Don't tell me I've kidnapped a CIA agent."

"Ex."

"Golly gee! That makes me feel better."

Then, before he could blink, she reached over the seat, locked his right wrist to her extended left, and pocketed the key.

"Sister, you are driving with your lights on dim."

"I am *not* a nun."

Cursing silently, he berated himself for his careless-ness. Never underestimate the enemy. Never. How could he have forgotten that golden rule of the secu-rity business? His biggest mistake was treating this Santa/bimbo/nun like less than the threat she posed.

"So, Luke, do you know any Mafia?"

Her totally off-the-wall question floored him for a moment. "No, do you?"

"Uh-uh. But I need to find some bad guys to rob. Real quick."

This Mother Teresa clone was not playing with a full deck. "Let me get this straight. You're going to pull another robbery, and you'd like to target the mob."

"I did *not* rob the Piggly Jiggly. I was just getting

back my money. That's not a robbery," she declared vehemently. "I would never rob honest people, not that I think Piggly Jiggly is all that honest. But I need cash, *desperately*, and that means I've got to find some bad guys."

He groaned. This was turning into the most bizarre nightmare. "Why do you need the money?"

She refused to answer.

"How much? I've got about fifty dollars in my wallet."

She sniffed indignantly. "That would be robbing."

He crossed his eyes with frustration. *How do I reason with a lunatic?*

"Besides, it's not enough. I need about five hundred dollars. And, take my advice, you don't resemble Brad Pitt when you cross your eyes. If fact, you look down-right homely."

Don't react. Be cool. She's just a dumbbell pretend nun. What does she know about good-looking men? "We could stop at an ATM machine to get more money. My bank will let me take out three hundred dollars at a pop."

"I told you I'm not going to steal from innocent people. If Julio hadn't stolen my car and purse with all my credit cards, I wouldn't have any problems at all. I could have cashed a check or used my own ATM or Visa card. Nope, I need bad guys."

He shouldn't ask. He really shouldn't. "Who's Julio?"

"Some teenage miscreant whose life won't be worth beans when I get a hold of him."

"Well, that explains everything. Listen, Ms. Claus, or Sister Claus . . . what's your name, by the way?"

She hesitated for a long time, and Luke practically heard her devious mind whirring sluggishly.

"Tiffany," she announced finally. "Tiffany Blake."

He let out a hoot of laughter. "Sister Tiffany?"

"I told you, I'm *not* a nun."

"Okay, Ti-fan-ny. Now that you've done your 'Tiffany does Piggly Jiggly' routine, what next?"

"Pull over here," she said abruptly. "That's where I'm going to pull my next job. Oh, this is perfect. Surely the people who run this place qualify as bad guys."

Luke swerved into the parking lot with a screech of brakes and gaped at the flashing neon sign in front of a corrugated metal building: "Sam's Smut Shop." A handmade posterboard next to the red door listed a menu of "triple X-rated videos, sex toys, peep shows." Then, "Body piercings and nude massages, by appointment."

"You're going to rob a porno palace?"

"Yep," she said with a bright burst of enthusiasm. "Good idea, huh?"

Oh, Lord! "Do you think the Christmas Curse is contagious?"

Chapter Two

"Trust me, this is not a good idea," Luke said, shutting off the car and turning in his seat to face her. "I don't think you realize the seriousness of what you're doing. Armed robbery is a felony."

"Only if I get caught," she boasted bravely. *Prison? Me? The worst thing I've ever done is overcharge a customer for an almond creme wedding cake.*

"Maybe you could convince a judge that the super-market owed you thirty-nine ninety-five, *if* you hadn't been carrying a loaded gun."

"I didn't know it was loaded."

"You didn't?"

"Of course not. I'm not an idiot. And stop looking at me like that."

"How am I looking at you?"

"Your eyes are crossing again. You'd better be care-ful, your face might freeze like that. Aunt Clara told us once about—"

"Aaarrrgh! Stop changing the subject."

"Listen up, you lunkhead. I didn't know the gun was loaded because Julio told me it was empty."

"Julio again? Never mind." He inhaled deeply. "The bottom line is that you haven't done anything *too* serious yet, providing I don't press charges against you for kidnapping, terroristic threats, auto theft, personal assault—"

"Don't forget loss of lottery ticket,'" she snickered. "And 'hair and age insult.'"

He let out a whoosh of exasperation. "You . . . can't . . . go . . . in . . . this . . . store . . . with . . . a . . . loaded . . . gun," he said through clenched teeth.

"Okay, I'll unload it." She turned the gun over to see how that might be done. Every movement she made jerked his arm along with her, like a puppet, because of the handcuff, but that couldn't be helped.

"Stop!" he cried. "Geez, don't ever point a gun in your face."

"Oops."

"Oops? Lady, you oughta be restrained for your own good." Shaking his head incredulously, he then told her, step by step, how to release the remaining bullets.

There were none.

"Damn! You've been ordering me around like a fool with an empty weapon."

"Whew! I don't know about you, but I'm relieved. I wouldn't have wanted to hurt anyone."

"You're smiling," he accused. "You knew all along that there were no bullets in the gun, and you let me shiver."

"Were you shivering? Good." She beamed with supreme self-satisfaction. *Put that in your macho pipe, Brad baby.* "Remember when I shot at the Little Debbie cake rack and accidentally hit the Buzzy Burp Bears?"

He was gaping at her as if she'd flipped her lid. "You were aiming for Little Debbie?" he sputtered.

"Yeah. Anyhow, I actually shot twice, and only the

first bullet came out. So, *voilà*, I knew the bullets were all gone."

His face turned purple, and he made a sort of strangled sound deep in his throat. Finally he choked out, "You are a certifiable dingaling. Don't you know that just because one bullet is missing in a chamber doesn't mean the gun is empty? Have you ever heard of Russian roulette?"

"Oh, my God!" She started to shiver herself with aftershocks at what she might have done. "This is the Christmas Curse to beat all Christmas Curses."

"You are dangerous. To yourself. Society. The world."

Tell me something I don't already know. "What's done is done. You're okay, I'm okay." She shuddered suddenly. It was getting cold in the car. "Let's move on here. Maybe I should have you park on the other side of the building while I go in," she said, thinking out loud. She wasn't going to let guilt override her plan.

"You're not taking me with you?"

"Of course not."

"Oh, please, *please* take me with you. Consider it a Christmas present."

"Why?"

"Because I *really* want to see you rob a porno shop."

"Wouldn't you be considered an accomplice or something?"

"Probably 'something.'"

"You're making fun of me, aren't you?"

"A little, but, hell, I've never met a robber-nun-Santa who was about to enter a den of iniquity."

"I am *not* a nun."

"Take me with you. Come on. You need someone to

protect you from yourself. And you never know what kind of creeps are in these places."

"Nope, I can't do it," she decided. "You'd call for help, or tackle me. How could I trust you?"

'I promise . . . on my mother's grave.'

"Is your mother dead?" Her face softened with sympathy.

"No," he confessed sheepishly, "but it's the most solemn oath I could think of." He studied her for a long moment. "I'd take odds that *your* mother is dead, though," he remarked in a gentle voice.

Jessica cautioned herself once again not to reveal anything to the over-observant lout. And she didn't want his pity or anyone else's. "I think I should lock you in the trunk."

That wiped the pity right off his face. "I don't have a trunk."

"Oh. Well, maybe I could duck-tape your mouth shut and your hands and legs together."

"Bondage now? Wow! Who's the pervert here?"

She made a tsk-ing sound of disgust at his innuendo.

"Besides, I don't have any *duct* tape handy. Are you going to rob a hardware store, as well as a supermarket, before you rip off the sex shop?"

"I did *not* rob a supermarket. Will you stop saying that?"

He just smiled infuriatingly. And, my oh my, he really did resemble Brad Pitt when he flashed that dazzling smile. A girl could be tempted, *easily*, into allowing him to plant those teeth on her neck and inhale about a gallon of blood.

"Why are you licking your lips?" the Brad-Dracula asked, smirking knowingly.

If she had a stake handy, she would have whacked him a good one. She had to admit, though, that even when he smirked, he looked pretty darn good.

"You smell nice," he said irrelevantly, leaning closer and sniffing. "Is that Giorgio?"

"No, it's Eau de Scared Silly."

He sniffed a couple more times, and the brute looked sexy even when he sniffed. "Oh, I see. Sort of a designer ripoff of Eau de Stupid?"

"Probably," she agreed.

In the end, Jessica had no choice but to let Luke accompany her after he practically swore a blood oath to behave, at least until they were back in the car. She didn't trust Luke outside her sight, and the blood oath thing gave her the willies, but . . . well, there was another teensy problem. She'd been digging in both pockets of her Santa suit for the past five minutes and was unable to find the blasted handcuff key.

"You're on your honor, Luke," she pointed out. *Do vampires and movie star look-alikes have honor?* "I'm accepting your word."

"Right," he said, and grasped her free right hand in his handcuffed right one, shaking. She felt the tingle of that warm touch up to her armpits. And other places, too. *Oh, boy!*

Then Luke jammed his beard and wig on, grinning at her the whole time. Lordy, there ought to be a law against men with killer grins like his.

"Hey, Tiffany, I just thought of something." He chortled mischievously as she crawled clumsily over the gear shift area between the seats so she could slide out through the driver's door with him. He didn't help her at all, watching with delight as her rump hung up in the air for a long moment before she righted herself. "Do you think this counts as a first date for us?"

She mumbled a foul word under her breath in answer as they exited the car and began to walk toward the shop. Snow was beginning to come down steadily, and the temperature had turned decidedly colder.

"Today is December twenty-third," the cad continued teasing. "You'll probably want to write it in your diary. First date. Luke. Porno shop."

This time she said the foul word out loud.

He laughed. "I could even clip off a lock of my hair for you to press between the pages."

She yanked on his chain then, hard.

Luke had no intention of letting psycho Santa babe commit another robbery.

He couldn't explain why he felt this protective urge to help a stranger. He just did.

Maybe it was her huge doe eyes that failed to hide abject terror. The woman was clearly frightened to death, and, even so, she insisted on pulling off a robbery.

Then again, maybe it was her absolutely sensuous lower lip (her upper lip wasn't too bad, either) that tugged at his long-deadened emotions.

He hoped it wasn't because the brave front this screwball put on reminded him so much of that day six years ago when he and Ginny had emerged from the doctor's office. They'd gone in expecting to hear good news—that Ginny was finally pregnant. Instead, the obstetrician had dealt her a staggering blow. She had advanced cervical cancer, and less than a year to live.

The look Ginny had given him when they'd hit the street had been filled with terror, but, at the same time, she'd had a desperate need to put on a brave front. Like this dingbat.

He'd been unable to help Ginny, but maybe he could help the dingbat.

Ginny's desperation had been understandable, but why did this squirrely bubblehead need 500 dollars so desperately?

Well, he'd soon find out.

Twining his handcuffed hand with Dirty Harriet's, he walked inside, inhaling deeply. *And it is Giorgio, I know it is.*

Jessica should have pulled her hand out of Luke's firm grasp, but he gave her strength, somehow. The feel of his pulse throbbing against hers, wrist to wrist, comforted and strengthened her for the formidable task she'd set for herself.

"Okay, let's do it," she said resolutely.

He squeezed her hand in answer, but she thought she heard him mumble, "Dumber than a doornail." She wasn't sure if he referred to her, or himself.

The guy behind the counter, presumably Sam—a gray-haired gentleman who was probably somebody's grandfather—nodded at them and went back to waiting on a teenage boy who was purchasing about a gross of condoms and a magazine titled *Nympho Nurses*.

Hundreds of videos lined one wall, and magazine racks covered the other. There were several aisles of glass-topped counters displaying every kind of paraphernalia from edible underwear to bizarrely shaped vibrators to body oils that heated up on skin contact.

To her annoyance, Luke picked up one of the latter bottles and examined it closely, reading the instructions on the back. "Hmmmm," he said aloud. Then the lech winked at her.

His wink—a mere wink—caused her heart to lurch and her breasts to swell. Even in a ridiculous Santa wig and beard, the guy was drop-dead gorgeous and utterly charming. Quickly she turned her face away, not wanting him to see her heated blush, or her attraction to him.

As her eyes scanned the room, Jessica smiled. If she'd entertained any misgivings about their drawing undue attention, wearing Santa outfits and handcuffed together, she'd worried in vain. A stereo speaker belted out old chipmunk Christmas carols, and the customers went about their business browsing the wares.

To her amazement, two other Santas cruised the aisles, one of them schnockered and the other eyeing a pair of padded handcuffs with a matching velvet whip—probably a Christmas present for his spouse. *Gawd!* There were also a sophisticated-looking yuppie couple—definitely lovers, by the seductive glances they exchanged repeatedly; a young guy in a jeans jacket, cowboy hat, and boots; and two twenty-something women who giggled as they handled a pair of red satin men's bikini briefs that played "Jingle Bells" when a string was pulled.

"Gee, this isn't as bad as I thought it would be," she whispered, tugging on Luke's handcuffed wrist. "We should pretend that we're regular customers until the shop empties out a little, don't you think?"

"Whatever you say, Tiffany. You're the boss."

"Hmmmph!"

She immediately changed her mind about the shop

not being so bad when she backed into Rita, a lifesize balloon of a nude, flame-haired woman with breasts the size of cantaloupes and red nipples resembling maraschino cherries. Two of the bimbo's plastic girlfriends, Bridget and Trish, stood next to her—a blonde and a brunette.

Do men really buy garbage like this? When the drunk Santa put his arm around the blond balloon's waist and hauled her up to the cash register, Jessica answered her own question. *Yep, they do.*

"Would you like a Bruce Balloon, honey?" Luke chuckled.

She looked where he pointed his free hand and saw a six-foot tall male balloon whose endowments were impressive, to say the least. Bruce. Jessica's eyes almost bugged out.

"Uh, I don't think so, *honey*," she responded, trying to appear casual.

Luke's devilish hazel eyes crinkled with mirth as he guided her over toward the video shelves and began to peruse the offerings nonchalantly. After flicking through *A-cup Cuties*, *Breaststroke*, *Porking Miss Piggy*, and *Hot to Trot*, he turned to the "legitimate" movie section. *Hah! There is no such thing as legitimate in this place.* There he snickered as he read the titles aloud. *Hannah Does Her Two Sisters*, *Forrest Hump*, *High Nooner*, *Close Encounters of the Lewdest Kind*, *Lord of the Fly*, *The Breasts of Madison County*, and *Three Days of the Condom*.

"Let's get out of this section," she urged.

"No, no, no." He rebelled as his eyes latched onto something new. "How about this, sweetie?" he asked brightly, shoving a video case in her face. *"Tiffany's Great Adventure."*

She made a gurgling sound of revulsion as her face heated up some more. At a sudden blast of cold air, her eyes darted to the doorway where the teenage boy exited, followed by the plastered Santa and the yuppie couple, who'd bought some assorted lotions and a video.

"Merry Christmas," the proprietor called out after them cheerfully. "Hope you have a great night. Ho, ho, ho!"

The other Santa followed soon after, purchasing nothing.

Okay, only three more to go—the two women and the cowboy. With any luck, there wouldn't be any new customers at this time of night.

"Have you ever tried these?" asked one of the women next to her. Her friend had moved to the register where she was paying for the Jingle Bells cock strap.

Me? Is she talking to me?

She was. "Have you ever tried these?" the woman repeated, holding up two eggs connected by a thin electric wire to a battery-operated controller which began to vibrate when she pressed a button. The woman twittered, and Jessica's mouth dropped open. She refused to look at Luke to see what he was doing.

"What *is* that?" she blurted out, and immediately regretted her loose tongue when Luke answered, "Love eggs."

She and the woman both looked at him, and he shrugged. "I read about them in a magazine."

"Sure you did," Jessica muttered under her breath.

But he heard her. "Hey, I haven't been in one of these places since I was a teenager. Not my style."

Soon after, the two women left the store, and the cowboy headed toward the back of the shop where a weary-looking woman dressed only in a black teddy, garter belt, and stiletto heels emerged through a set of swinging, western-style doors. She was crooking a long painted fingernail toward the cowboy, who shuffled back with a puppy-dog grin. Jessica wasn't sure if it was the dude's turn for a nude massage or a body piercing.

No matter. That left her and Luke alone with the proprietor.

"Can I help you folks?" the old guy asked. "Great handcuffs, by the way."

Jessica was about to pull out her gun when Luke pinched her fingers in warning and handed the owner a bottle. "Yeah, I'll buy this."

She hadn't realized he still carried the warming oil.

"That'll be nine ninety-five."

One-handed, Luke fished out his wallet and laid a ten-dollar bill on the counter.

Okay, this is it. Now's the time. Oh, geez, oh, geez! Jessica reached in her pocket for the empty pistol, but in the process accidentally elbowed a display on the counter. To her horror, she knocked over a sort of vibrator thing with a huge wiggly tongue on the end, which began to jiggle madly. With two fingers, she distastefully tried to pick the thing up and turn it off, but it shimmied away from her, right off the counter to the floor. She dropped down to her knees, pulling Luke with her, and tried to catch the obscene object.

Luke and the shop owner were laughing hysterically at her antics. Angry now, she gave the thing a kick, which shut it off.

When she stood up, shaking with mortification, her

cap and wig slipped and her long hair billowed out in a flaming explosion midway down her back.

Luke gaped at her as if someone had just handed him a bomb. "I can't believe it! You look like Little Orphan Annie," he exclaimed, fingering one of the corkscrew curls—the bane of her life. At least he'd stopped laughing at her.

The fact that he added, "You're beautiful," came too late. Comparing her to Little Orphan Annie was not a compliment in her book—not now, and not when she'd been a real orphan. And there was no way she was beautiful with her wild mop of red hair. No way!

She fought the tears that filled her eyes. Angry with herself and Luke, she jerked out her revolver and started to aim it at the guy behind the counter, who was holding his sides as he continued to howl. With a quivering voice, she shouted, "This . . . is . . . a . . . stick—"

"No!" Luke roared, and with one swift motion he hefted her into the air and over his shoulder, the gun dangling from her fingers. As he headed toward the door with his free hand clamped over her struggling behind, he informed Sam the Sleaze, who'd just noticed the gun and was making hyperventilating noises, "Don't worry, this is a game my wife likes to play every Christmas."

Sam expelled a wheeze of relief. "Hey, I see this kind of thing all the time. It's the curse of my business."

"I'll give you a curse," Jessica raged.

"Merry Christmas," Luke laughed.

"Ho, ho, ho!" Sam chortled.

* * *

"You scum! You slimeball! Put me down. Right now. I can't believe you did this. Oooh, oooh, this is awful. I needed that money. You don't know what this means."

Kicking and screaming and thrashing, she pounded his back with her free hand. She dug her fingernails into the palm of his cuffed hand. She landed a pointed toe on his thigh.

"Ouch!"

Finally he set Little Orphan Tiffany down next to his car, and immediately raised both her flailing arms over her head and held them on the car roof by the wrists with his cuffed hand. He pressed his lower body against hers to keep her from escaping or doing him more bodily harm, not an easy task with both of their pillow-bellies.

Angry himself now and sick of this game which had gotten way out of hand, he tore off his disguise, tossing the cap and beard and wig to the snow-covered ground. Then he yanked off her beard. Finally he got his first good gander at his surprising Santa.

Time seemed to stand still.

An ethereal silence surrounded them as snowflakes as big as golfballs came down, landing with feather lightness on her mane of curly red hair, in her eyelashes . . . on her parted lips.

She no longer struggled. In fact, she stared at him with equal awe.

Tears burned in his eyes for reasons he couldn't explain. All he knew was that the tight knot surrounding his heart—a knot he hadn't even realized was there—began to unravel. And he felt as light as the snowflakes caressing his face. And hopeful.

It was so strange.

"Are you an angel? A Christmas mirage?" he murmured. Lowering his lips toward hers—those luscious lips that had drawn him from the start, he sighed.

Instead of protesting, she arched upward, meeting him halfway. "I'm no angel."

"Thank God."

Against his lips she whispered, "I'm not really a nun, either."

"I know," he smiled, then repeated, "Thank God."

"You shouldn't kiss me," she demurred even as she parted her lips. "My Christmas Curse might rub off on you."

"Rub all you want, babe," he growled, grinding his big belly against hers. "I'm cursed already."

"What's that hard thing?" she asked suddenly.

He laughed.

"Not *that*. Under your jacket."

"A bulletproof vest."

She raised a brow. "So, you weren't afraid of me at all."

"Oh, I was afraid of what you'd do. I still am."

She smiled enigmatically, as if he'd better be.

But he couldn't think about that now. All he could think about was this tempting redhead in his arms.

Cupping her jaw with his free hand to hold her in place, he slanted his lips over hers, shaping her for his kiss, relishing the contrast of cool lips and hot breath. Hard and demanding, soft and cajoling.

She whimpered.

He groaned.

Powerful, bone-melting sensations overwhelmed him. Suddenly he wanted so many things, and they all seemed to revolve around this woman—this stranger.

Pulling away slightly, he studied her face—misty eyes locked with his in question, mouth already swollen from his kisses. Their warm breaths, panting, frosted in the cold air between them. Hearts thudding in unison, they tried to comprehend what was happening.

In that instant, he understood. Blood hammered in his ears as the realization hit Luke like a thunderbolt.

I love her, he thought, disbelieving, at first. Then he smiled, happier than he'd been in ages. *I love her.*

He'd never believed in love at first sight before. He did now. *I love her.* He couldn't stop saying the words in his head.

Should he tell her?

No, not yet. He didn't want to scare her away. Besides, he needed more time to think. He rolled the words around in his mind with a joyous relish: *I love her.*

"I feel weird," she said, as if reading his mind.

"So do I, babe. So do I."

She blinked at him. "It must be the Christmas Curse."

He shook his head vehemently. "No, it's a Christmas Miracle."

Chapter Three

"Are you still cold?" Luke asked the shivering woman next to him as he pulled out onto the highway. Lord, how he wanted to stop the car and take her in his arms, but he didn't have the right . . . *yet*. She already appeared scared to death of him. Instead, he turned up the heat.

Jessie—that was the name of the woman he loved, Jessica Jones . . . she'd just told him so—shook her head and bit her bottom lip in concentration. She was probably planning another heist. Perhaps a cathouse this time, he thought with a chuckle. *God, I love her.*

Or maybe she was having second thoughts about their killer kiss.

Uh-oh. No, he wouldn't let himself think that. Now that he'd found a woman he could love, after all these years, he wouldn't let her go. She would love him. He was determined.

But he was nervous, too, and that was something new for him. For the past five years, ever since Ginny died, he'd had more women than he could handle. But he hadn't cared about a single one of them.

Now that he did care, would he be rejected?

Luke clenched the steering wheel tighter. He had to believe that everything would work out all right. God didn't hand out miracles and then yank them away. Nope, all he needed was a little time.

Luke considered his next move as he drove back to the Piggly Jiggly parking lot. Jessie insisted she had to get the van and return to "Clara's House," mission unaccomplished. Alone.

Hah! Not if I have anything to do with it.

He could barely see through the wildly swinging windshield wipers which couldn't keep pace with the falling snow. It would be a white Christmas this year, after all, if this blizzard kept up. He'd already tried using the storm as an excuse to keep Jessie with him, but she'd refused adamantly, pointing out that the van had snow tires.

Luckily they'd been able to find the handcuff key under the back seat floor mat, after some amusing calisthenics necessitated by their bound wrists. Amusing to him, at least. In the close confines, with all her squirming, he'd gotten a real good idea of what kind of body his Santa babe hid under her suit—tall, curvy, not too lean. Perfect.

So now he and Jessie sat unattached for the first time in hours. And Luke felt as if a mile separated them, not three feet.

He reached over and twined his fingers with hers.

Startled, she glanced first at their linked hands, then at him, questioning. He hoped she got the silent message he was unable to speak out loud, just yet.

Fear flashed through her wide doe-brown eyes for a moment—of what, he wasn't sure—but he suspected she was about to pull away.

"Don't be afraid of me, Jessie," he said, his voice husky. "I won't hurt you."

"But I might hurt you," she said in a voice laden with regret. "I'm cursed. And it's Christmas. I don't stand a chance. Neither do you. You'll be better off when you're rid of me."

He squeezed her hand. "Maybe the trick is to replace your Christmas bad luck with good luck. You know that saying 'When someone hands you a bag of bones, make soup.'"

"Don't you mean lemons, and lemonade?"

He scowled at her interruption and went on. "Treat our meeting as a miracle instead of a curse . . . oh, hell, I'm not very good with this kind of stuff. I have all these thoughts and feelings inside, but they just don't come out right." He ducked his head in embarrassment. "I'm not very good with words."

She squeezed his hand back, and he thought his heart would explode with happiness. "You're doing just fine," she assured him.

"I still say we should go to my place. It's only fifteen minutes from here. You could warm up, and—"

"No, I've got to get back. Sister Clara will be frantic."

"Sister? I thought she was your aunt."

"I call her aunt, everyone who lives at 'Clara's House' does," she said, waving her free hand dismissively. He was holding on to her other hand for dear life.

He frowned. "You live at 'Clara's House'? An orphanage?"

"No. Of course not. But I used to. Besides, it's not really an orphanage. It's sort of a foster home for incorrigible kids."

Now, that was a revelation. Jessie had been an orphan, and incorrigible. His lips twitched with humor. He could understand the incorrigible part. "You mean juvenile delinquents?"

"They don't call them j.d.'s anymore. Politically incorrect." She smiled at him shyly, and Luke could hardly speak over the lump in his throat. Who would have thought that he'd fall in love so quick, so hard?

"What do you do for a living, Jessie?" he asked finally when he got his emotions under control.

She regarded him mischievously, giving him her full attention now. "So you're finally convinced I'm not a nun?"

"Babe, nuns don't tongue kiss," he replied and winked at her.

He could see a blush bloom on her cheeks. Still, she gave him a slick comeback. "Kissed a lot of nuns, have you?"

How lucky could a guy be? A gorgeous redhead. And a sense of humor, too. He was going to light a few thank-you candles the next time he went to church.

He released her hand and wagged a finger at her. "You're changing the subject. What do you do for a living, besides burglary?" Then he immediately took her hand again. He wondered idly what she'd do if he tried to pull her over onto his lap. Or stopped the car to kiss her again . . . and again . . . and again. And unbuckled her belt, and . . . *oh, brother!* About 50,000 of his testosterone were revving up for the start signal.

"I didn't rob . . . oh, never mind," she said huffily. "I don't suppose you'd buy Avon Lady?"

"Hell, why not? You've hit me with Santa, nun, and gun moll so far. There isn't anything else you could do that would surprise me." *Except maybe jump onto my lap, uninvited. Yeah! I should be so lucky.*

"I'm a wedding caterer."

"Say that again."

"I bake spectacular wedding cakes . . . the best al-mond creme, ten-tier cake in the country. And I supply gourmet food for wedding receptions."

"Here in Philly?"

"No. I'm from Chicago."

Whoa! Red flag! That posed some logistical prob-lems. Long-distance dating and all that. Well, no problem! He'd skip the dating and get right down to the serious stuff. *Hmmm. I wonder how long I can wait before I propose? Oops! First, I've got to tell her I love her. Then I can ask her to marry me and move to Philly. Betcha I could do that all in one shot. Yep, that's what I'll do. I love you, let's tie the knot, wild sex, wedding. Or maybe I could reverse the order. Oh, yeah! Wild sex, I love you, wild sex, let's tie the knot, wild sex, wedding, wild sex. Whatever.* He could barely wait.

"Why are you grinning?" she asked.

"You don't want to know, sweetheart," he chuckled. *Yet.*

"If you're remotely considering sinking your teeth into my neck and sucking blood, forget it. I have a twentieth-degree black belt in karate."

He shook his head like a shaggy dog to clear it. Sometimes her train of thought confused him. Then he understood. She was associating him with that movie *Interview with a Vampire*. And he probably had been ogling her as if he'd like to suck a few body parts, except his preference would be a bit lower than her throat.

"You're smirking again."

"I don't smirk. That was a lascivious smile."

"Looked like a smirk to me."

Then he thought of something else and he hooted at her, "So, you do think I resemble Brad Pitt."

"Well, maybe an older version," she conceded with a sniff.

He lifted their laced fingers to his mouth and kissed her knuckles. He couldn't help himself.

Instead of resisting, she sighed. That's all. Just a sigh.

The 50,000 testosterone split and multiplied into an orgy of anticipation. He didn't think he could wait another five minutes before kissing her again.

But then, still another thought occurred to him, and his heart began to race with anxiety. "You're not married, are you?"

"Almost, but not quite."

"Almost? Almost? What do you mean 'almost?'" His chest constricted so tightly he could scarcely breathe.

"I got jilted two weeks ago by my fiance, Burton Richards the Third. Burt and I were engaged for a year, but he just discovered that the trust fund I got on my thirtieth birthday isn't quite as large as he'd anticipated."

Luke let out a whoosh of relief. "That's too bad . . . about you and Burp," he said sweetly. He felt like pumping his fist in the air with the victory sign.

"Burt," she corrected, then shrugged. "It's just as well. I didn't like him much toward the end anyhow. He played golf a lot," she confided.

Luke made a note never to play golf again.

"I should have known better, of course, knowing as I do that all men are scumbags."

"I beg your pardon."

"You wouldn't believe how many men—engaged and married men—hit on me even as I'm making preparations for their weddings. The louses! One bridegroom even cornered me at his reception, offering me a quickie."

I've got a lot of backup work to do.

"Well, I've learned my lesson from Burt. I'm never getting married now."

Yep, lots of backup work.

"Maybe I'll become a nun."

Over my dead body.

"So, how about you?" Jessica asked. "Are you married?"

How could she ask that question so calmly, as if she couldn't care less either way? Luke decided she was just playing it cool. Her heart was probably doing a high-speed tap dance, just like his.

"No, not anymore," he said, and was astonished that the usual pain didn't accompany that statement.

"Divorce?"

He shook his head. "Ginny died five years ago of cancer." And with those words, a door slammed shut on Luke's past. Oh, it wasn't as if he'd ever forget Ginny. How could he? They'd been sweethearts since junior high. But she was dead, and somehow, someway, his new, fantastic feelings for Jessie suddenly gave him permission to go on living . . . not just in meaningless one-night stands, but with a forever kind of commitment.

"Oh, Luke, I'm so sorry. I shouldn't have pried."

"That's okay. She's been gone a long time. Anyhow, tell me why you're here.

" 'Clara's House' is in the Poconos, and—"

"The Poconos! The Poconos! That's two hours from here. What were you doing in Philly at midnight?"

"I had to go to Aunt Clara's 'mother house' in the city. Clara's a retired nun; but she still has ties to her religious order. Anyhow, after I'd completed my errand, the sisters talked me into playing Santa following their Christmas recital. On the way back, I decided to *handle* Aunt Clara's problem at the Piggly Jiggley."

It should have made sense. It didn't. "I meant, what are you doing so far away from Chicago to begin with?"

"Oh. I came here two days ago when I got an SOS call from Aunt Clara. She broke her leg, and she needed my help to keep her foster home together through the holidays."

"I don't understand."

"Aunt Clara operates a group program under state regulations. If they found out she was incapacitated, they'd withdraw her funding and split up these kids quick as spit. She was especially concerned about them missing Christmas together. Not that it's going to be much of a Christmas now." Her expression drooped dolefully.

"Because you weren't able to get any money?" he concluded, finally understanding.

"Yep. I would have been all right if Julio hadn't ripped me off this afternoon, but now . . ."

He cursed under his breath.

"Julio stole all the money Aunt Clara had for Christmas gifts, as well. It's going to be a mighty bleak holiday for those kids." She straightened her shoulders with resolution. "But they're used to disappointment. They'll survive. We . . . I mean *they* . . . always do."

There was a world of hidden meaning in Jessie's words. How many disappointments had she had as a child? As an orphan? How many bleak holidays?

Well, he'd be damned if she'd have another.

"This is the turnoff for the Piggly Jiggly," Jessie reminded him. "Just a few more minutes and you'll be rid of me."

Warning buzzers went off in Luke's head. He had to think fast. How could he keep Jessie with him? Time. He needed time.

"Duck!" he shouted.

She jerked her head toward him in surprise. "What?"

"Hurry, get down on the floor. The parking lot is loaded with cops. Frank must have reported your heist to every precinct from here to New Jersey."

Jessie dropped down into a curled-up ball in the cramped floor space, and he threw the two pillows they'd taken from their bellies on top of her. Then he surveyed the deserted parking lot with a wide grin.

"Whatever you do, don't lift your head or your butt is gonna land in jail." *And a very nice butt, it is, too,* he noted, glancing down at her.

"Oh, geez, oh, geez! What am I going to do now?"

"I guess I'll just have to drive you to 'Clara's House,'" he said with an exaggerated sigh. "No, no . . . don't worry about inconveniencing me. It's the least I can do for those poor orphans." He patted the pillow over her upraised behind, barely stifling the chuckle of satisfaction that rippled through him.

"But what about the van?" she groaned. "Can you turn down the heater? I'm melting here. Oh, good grief, maybe I should just turn myself in, beg for mercy."

"Nope," he said in a rush, "you can't do that. Philly cops are notorious for being hard-nosed. Mercy isn't in their vocabulary. They'd probably put you in a cell with . . . Mafia hitmen or something. Do a strip search . . . naked, body cavities, delousing, the works."

She groaned again.

"You can come back and get the van after Christmas," he advised. Interpreting her silence for assent, he added, "Is there anything you need from the van? Maybe I could slip in unnoticed."

"I don't know. I can't think here. It's about five hundred degrees under this blower. Yeah, you'd better get the boxes."

"Boxes? What boxes? How many boxes?"

"About fifty."

Fifty? he mouthed silently. "What's in them?"

"Fruitcakes."

An hour later, Jessica sat in the car in front of an all-night Uni-Mart convenience store, sulking. "I still don't see the harm in my going inside. I promised Aunt Clara to bring back bread and milk. Criminey, don't you think you're being a mite overcautious?"

"Nope, you can't be too careful," Luke said. "Lots of these convenience stores have police radios behind the counter. There might be an all-points bulletin out for you."

"Sixty miles away from Philly?" she scoffed.

"Just sit tight, toots," he said, chucking her under

the chin. "I'm perfectly capable of buying bread and milk." He peered down with disgust at the bills and change she'd shoved with stubborn pride into his hands. "Even thirty-nine dollars and ninety-five cents' worth."

"Don't spend it all on bread and milk, you fool. Buy some peanut butter and jelly, too. I've got to make this money stretch till Tuesday, the day after Christmas. Then I should be able to call my bank."

"Just how many kids are at this house?"

"Four . . . five when Julio is there."

"How old are they?"

"Eleven to fourteen. Julio's the oldest."

"Let me get this straight. You expect kids that age, who suck up food like human vacuums, to live on peanut butter and jelly sandwiches for the next two days? Over Christmas?"

"And fruitcake. Don't forget the fruitcake."

"How could I?" he said with a moan. Despite their both protesting that they hated fruitcake, they were so hungry they'd polished off half of a three-pound ring so far. "Whatever possessed those nuns to send fifty fruitcakes?"

"They had a fund-raiser that fell through. I guess they sold less than they expected."

"Exactly how many of those lead sinkers do they have left?"

"Five hundred."

His mouth dropped open in amazement. Then he burst out laughing. "Tell me a little something about these kids."

"Well, Julio you already know about. He's fourteen,

half Puerto Rican, half black, and street smart to the nth degree. He's been arrested for everything from grand theft auto to dealing marijuana. You'd like him, though. He could charm the socks off a snake."

"Sounds delightful."

"Darlene is next. She's thirteen, going on thirty. Sexy as hell and headed straight for a life of prostitution if someone doesn't help her soon." She laughed. "Yesterday she pierced her own navel, and she tried to talk me into doing the same."

"Did you?"

She cast him a rueful glance. "Hardly. Robbing porno shops is as adventuresome as I get."

He grinned. "Who's next?"

"Henry is thirteen, too. The next Bill Gates, or so he thinks. He knows everything there is to know about computers. In fact, you'll soon know what he wants for Christmas—a computer system with a CD-Rom—not that he'll get such a pricey item, unless there's a real Santa Claus."

"He doesn't sound too incorrigible. What's he done?"

"Credit card fraud. Illegal hacking. The last scam he pulled off netted him ten thousand dollars. Not bad for a thirteen-year-old, huh?"

"Is your Aunt Clara a saint or what? No sane person would take on all these hopeless cases."

"They're not hopeless," Jessie asserted defensively. "All they need is help."

"Sorry," he apologized. "Go on."

"Kajeeta is twelve. Poor thing. She's . . . well, she's overweight, but she has this dream of becoming a singer and dancer, like Janet Jackson. No one has the heart to tell her it's probably a hopeless dream. Anyhow, Kajeeta refuses to go to school. The other kids make fun of her. She's continually being called into court by school probation officers. Foster parents don't want her, too much trouble."

He nodded. Sounded like a great bunch of kids so far.

"Then there's Willie. He's eleven." She smiled. "His orange hair and freckles will fool you. He's a compulsive shoplifter. And he's going through this Ninja phase right now."

He raised a brow.

"He does karate moves . . . all the time. Seems like he can't even go to the bathroom without Kung Fuing along the way." She stared out the window, deep in thought. Then she seemed to shake herself back to the present. "We're wasting time here. Am I going into the store or are you?"

"I am. But how about soda and snack food for the kids?" he suggested.

She raised her chin. "I can't waste money on junk food. We'll get by. Just buy four loaves of bread, four gallons of milk, a jar of peanut butter and a jar of jelly," she said inflexibly, "or I'll do it myself."

He gave her a condemning glare and slammed out of the car, storming into the store. He'd left the wipers on, so she was able to watch him through the well-lit store window, even through the blinding snow. He said something to the teenage girl behind the counter, and she smiled up at him as if God had just walked into her store. Or Brad Pitt.

She couldn't blame the girl. Jessica felt all warm and fuzzy inside when she looked at him herself. Actually, she'd felt more like hot, hot, hot, especially when he'd kissed her. No one, *no one* had ever made her feel like that.

This night was probably just a lark for him. He was humoring some crazy woman who'd pulled a loaded gun in a supermarket, kidnapped him, then tried to rob a porno shop.

She groaned aloud. It sounded awful when she played it back in her mind. Heck, it *was* awful. Her brain really must have splintered apart to have tried such foolish stunts. But she was desperate. How was she ever going to provide a Christmas for those kids who depended on her? In a way, she was letting them down, just like so many adults had let her down as a child when she was shifted from one foster home to another . . . until she'd found Aunt Clara.

Well, enough maudlin thoughts. Her Brad-savior was returning, loaded down with two grocery bags in each arm. She leaned over to press the automatic rear door release.

Even that short walk from the front door of the Uni-Mart to the rear of the car resulted in his being covered with snow. To her surprise, he didn't immediately enter the car, though. He went back in the store twice more, returning with six more grocery bags.

When he finally slid into the front seat, she lit into him. "I told you to buy four things. What's in all those bags?"

"My stuff," he said, latching his seat belt and backing out of the lot. His jaw squared mulishly.

"Stuff? What kind of stuff?"

"Snack stuff. Food I can eat while all the rest of you are scarfing down fruitcake."

She narrowed her eyes suspiciously. "You aren't going to be at 'Clara's House' long enough to see anyone eat fruitcake. You're turning right around after you drop me off, and going home."

He slanted her one of those "wanna bet?" looks, but said nothing.

"Luke?" she persisted.

He sucked in a deep breath and glowered at her as he drove along the deserted highway. It must be three A.M. by now. "Jessie, you can't possibly think I'm going to return tonight. I'm exhausted. We're in the middle of a blizzard. Do you want me to have an accident?"

"No, but . . ." Little alarm bells were ringing all through her body. She wasn't sure how much exposure she could take to this guy, how long she could resist the attraction.

"Surely your Aunt Clara has a sofa or something where I can crash for the night." He fluttered those feather-duster lashes at her. It was a ploy he'd probably perfected over the years to suck in susceptible women . . . like her.

She immediately felt guilty for her lack of charity, especially since Luke had gone out of his way to help her. And it wasn't as if "Clara's House" didn't have plenty of room. The old gingerbread Victorian had three stories and about eight bedrooms. "Oh, all right. But just for one night."

She could have sworn he murmured under his breath, "That's all I need." But when she scrutinized him closer, he stared straight ahead. Innocent as a cobra. Or a blood-sucking vampire.

* * *

The next morning, Luke awakened in a third-floor bedroom of "Clara's House" to a wet tongue tracing his lips. His morning hard-on shot up like a rocket.

Wow! What a wake-up call! He hadn't expected his plan to work this fast. He must have more charm than he'd realized. It appeared as if the wild sex was going to come sooner than he'd expected.

With a growl, he reached up to pull Jessie into bed with him.

And she growled back.

Rather, *it* growled. A huge yellow dog was standing next to the bed with its long tongue hanging out. *Fred*, he concluded immediately. Jessie's randy mutt.

Yech! was his next thought as he realized the dog's tongue had been lapping his mouth. He'd probably get ringworm or something.

He stood and stretched with a loud yawn. The house seemed awfully quiet. Checking his watch, he saw that it was already nine o'clock.

No one had been awake when they'd arrived the night before at four A.M. So Jessie had worried in vain that Aunt Clara would be frantic about her safety. They'd brought the grocery bags and boxes in from the car without awakening anyone and gone immediately to bed.

Jessie had made a point of putting him on the third floor with the boys. Her bedroom was a floor below. No problem. She didn't stand a chance now that he had time on his side. *Wild sex, here I come.*

First things first. He wasn't sure which screaming body organ needed the most attention, his empty stomach or his full bladder. He opted for the bathroom first, with Fred padding after him like a shadow. "So, Fred, knocked up any poodles lately?"

"Woof, woof."

"You old dog, you!"

After leaving the bathroom, whose antiquated plumbing clunked and sputtered in protest, he headed downstairs where he heard chattering voices coming from what he assumed was the kitchen. He was about to push open the closed door when he paused.

"Where did you get those Frosted Flakes?" he heard Jessie's voice ask shrilly.

"They were in the grocery bags," a small-boy voice answered.

"Well, don't eat them. They belong to our guest, Luke Carter. And he's leaving."

"But I already put milk on them," the kid whined. "And there's three other kinds of cereal, too. How's he gonna eat all this stuff himself? Is he fat?"

There was a long silence, for which Luke planned to punish Jessie later, before she answered simply, "No."

But the kid didn't give up. "Besides, how's this Luke dude gonna leave now? There's three feet of snow covering his car. And I'm not shoveling that driveway again. It's a mile long."

Three feet of snow? He smiled. God, or someone, was on his side.

Jessie groaned. Apparently she didn't consider the snow a heavenly blessing. *Yet.*

"Do you think he knows anything about karate?" the kid went on to the accompaniment of slurping noises.

It must be Willie, the eleven-year-old Bruce Lee clone Jessie had described.

"Oh, you are such a toad," a girl's voice said. "Karate, karate, karate . . . that's all you think about."

"Yeah, at least I'm improving my body. You give yours away like lollipops, Darlene. You are a slut. S-L-U-T."

"I'm gonna kill you, you little twerp."

"Put down your knife, Darlene," Jessie cautioned.

Well, enough eavesdropping for now. Luke pushed open the kitchen door and saw four stunned kids gaping at him, and one not-so-pleased adult woman.

"Oh, my Gawd!" a young girl wearing enough makeup to plaster a wall exclaimed. *Darlene.* "It's Brad Pitt. Aunt Jessie brought home a movie star."

On the other side of the table, a fat black girl with buck teeth was inhaling Pop Tarts as if they might disappear. *Kajeeta.* She scrutinized him from head to toe, found him not so interesting, and went on eating.

Another boy, wearing wire-rimmed spectacles and a condescending expression, was reading the back of the Frosted Flakes package, reciting the ingredients. He wore a catalog picture of a computer taped to his forehead probably as a Christmas hint. *Henry, aka Bill Gates.* He swept Luke with an appraising look, taking in his well-worn jeans and ratty black T-shirt, before asking, "How many credit cards do you have?"

Luke stifled a laugh.

Then a skinny little kid with orange hair, about two zillion freckles, and ears that could propel an airplane—*Willie*—piped in, "Wanna see my numchucks?" He waved a hand in the air, holding a pair of foot-long black sticks connected by a small chain—*nunchakus.*

Jessie glanced with horror at each of the kids, then

him, before laying her head down on the table in resignation.

He plopped down in the chair next to Jessie, patted her shoulders, then beamed at the kids. "Hi, I'm Luke. You can call me Uncle Luke. Your Aunt Jessie and I are gonna get married soon. You're all invited to the wedding."

Chapter Four

A half hour later, Luke was outside helping Willie and Henry and Kajeeta shovel the driveway, which indeed seemed about a mile long and three feet deep in snow. And the flakes continued to come down steadily. *Thank you, God! I'm trapped.* Darlene was inside, probably painting her toenails or something equally important. Fred was rolling in the snow like an orgasmic lunatic. He probably smelled female dog scent in the buried grass.

After Luke had made his amazing wedding declaration in the kitchen—it had amazed even him—Jessie had sputtered at him unintelligibly for several moments before hissing, "We have to talk . . . in private. You dolt!"

He was pretty sure she didn't have wild sex in mind. So he took his cue and hightailed it outside to shovel his butt off. With any luck, Jessie would cool off before he went back inside.

"Do you have a computer?" Henry asked him, jolting him back to the present as he pushed his foggy glasses up on the bridge of his nose for the umpteenth time. The colors from the computer on his forehead were bleeding down his nose and onto his cheeks from the wet snow. He looked ridiculous.

There were teenagers in the world today buying

guns and drugs, Luke thought. All this boy wanted was a lousy computer.

Luke felt like crying.

Or hugging the kid.

Or driving to the nearest Computer World and buying him whatever equipment he wanted. Which was impossible with the roads blocked by the storm. Not that Jessie, with her raging pride, would ever allow him such an extravagant charity.

"Yeah, I have a computer," Luke finally answered. "Nothing fancy. Just an IBM home system."

That was all it took. Henry spat out one question after another about megabytes and rams and high-tech software programs, none of which Luke was able to answer. He scarcely knew what a cursor was.

"Hie-yah!" Willie yelled as he attempted a flying side kick, landing with a thud on his well-padded bottom. The Karate Kid he was not. Slack-jawed, Luke watched as the youngster dusted himself off, then waddled over, wearing so many layers of clothing he looked like a roly-poly bear, with only his eyes and mouth visible under a wool cap and scarf. "I'll show you my moves if you show me yours," Willie said right off.

Luke choked.

"Give me a break!" Henry said, and tramped away to the other end of the driveway to shovel, muttering, "Not that again!"

"I beg your pardon," Luke squeaked out to Willie, who was staring up at him, avidly awaiting his answer.

"I'm plannin' on getting my black belt in karate, but I'm havin' trouble with some of the moves," Willie explained, meanwhile poking out his tongue to catch snowflakes in little-boy fashion.

Oh! The boy is talking about karate moves. Whew! I shoulda known. Luke caught himself poking out his own tongue to catch snowflakes.

"So, are you into karate? Do you have a black belt? Huh?" Willie persisted. "Betcha you do, lookin' like Brad Pitt and all. Betcha you learned all the moves early on, to impress the chicks and all. Like Chuck Norris."

Oh, my God! More like the Ninja turtles.

"How come your eyes are crossed? You look really weird when you do that. Aunt Clara says your face might freeze forever and ever if you make faces. You're not gonna teach me any karate moves, are you? Grown-ups never have the time for kids," he grumbled. Throwing down his shovel, he stalked toward the house.

Kajeeta huffed up the slight incline from the bottom of the driveway, and Luke braced himself. What was this? Trial by kid?

When the girl drew near, Luke got his licks in first. "I've got to make a telephone call. Can you finish this small section?"

"Phone's disconnected," Kajeeta panted out. If Willie had looked like a roly-poly bear, Kajeeta resembled a huge, mutant peach in her oversized, pale orange, one-piece snow suit.

"Huh?"

"Willie was makin' so many 900 calls to one of those karate hotlines, he ran the bill up to two hundred dollars. Aunt Clara refused to pay, and Ma Bell cut us off."

Oh, great! Good thing I have a cellular phone in the back of my car. I can't let Jessie know about that, though. Nope. She'd probably call a helicopter service to air-evac me out.

"I want to be a dancer someday . . . and a singer," Kajeeta informed him out of the clear blue sky.

Her comment had no relevance whatsoever to anything, not that Willie or Henry's questions did, either. Hell, were these kids so lonely for company that they'd spill their guts to any stranger?

Yes.

"Do you think I have a chance?"

"Everybody has a chance," he assured her, and he meant it.

She beamed at him as if he'd handed her a million bucks.

These kids of Clara's, who clearly had emotional problems, tugged at Luke's heartstrings. "If you don't dream big, it's not worth dreaming at all," he continued with a catch in his voice. "And there isn't anything in the world a person can't have if they want it badly enough."

He kept his fingers crossed behind his back as he spoke because he sure as hell wanted Jessie. And he didn't want to believe there was any chance he couldn't get her.

But how did he convince her?

Wild sex, he decided with sudden, pure male insight. Yep, that made sense. He was great in the sack, if he did say so himself. All he had to do was seduce Jessie into his bed. Then he'd convince her that he was her Christmas Miracle, not her Christmas Curse.

He handed his shovel to Kajeeta, who was still rambling on about her dreams and Weight Watchers and dance lessons and menstrual cramps and God only knew what else. He started toward the house, a determined glint in his eye.

A little niggling voice in his brain suggested that perhaps he ought to try convincing Jessie of his love first, but another part of his body, down a lot lower, moved. It actually moved. And he could swear it said, *wild sex, wild sex, wild sex*.

Who was Luke to argue?

No sooner did Luke hang up his coat on a wooden peg in the kitchen than Jessica grabbed the infuriating man by his ponytail and dragged him into the small, closet-like pantry, locking the door behind her.

"Ouch!" he complained.

She released him and planted a hand on each of her hips, clad in a pair of skintight jeans. Her suitcase was in the car Julio had stolen, so she'd had no choice but to wear a pair of Darlene's jeans and a T-shirt that read "Born To Be Wild." It was all part of the Christmas Curse, of course.

Luke was grinning at her.

She shoved him hard with a palm against his chest. "I could kill you for telling those kids such an outrageous lie about our marrying."

He didn't budge an inch. "Now, Jessie—"

"And stop looking at my hips. I know they're too big. You don't have to . . . oomph!"

He hauled her flush against his body and leaned back against the counter top. "Your hips are perfect," he rasped out. Then, before she could react, he spread his long legs and pulled her even tighter into the cradle of his thighs.

Jessie saw stars as the most incredible sensations shot like wildfire through her instantly attuned nerve endings. She forgot why she was so mad at Luke, why she'd shanghaied him into the pantry, why she wanted him out of her life. Heck, she forgot her own name.

He gripped her head in both hands. "How do you

feel about wild sex?" he growled just before his mouth swooped down and captured her lips, silencing any protest she might have made.

Wild sex? She would have said, "I hate it" or "How dare you!" or "Huh? What's that?" or "Yesyesyes," but she was incapable of coherent speech. She couldn't talk at all. She was reduced to a whimpering vegetable as Luke devoured her mouth, alternately hard, then soft, pressing and sucking.

She barely recognized the mewling, guttural words of encouragement emitting from her. And when he forced her mouth open with his thrusting tongue, he filled her with such exquisite longing that she drew deeply on him.

He made a raw sound deep in his throat, and she exulted.

The smell of spices surrounded them—cinnamon and basil and cloves. From outside, she could hear the muted, distant laughter of the children. Upstairs in Darlene's bedroom, a Madonna tape blasted out suggestive lyrics in a thrumming rhythm. But all Jessica could think of was the delicious feel of her body pressed up against Luke. Of his lips nuzzling her neck, whispering sweet, sinful things.

Like magic, his fingers slid up under the back of her T-shirt and deftly, with a mere flick, released the catch on her bra. She pulled back to protest, or was she arching her back in invitation? It must have been the latter, because it felt so right when his big hands moved around to the front and cupped her breasts high, from underneath, so that his mouth could take first one aching nipple, then the other through the thin fabric, and suckle deeply.

Her legs trembled all the way down to her wobbly ankles, but he held her firmly in place with his powerful thighs. His hands framed her hips, then moved in a wide caress to palm her bare buttocks.

My bare buttocks!

When had the brute unbuttoned her jeans and pulled down the zipper? When had he slipped his devious hands inside the back of her panties?

Had she lost her mind completely, letting herself be seduced by a too smooth Brad Pitt clone? Had the Christmas Curse totally blindsided her this year?

She tore her lips from his.

Chest heaving, Luke looked down at the precious woman in his arms, who was stiffening with resistance by the minute. His foggy brain fought through the blistering arousal that consumed and disoriented him.

"No," Jessie said in a small voice, but her fingers still dug into his shoulders. Luke also noticed the sexual glaze that misted her honey eyes and the deep pants that came from her parted, kiss-swollen lips.

He hadn't lost her yet.

Wrapping his arms tightly around her waist, he walked her to the opposite counter, sitting her rump on the edge. Before she could blink, or even think of saying "no," he swept her jeans and panties down her parted legs and pulled them off her sneakered feet, which dangled a foot from the floor.

She looked down at herself, naked from navel to calves, with obvious incredulity. Before she could bolt, Luke tilted her chin upward and held her eyes in a coaxing caress. He fished a foil packet from the back pocket of his jeans just before dropping them and his boxers to the floor.

"Please," he whispered and guided her hand to him.

She didn't resist. Instead, in a daze, she ran her fingertips over him lightly, in awe, before taking him in both hands.

He closed his eyes as an explosion of bright lights went off in his head. When his pulse slowed down to breakneck speed, he gently grasped her hands and placed them on his shoulders.

"We shouldn't," she said softly, even as she pulled him closer and spread her legs wider in welcome.

"We should," he insisted, nipping her neck and looping his hands under her knees, dragging her tush even farther out on the edge of the counter.

"I'll be sorry later . . . you'll be sorry," she moaned, and wrapped her legs around his waist.

"No . . . never," he grunted as he eased himself into her tightness. She clenched him spasmodically, and he feared he'd come, way too soon. For long, long moments, forehead to forehead, imbedded fully, he waited out her first orgasm.

When she sighed, finally, he smiled and pulled away to examine her blushing face.

"Oh, Jessie, I love you."

Her face paled with shock.

He hadn't meant to say the words yet. They just came out.

"No. No, you don't. You're just like all men. You think you need to say . . . o-o-oh!"

To stifle her protests, he'd pulled out, then stroked back in. Once, twice, three excruciating times.

"I love you, Jessie. Believe that." This time when he filled her, he twisted his hips, side to side.

She began to keen with the beginning of another climax, but he wanted to slow her down. "Look at us," he urged her. Her half-lidded eyes moved in the direction he pointed, and widened with the same wonder he felt. Highlighted by the winter sunshine streaking through the single window in the pantry, fine red curls blended with his dark, crisp pubic hairs where they were joined, creating an erotic picture, like silken threads in a tapestry.

A tear slipped down her cheek. "We're beautiful together," she whispered.

"Yes," he agreed thickly, and allowed himself to succumb to the overpowering need he had for her. This time when he withdrew and plunged into her, she rippled around him. And each time he stroked, and stroked, and stroked, he repeated, "I love you."

She no longer protested his love words. Maybe she believed him now. Then again, maybe she was as swept away as he was by the most explosive orgasm of his life. With blood roaring in his ears, and bells ringing, he reared his head back and cried out his release, pummeling into her one last time.

Jessie shuddered from head to toe and hung onto him fiercely, crying out, "Oh, oh, oh, oh, oh, oh. . . ."

Even when the racking shudders no longer shook them both, Luke still heard bells ringing. He had to give himself a mental pat on the back. When he'd planned *wild sex*, he'd never imagined that it would happen so soon or that it would be as spectacular as what he'd just experienced . . . bell-ringing and all that. He must be even better than he'd always thought.

"Oh, my God! It's Aunt Clara," Jessie said with horror.

"What about Aunt Clara?" he said, bemused, giving her luscious lips a quick kiss as he eased himself out of her body.

His first clue that he was in big trouble came when she punched him in the stomach, just before she slid to the floor and jerked on her panties and jeans.

"Ooomph!" he said in delayed reaction to her punch, although it didn't really hurt. "Why'd you do that?" He decided to pull up his own pants, as well. Odds were against a repeat performance anytime soon.

"Because you seduced me, you creep. Because you made love to me in Aunt Clara's pantry, for heaven's sake. Because Aunt Clara's bell has been ringing forever, and I've been down here engaging in a world-class wall-banger."

Well, at least she has the good taste to recognize world class when it hits her like a ton of testosterone. Then, *so that's what the bell ringing was?* But he didn't voice his thoughts. Instead, he remarked, "I wasn't the one who dragged you into the pantry by the hair looking for wild sex. You seduced me, babe, not the other way around. Not that I wasn't willing."

He reached for her and she slapped his hands away.

"Wild sex! That's what you mentioned when we came in here. Yes, you did, you said something about wild sex just before you kissed me. I heard you. Don't deny it. You deliberately seduced me."

"Whatever." He was in too good a mood to argue. "When can we get married? I mean, will you marry me?" *Oh, boy, I'm getting this love stuff all out of order. Probably because I'm horny again. Just looking at all that wild red hair makes me hot. I wonder what she'd think if I suggested . . . oh, boy. Slow down.* "Jessie, honey," he started over, "I love you. Will you marry me? Tomorrow. Or the day after that?" *And can we go have wild sex again? Now? Maybe in that antique bathtub on the third floor.*

"Love? Love?" she sputtered. "You are driving with two bricks short of a full load. And stop leering at me. You're not touching me again."

Wanna bet? "Leering? I don't leer, babe. That look you see in my eye is a promise." He jiggled his eyebrows at her and reached around to unlock the door. Aunt Clara's bell was jingling to beat the band.

No sooner did he open the door than he saw Willie, openly eavesdropping. Willie took in the appearance of both of them, then did a little victory dance, karate style, around the kitchen.

"Oh, Lord!" Jessie said and scooted away, down the hall and toward Aunt Clara's incessant bell-ringing.

He looked at the freckle-faced twit and knew that Jessie had deliberately abandoned him to the adolescent Bruce Lee. Probably her idea of just punishment.

"So, did you boink Aunt Jessie in the pantry?" the kid asked unabashedly.

Luke looked down to make sure he hadn't left his zipper undone. Everything was in order. He sliced a glare at the curious boy, warning, "Willie, that's enough."

He started down the hall, following in Jessie's tracks, but Willie bird-dogged right after him, throwing in a few side kicks and an occasional grunt of "Uut" along the way.

"I need a bong pole. How big is yours?"

Luke's step faltered.

"Will you help me make one out of Aunt Clara's broom? A bong pole's supposed to equal your height, but I think a broom handle will do for me. Don't you? Huh? Will ya help me? Huh?"

"No." Luke was already climbing the stairs, and Willie padded after him doggedly. No, that padding sound was Fred. Somehow they'd picked up Fred along the way.

"No?" There was a long silence following his disappointed question, and Luke walked down the second floor hall toward a bedroom where he heard voices. He'd thought he lost the kid until Willie asked, "How old were you the first time you did *it* to a girl?"

Luke stopped suddenly, and Willie and the dog ran into him with a yelp and a bark.

"Listen, Willie," he said, hunkering down. "You can't ask those kinds of questions of complete strangers."

Willie's face and big ears flushed bright red and his eyes filled with tears. "I don't feel like you're a stranger."

And Luke felt like a rat. Hell, the kid was asking a normal question for a boy his age. But usually it was addressed to a parent . . . a dad. Which Willie didn't have.

"Okay," he said, taking a deep breath and wondering how he'd gotten himself into this predicament. "I was fourteen the first time."

"Fourteen! Fourteen!"

Luke stood, laughing, and rumpled the boy's hair as he continued toward Aunt Clara's bedroom. He heard Willie mutter as he skipped back down the stairs, "Did you hear that, Fred? Fourteen! Uncle Luke musta been retarded or somethin'. Guess lookin' like Brad Pitt doesn't mean everything."

* * *

Aunt Clara took one look at him when he entered the bedroom and exclaimed, "Thank the Lord! He sent me a miracle."

Luke cast Jessie a knowing smirk that said clearly, "See, I am so a Christmas Miracle."

Jessie was sitting on a straight-backed chair next to the bed, talking to a sixtyish gray-haired woman with one leg encased in a white cast from toe to thigh.

"Aunt Clara, this is Lucas Carter, the man I told you about who helped me last night when the van got stuck in the snow."

Luke arched a brow at Jessie as he moved around to the other side of the bed. *Lying to a nun now, are you, Jessie? Tsk-tsk!* He leaned down and ignored the hand Aunt Clara extended to him, giving her parchment cheek a light kiss.

It was the right thing to do, he could tell immediately. She literally glowed as she took his right hand in both of hers and drew him down to sit on her bed.

"I'm so pleased to meet you, Aunt Clara . . . I hope you don't mind my calling you Aunt Clara . . . I feel as if I know you already."

"Of course not, my boy." Still holding his hand, she studied him intently before nodding, as if answering one of her own silent questions. "So, Darlene tells me that you plan on marrying my sweet girl, Jessie."

Jessie gasped and turned greenish. Probably all that fruitcake she'd consumed.

"Yes. Yes, I do," he said firmly before Jessie could say different. "Jessie doesn't think I'm serious, but I am."

"I am *not* going to marry him," Jessie told Aunt Clara when she finally regained her voice. "We hardly know each other." With that, she shot Luke a glare, daring him to contradict her. At the same time, her face turned from green to a pretty shade of pink—a nice contrast to all those unruly red ringlets—as she remembered just how well they did know each other.

"Well, I don't know if the length of time two people know each other is a true indicator of feelings," Aunt Clara opined.

I love this old bird. "Right," Luke intervened quickly. "Look how long she knew Burp, and they were a mismatch from the get-go. Why, he even played"—he made an exaggerated shiver of distaste—"golf."

"His name is Burt," Jessie stormed.

Aunt Clara snickered behind her fingers.

"And you and I are the mismatch," Jessica railed. "Geez, Brad Pitt and Little Orphan Annie!"

"Who's Brad Pitt?" Aunt Clara asked.

Luke and Jessie both gaped at her, wondering what world she'd been living in the past few years.

"I'd like to get married real soon," Luke went on, ignoring Jessie's hiss of warning. "How soon do you think it will be before you're out of that cast, Aunt Clara?"

"Well, the doctor said I could have a soft cast next week," she said tentatively.

"Gol-ly," he said contemplatively, tapping his chin. "I don't know if I can wait that long." He turned to an outraged Jessie. "What do you think, honey? Can you wait for a whole week?"

"Lucas, I just knew when I saw you walk through that door that you were the answer to my prayers," Aunt Clara said, smiling at him.

He'd like to be the answer to someone's prayers, although not a nun's. But Jessie didn't look much like she was in the mood for praying. In fact, her eyes were crossed. Someone ought to tell her about faces freezing and stuff. Perhaps he should call Willie.

"You are the worst Christmas Curse I've ever had," Jessie gritted out at him.

Aunt Clara gasped at her harsh words, and Luke felt a little twinge of hurt, as well.

"Jessica Jones, what an awful thing to say! I brought you up better than that." Then Aunt Clara's frown melted away as she confided in a softer voice, "I was praying this morning for a Christmas Miracle. Who are we to question the answer God gives us? A miracle is a miracle."

Aunt Clara and Jessie looked at him then—him, the miracle.

Aunt Clara beamed.

Jessie's honey eyes threw sparks of disbelief.

Luke wondered how soon till he could have wild sex again.

Chapter Five

Later that afternoon, they were all in the living room, decorating a huge blue spruce tree that Luke and the kids had dragged in from the woods behind the house. Christmas carols played on the radio in the background, interrupted repeatedly by storm warnings.

Aunt Clara was reclining on the sofa in front of the fireplace where Luke had carried her two hours ago. She gave them gentle instructions as to which ornament went where while her knitting needles clicked away at one of her perpetual afghans.

"Are you still mad at me, honey?" Luke said close to Jessica's ear, causing her to jump about two feet.

"Criminey, do you have to sneak up on me all the time?" she snapped.

She'd been avoiding the rascal all day, along with his knowing looks, his disarming smiles, and "accidental" touches. Luke had laughed, and stalked her just the same.

She couldn't believe she'd actually made love with a man she'd met the night before. She hadn't been thinking. It had happened too soon. It shouldn't have happened at all.

She had to get rid of the tempting hunk soon or lose her sanity. Or something worse. Her heart.

"What do you call a nun with one leg?" he asked with a glimmer of humor in his flashing eyes, slanting a glance at Aunt Clara to make sure she didn't overhear.

A joke? She tried to look at him disapprovingly.

"Hopalong Chastity."

She giggled reluctantly, and Luke used that opportunity to put an arm around her shoulder and squeeze her close.

Despite the thrill of excitement engendered by that slight embrace, she ducked and escaped, putting several feet between them.

He chuckled.

"Maybe you can still leave tonight . . . if the roads get cleared," she suggested.

Why did her heart constrict at the possibility? He'd have to leave sometime. If not tonight, then tomorrow. Everyone she'd ever loved left eventually. He would, too.

Not that I love him.

And there he went again, looking at her with such hurt, and longing, in his beautiful eyes. He did it every time she rebuffed him.

It's not as if he really loves me.

But what if he did?

"No way!" Willie protested. "Uncle Luke can't leave tonight. He's makin' Philadelphia cheese steaks for dinner."

That was another thing that made Jessie mad. No one would eat her peanut butter sandwiches. They were scarfing down all the junk food Luke had bought, including minute steaks and rolls for a Christmas Eve dinner. He must have spent a hundred dollars in that Uni-Mart.

And Aunt Clara wasn't even protesting that they would miss *Vilia*, the traditional Slovak Christmas Eve dinner she always prepared, where everyone must taste at least twelve of the many dishes assembled, presumably in honor of the twelve apostles. The merry meal always included, at the least, the core items of *oplatky*, the Christmas communion wafers dipped in honey; *bobalky*, braided homemade bread; red wine; *pierogies*, the little cheese-stuffed pies; several kinds of fish; mushroom soup; poppyseed rolls; sauerkraut; nuts; and fresh fruit.

Well, she had to give Luke credit. In the spirit of improvisation, he was putting together a new-age *Vilia* supper, complete with Philadelphia cheese steaks, Frosted Flakes, Fruit Loops, peanut butter and jelly sandwiches, Hawaiian Punch, and fruitcake, of course. And everyone—all the kids and Aunt Clara—acted as if everything was hunky-dory.

Was she the only one worried to death about the Christmas Curse, and the kind of holiday disaster that loomed this year?

"You can't make Uncle Luke leave. He's gonna show me how to dance the Philadelphia Stomp later tonight," Kajeeta said, interrupting Jessica's dismal thoughts. Kajeeta peered up shyly at Luke for confirmation.

"Yep," he told Kajeeta, and then caught Jessica's skeptical frown. "And if you're real good, sugar, I'll do the two-step with you." He winked suggestively and whispered *sotto voce*, "Re-e-eal slow. After the kids have gone to sleep."

"In your dreams!" she said haughtily. But already he'd planted some tantalizing pictures in her mind. The Christmas-tree lights flickering in the darkened room, fireplace roaring, soft music . . . *Get a grip, girl.*

"And Luke said he would French braid my hair," Darlene added, having just condescended to join the group.

Everyone gawked at Luke, astounded.

He shrugged with a sheepish grin. "Hey, my sister Ellie made me do her hair when we were kids. She was bigger than me *then*, and considered me her personal slave."

Everyone laughed at the image of Luke being forced by his sister to be her slave.

"Aunt Jessie, you oughta hang onto this guy," Henry added in the end. "He's a lot better than that Burp fellow you brought here last year."

She started to tell Henry that his name was not Burp, but all the kids were having such a good time. And besides, the name Burp suited the jerk much better than Burt, anyhow. So she joined in the good-natured ribbing.

"Tell us about your work," Aunt Clara asked Luke, her nimble fingers moving the knitting needles in an intricate pattern as she spoke.

Luke was on a ladder putting a star atop the tall tree.

"Yeah, did you ever bodyguard anyone famous?" Henry asked as he helped to brace the shaky ladder.

"Sure. All the time," Luke answered, tilting his head this way and that until he positioned the star just right. "Even Bill Gates one time," he told a flabbergasted Henry as he descended the ladder and folded it, preparing to take it out to the kitchen. "He hired me and four other guys to accompany him to Japan. It was a time when there was a lot of anti-American sentiment there."

Henry was gazing at Luke as if he were God.

"And I just came back yesterday afternoon from working a Janet Jackson concert at the Spectrum in South Philly," he told a *very* impressed Kajeeta as he passed en route to the kitchen.

When he reentered the living room, all the kids jumped on him with eager questions.

"Do you *really* know Janet Jackson?" Kajeeta wanted to know.

"Well, I wouldn't say we're friends. But, yes, I've met her and worked for her."

"How about movie stars?" Darlene asked.

"Yep. Lots of movie stars, like Bruce Willis, Sharon Stone, Antonio Banderas, Kim Basinger. And rock stars. Once I guarded Madonna . . . now, that was a trip," he recalled with amusement. "Even Michael Jackson, though he usually has his own private security team."

"Did you ever bodyguard Chuck Norris?" Willie wanted to know.

Luke shook his head negatively. "Mostly I work for politicians—those who aren't high up enough to qualify for CIA protection, and corporate bigwigs traveling in third world countries."

"Wow!" the kids sighed.

Luke addressed Aunt Clara then, seeming to give her a special silent message. "Once I even guarded Mother Teresa."

"O-o-oh, Luke," Aunt Clara breathed. Her simple words said loud and clear that she thought Luke was the answer to her Christmas prayers . . . sent special delivery by God, via Mother Teresa, no doubt.

Jessie felt the happiness and Christmas spirit swell around her, filling the room, but it was a sham. Because these kids still believed . . . perhaps not in Santa Claus . . . but in miracles. And there was going to be no miracle when they came downstairs tomorrow and found no gifts.

"Stop worrying, Jessica," Aunt Clara said softly with uncanny perception, sensing her distress. "For once in your life, trust. Especially at Christmas time, let yourself believe that good things can just happen."

"Hah! The only thing that ever happens to me at Christmas time is my Christmas Curse," Jessie grumbled.

"Now, Jessica, I have never believed that nonsense."

Henry distracted Aunt Clara then, wanting her advice on some tinsel that had become tangled.

"Have some more fruitcake," Luke urged, pressing a too-big hunk against Jessie's mouth. Lord, the man must be part Indian the way he crept up on her unawares all the time.

"I don't want any more. I hate fruitcake. And I'm not hungry," she insisted, which gave Luke the opportunity to shove the huge morsel in her open mouth. "Glmph."

He kept his fingertips on her lips an intimate second too long, and his smoldering eyes told her he had a hunger of an entirely different kind. Leaning close, he whispered, "Are you ready for some more wild sex?"

She chewed quickly so she could answer him, but he laughed again and moved away.

Willie ambled up with a calculating gleam in his eyes. "So tell me, Aunt Jessie. How old were you when you lost your virginity? Uncle Luke was fourteen."

She began to choke as the blasted fruitcake went down the wrong throat passage. When she finally recovered, after drinking a glass of Hawaiian Punch—another of Luke's purchases—her gaze shot across the room.

Luke threw his hands out hopelessly.

Meanwhile, Willie karate-chopped a fruitcake in half.

Jessica couldn't remember when the Christmas Curse had ever been so bad.

It was close to midnight before all the kids were nestled in their beds. Aunt Clara had retired soon after their absolutely wonderful Christmas Eve dinner—the best any of them had ever experienced. Jessica was about to call it a night herself, but first she had to take Fred out for one last nature call.

"I'll take him," Luke offered, coming down the hall from the kitchen where he'd just gone to put away the last of the leftovers and turn out the lights. "I need to make a few more phone calls."

"Thanks. I'm really beat." Then his words sank in. "Telephone calls?"

"Yeah, I have a cellular phone in my car," he admitted.

She was too tired to be angry with him anymore. "You rat," was the best she could come up with.

"Hey, I have to have a cellular phone in the car at all times, in case of emergency. The nature of my business, you know. Besides, I had to call my sister Ellie to go get my laundry from the laundromat, didn't I? Did you really think I would have gone with you so willingly if I knew I was losing a couple hundred dollars' worth of clothes?"

Jessica wasn't sure what she'd been thinking at the time. Or if she'd been thinking at all.

More important, Luke looked really worried now as he pulled on his jacket with Fred running circles of anticipation around his legs.

"What's wrong?"

"Jessie, I thought I was going to be able to pull off a Christmas surprise for you. I called my sister earlier today, like I said, and . . . well, a few other people. But even with the storm finally stopping tonight, I just don't think I'll be able to get any gifts here by tomorrow morning with the roads the way they are. It looks like there really won't be any gifts when the kids wake up. I'm sorry."

Tears welled in her eyes, and her throat closed over. "Oh, Luke. You did that for these kids?"

"No, Jessie, I did it for you," he said, stepping closer.

She'd been skittish all day every time Luke got near her, but now she opened her arms for him and hugged him warmly. "Thank you. No one's ever done anything so nice for me before."

He smelled like wood smoke from the fireplace, and evergreen boughs, and fruitcake. She smiled against his neck—the brute smelled like fruitcake. And she was developing a compelling taste for fruitcake, darn it!

He pulled back slightly. The fingertips of one hand brushed some unruly ringlets off her cheek, then trailed down to her throat, resting lightly on the pulse point. He gazed at her somberly as his head descended . . . one infinitesimal inch at a time. She angled her lips to meet his kiss.

Unlike their earlier, frenzied touches, Luke acted as if he had all the time in the world now. Gently, gently he laid his lips on hers, exploring, coaxing

All of Jessica's senses heightened. She felt the heat of Luke's body. She heard a Mormon Tabernacle Choir rendition of "Silent Night" on the radio in the background, more beautiful than the highest heavenly hosts. The fire crackled a seductive lure. The glittering lights on the tree outshone the very stars in the night sky.

Jessica never knew a kiss could be so expressive. And there was no doubt in her mind that Luke was using this gentle kiss to convey all the emotion she refused to recognize. With its shifting, changing textures, its feathery pressures and strokes, Luke's kiss perfected all the nuances that a man's lips could wield on a woman.

He's showing me that he loves me.

Jessica scrunched her eyes closed tight at the wonder of it all.

And, God help me, I love him, too.

Cupping her face in both hands, Luke looked her fully in the eyes. The dog practically crossed its legs, yipping near their feet. "Wait for me, Jessie. We need to talk."

She nodded, too benumbed to speak.

"I'll be right back," he said huskily over his shoulder. His hand was on the doorknob when a car horn blasted loudly, coming up the drive. Luke turned to her in question.

She shrugged, unknowing.

They both stood on the porch, shivering, watching the red car come barreling up the drive at breakneck speed, way too fast for the snowy conditions. It fishtailed in the turn-around area before the steps.

"Oh, this is too much!" Jessica exclaimed as a tall, lean teenager in a black leather jacket and cowboy boots emerged from the driver's side, grinning smugly.

"Is it . . ." Luke began to ask; ". . . could it be . . . ?"

"Julio."

"*Feliz Navidad*, everyone," the witless kid called out, as if he hadn't disrupted the lives of a whole bunch of people . . . in fact, ruined their Christmas. Jessica clenched her fists at her sides, counting to ten before she ripped him limb from limb.

That's when Luke tugged on her sleeve, pointing incredulously at the armloads of gaily wrapped packages Julio was grabbing from the back seat of Jessica's car.

"I'm gonna kill him," she gritted out.

Luke wrapped both arms around her from behind, locking her in place. "Slow down. Give him a chance to explain. Then let me kill him."

"Hi, Aunt Jessie," Julio said breezily as he walked by them, big as you please. "Don't just stand there like an icicle. Bring some packages in."

"Now, Jessie. Now, Jessie," Luke cautioned, "he's only a kid."

As Luke dragged her by the hand down to the car and started loading packages in her arms, she pointed out, "That *kid* let me think I was carrying an empty pistol. That *kid* stole my purse and"—she glanced at the dozens of gifts piled in the back seat—"oh, damn, he must have maxed out my credit cards."

Julio was back, beaming up at both of them as if he were a teenage Hispanic Santa Claus. "I did good, didn't I, Aunt Jessie?"

Luke jammed a package on top of the pile in her arms, blocking her face before she could answer.

"I even got a laptop computer for Henry. Boy, are those things expensive. You really should get a larger maximum on your Visa card, you know."

Jessica walked stiffly into the house, counting to ten, then twenty, trying to avoid her inevitable explosion. Behind her, she heard Julio ask Luke, "Who are you? Aunt Jessie's new boyfriend? Man, I hope you're better than that dweeb she was shakin' the sheets with before. Think his name was Burp."

"I think I'm gonna like you, Julio," Luke chortled. "What'd you get for Kajeeta?"

They'd entered the living room and were arranging the gifts under the tree.

"Ballet and tap shoes. And dance tights. But, man oh man, was it hard to find them things in an extra-large chunky size! I got Willie a bong pole, one of those stupid karate pajama outfits, and a Ninja turtle tape. And I bought that bad-ass Darlene a Walkman and a big carry-case of Revlon makeups. Now she can be a high-class slut instead of a low-class bad girl." He grinned at Luke, then fake-punched him in the arm to show he was teasing.

Then Julio added the topper. "Hey, anyone ever tell

you that you look a little bit like Brad Pitt . . . except older?"

Jessica did laugh then. The whole situation was so ridiculous. But there would be a Christmas after all. She was still angry with Julio—furious actually—but he'd delivered their Christmas miracle. And for that she had to be thankful. So she couldn't kill the messenger tonight, but tomorrow, *tomorrow* she would give him holy hell.

"I'm starved. I don't know how women do it. Shoppin' their booties off all the time. Man, it wipes a guy out. Is there anything to eat?"

"Fruitcake," she and Luke said at the same time.

A short time later, Jessica exited the bathroom and was shuffling along in her furry bunny slippers and flannel nightgown toward her bedroom. The house was silent now, except for the occasional creak of its aged "bones" and the whistling wind outside. Pleasantly exhausted, she mused that it had been one of the best Christmas Eves of her life, despite that misguided brat, Julio. And she had Luke to thank for it all.

So she shouldn't have been surprised when she opened her bedroom door to see him lying on her bed. The light of the bedside lamp reflected on his sensually posed, half-reclining body propped against the headboard with two pillows, arms folded behind his neck.

Shirtless and barefooted.

Wearing a pair of jeans that were already enticingly unbuttoned at the top.

Every hormone in her body began to tango.

"Luke," she squeaked out, "you can't come in here. Aunt Clara's in the next room."

"So I guess you'll have to be extra quiet when you—"

"Don't say it," she hissed.

"Nice slippers," he remarked as she stomped closer. Then he gave her voluminous nightgown a sweeping assessment. "Sexy negligee, too."

"Oh, get out of here."

"What? You don't want my Christmas present?" He held out a small package wrapped in Frosty the Snowman paper.

She eyed the gift suspiciously, trying hard not to notice the corded sinews ridging his extended arms, the hard tendons ridging his abdomen, the bulge ridging his . . .

Luke chuckled, and she averted her blushing face, taking the gift he tossed into her hands. He was sitting up now, watching her intently.

"God, I love your hair," he said in a husky voice.

She put a hand to the unmanageable curls, which she hated, and her knees felt weak and buttery under his hungry gaze.

"Can I brush it? *Later?*"

Her knees did buckle then. She had to hold on to the bedpost for support.

"Open your gift, Jessie," he urged.

"But I didn't buy you anything," she said with a moue of embarrassment.

"No problem! This gift's for both of us." A twinkle of mischief, not to mention dark, hard-core arousal, in his deep hazel eyes turned her suddenly alert.

That's when she began to suspect what the rogue

had given her. A flutter of excitement teased across her skin as she unpeeled the paper. "Oh!" She put the tips of one hand to her parted lips as she gaped, open-mouthed, at her gift.

The bottle of skin-warming oil.

Chapter Six

"Oh, my!" she gasped, the bottle feeling sinfully hot in her hand.

"I'll second that." He threw his long legs over the side of the bed and stood. Then, boldly holding her eyes, he unzipped his jeans and let them fall to the floor. He wore no underwear. Stepping out of the pant legs, he drawled in a thick, thick voice, "It's peppermint flavored. Do you like peppermint, Jessie?"

She couldn't speak at first, overwhelmed by the beauty of this man . . . this man she'd come to love in such a short time. "I love peppermint," she whispered.

He stood statue-still, five feet away from her, exuding virility. Chiseled bones created stunning curves and planes in his marvelously sculpted face. His hair was clubbed back at the nape, as usual, with a dark rubber band. Not an ounce of excess fat marred his well-toned body, from wide shoulders, to rippled abdomen, to narrow waist and hips, to flat stomach, to . . .

Something primal quickened deep inside her.

. . . to his erection, which stood out in rampant declaration of his need for her . . . his carnal intentions.

Breathlessly she waited for his next move.

There was none. Except for a slight tilt of his head. And she understood what he wanted.

Jessica was not used to this kind of foreplay. Oh, she'd had lovers before . . . not a lot, but a few. And she'd enjoyed sex some of those times, though the men she'd known were usually the aggressors, and she a docile participant. Willing, but never the seducer. Always the seducee.

Luke was insisting on more from her. Much, much more.

Do I want to make love with him?

Oh, yes!

Do I want to please him?

Definitely!

It would only be this one night.

Of course.

Then he'll leave.

They always do.

One night.

"Jessie," Luke hissed. A single word. Raw and soul-wrenchingly impassioned.

She kicked off her bunny slippers.

He smiled.

She released the ribbon of her ponytail and let her hair spill out over her shoulders and down her back.

He sighed.

Clutching the fabric of her nightgown, she began to draw it slowly upward, exposing first her calves and knees and thighs.

His smoldering eyes followed the hem.

She paused at the juncture of her thighs, took a deep breath to overcome her innate shyness, then drew the nightgown up to her waist.

His lips parted as his eyes locked on that part of her.

His ragged breathing was loud and heavy in the silent room.

Licking her dry lips, she gathered courage and pulled the garment the rest of the way upward, over her head.

"Oh, Jessie."

Hunger. His eyes devoured her with a primitive hunger that almost frightened her with its magnitude. His erection was even larger than before, turgid.

He crooked his fingers, coaxing her closer.

She moved halfway.

He closed the distance, still not touching her. Just looking. Then he held a hand out, palm upward, and she realized she still held the warming oil clenched in her hand.

Already, before he'd even touched her, Jessica was fiercely aroused. She didn't know if she could stand to wait. She might splinter apart, way too soon

Taking the bottle in his hand, he unscrewed the lid and sniffed deeply, grinning at her—a teasing grin of anticipation. Then he winked with wicked promise.

For the first time in her life, Jessica felt like swooning.

Shaking a drop of the slick oil onto his forefinger, he traced her lips, parting them. The pungent odor filled the air, and the flavor of candy canes teased her taste buds. Almost immediately, she forgot about the taste and smell, however, as her lips and tongue grew warm, throbbing with an odd heat.

He kept his body a good foot away from her. When she reached out to embrace him, he shook his head, pressing her arms to her sides. "No, sweetheart. Not yet. I want the sensations to center only on the oil. And the erotic places I touch."

Places? She groaned.

"How does it taste, Jessie?"

"Wonderful."

"How does it feel?"

"Tingly."

He laughed. "Can you feel the heat?"

"Ye-e-es," she breathed.

"Are you sure?" he said, his neck craning forward. "I'd better check." With the tip of his tongue, he traced the outline of her lips, then the seam. "Open for me," he demanded, and, before she'd barely complied, his tongue was filling her mouth, exploring. Stroking, in and out. Stroking. "Ummmm, delicious," he murmured against her, his mouth covering hers wetly.

"I can't stand it," she cried at last as her bones turned to jelly with the intense waves of excitement sweeping from her heated lips to her breasts and downward. Yes, downward.

"Good," he rasped out, and turned her so her back was to him, her head lolling on his right shoulder. His steely erection pressed against the cleft of her buttocks. Gently drawing her hair off her face, he anointed the pulse point at the curve of her neck. When it, too, turned warm, he nipped the spot with his teeth, then soothed the abused skin with slow licks of torture.

She tried to turn. "I want to hold you. I want you to hold me."

"Not yet. Put your hands behind my neck," he urged. Then he sketched an oily line from her armpits to her hips on either side, over to the center where he rotated the tip of his forefinger in her navel, then up through the middle of her body to her collarbone. A hot pulse followed wherever he touched, like a line of ignited dynamite powder. He did the same to the backs of her knees, and the insides of her thighs, even the sensitive arches of her feet.

Next he poured a more generous amount of the fluid on one of his palms and rubbed both palms together. He used the wide, callused surfaces to paint her breasts—under, around, the tops, everywhere but on the aureoles or taut peaks where she wanted the heat most. With a mewling cry, she attempted to guide his hands to the aching nipples, but he resisted, chuckling.

"Come," he said, taking her hand and pulling her to the side of the bed. He seated her on the edge and placed several pillows at her waist, forcing the backward. Her elbows were braced on the bed and her breasts were arched high—a continual vibrating thrum in their warm depths. Then he parted her legs and knelt on the floor between her thighs.

"Luke, no. I don't like this. I feel expos—oh . . . oh!"

Finally he was attending to her nipples, drizzling the warm oil around the aureoles, then over the pebbled points themselves. She let out a soft cry as the area turned immediately hot and pulsing.

"Shhh, babe. Just a little longer," he crooned, leaning forward to take her right breast deep in his mouth, suckling rhythmically, while the palm of his left hand drew wide, pressing circles on her other breast.

She tried to rear up off the bed.

He wouldn't let her.

She tried to buck him away with her hips.

He wouldn't budge.

Then he reversed the positions of his mouth and hand.

And she became a keening mass of quivering arousal. Her skin and nerve endings heightened to the point of ecstatic meltdown. She had no control over her flailing hands and trembling thighs.

In that condition, she was scarcely aware that he'd pulled back and was streaming the erotic oil between her legs.

"Oh, no! No, no, no," she protested as she felt the waves of an overpowering climax began to ripple from her womb, down through that hot channel that he was lubricating with the oil on two fingers. When he lowered his head, still with his fingers inside her, and took the nub in his lips, sucking softly, she gave up the fight.

Tears were streaming down her face.

Luke noticed and stopped, sitting back on his haunches. His lips and fingers were slick from the oil, and her.

"Are those happy tears or sad tears?" he asked with concern.

"Happy tears, you brute."

"Good," he growled, standing, and looped his hands under her thighs, lifting her tush off the bed. Then he bent his knees, entering her with a slow, slow, slow upward stroke.

Before he'd fully penetrated, she climaxed around him with violent spasms of pure, shattering pleasure.

When she finally emerged from her delirium of

satisfaction, she lifted her lashes slowly to see Luke still poised above her. Perspiration beaded his upper lip and forehead. A muscle twitched at the side of his compressed lips.

"Kiss me, Luke." She strained her face upward.

With a grunt of sheer male surrender, he lunged into her and brought his mouth down on hers, hard and openmouthed. Then, in a frenzy of movement, he tossed the pillows aside, lifted her hips, and slid her to the middle of the bed.

Jessica tried to caress his shoulders and back, to return his rapacious kisses, but Luke was too out-of-control. His hands and mouth were everywhere, caressing, plucking, sucking, biting, kissing, pressing, pinching, licking.

And her body, which should have been confused by all these conflicting messages, filled with the sweetest burn in the world, overflowing with liquid pleasure which moved closer and closer to the boiling point.

Abruptly, he stopped.

Panting for breath, he rolled them on to their sides, and lifted her topmost leg onto his hip. Unbelievably, he filled her even more completely.

"Jessie," he gasped out, waiting till her lashes fluttered open. When he had her full attention, he whispered, "Can you feel my love flowing? From here"—he pressed a palm against his chest—"down to here?"—he touched the place where they were joined, and Jessica almost exploded with utter ecstasy. "And up inside you"—he moved out and then in for emphasis—"to here?"—he breathed, resting his fingertips against her heart."

"Oh, Luke, don't spoil this by speaking of love. I don't need the words. Really." She tried to kiss him into silence.

He tore his mouth away angrily. "It's love, Jessie. Even if you won't admit it."

Then, with an efficient movement, he rolled over and she was on top of him, straddling his hips.

"If you can't say the words, show me, Jessie," he coaxed. "Love me with your body."

And she did. Oh, how she did!

Jessica hadn't known she had the expertise to make a grown man cry for mercy.

She did.

Jessica hadn't known a woman could climax, over and over, and still want more.

She did.

Jessica hadn't known there were so many erotic points on a man's or a woman's body.

She did now.

Jessica hadn't known a man could control his impending orgasm so stoically.

Oh, boy, did she know now.

Despite her protests, Luke kept repeating, "I love you. I love you. I love you . . ."

She never said the words, but her body did. And, for Luke, that seemed to be enough for now.

Later, but not so much later, they lay under Aunt Clara's handmade quilt, caressing each other softly. Luke gazed down at Jessica and considered himself the luckiest man alive. How had this magic landed in his lap? What miraculous power had put him in the same place as Jessie last night?

He clutched her tighter, overcome with emotion,

and whispered soft words of endearment. Jessie whispered back. Nice words. Complimentary words, though not the ones Luke wanted to hear.

His heart tightened painfully, but he forced himself not to become grim. He knew she loved him, and he understood his Little Orphan Jessie a whole lot better now. Her insecurities. Her fears. Her Christmas Curse, he thought with a silent laugh.

He could wait.

A woman like her would need proof of a man's staying power—and he didn't mean that in the sexual sense. He was staying, for good, no matter what she thought.

For now, he had other things on his mind.

Putting a forefinger under her chin, he tilted her face upward. Immediately, he saw the wariness in her honey eyes. She thought he was going to pressure her on the love and marriage issues.

"So how do you feel about peppermint sticks?" he asked.

"What?" she asked with suspicion.

"Peppermint sticks. Do you like to . . . lick them?"

"Sure, but I don't understand—"

He kicked the quilt off, looking pointedly at his upraised "stick," then over to the bedside table where the bottle of peppermint warming oil stood in waiting.

They both laughed then.

But not for long.

"Why do you and Uncle Luke smell like candy canes?" Willie asked Jessie the next morning, peering up for the first time in an hour from his Ninja turtle tape.

Scraps of Christmas wrapping paper surrounded him
and were scattered across the living room.

"Who has candy canes? I want a candy cane," Kajeeta whined as she pirouetted across the room in her
new flame-red tights.

Even from across the room, Luke saw a rush of pink
stain Jessie cheeks. And her eyes—her soulful eyes—
met his reluctantly, then darted away in embarrassment.

Was she embarrassed by Willie's impudent question, or about the incredible things they'd done to
each other last night?

He'd left Jessie's bed near dawn, not wanting her to
be caught in a compromising situation by any unexpected visitors. She'd been asleep when he slipped out,
and he hadn't talked to her in private since then. Surely
she didn't take his considerate departure as a mark of
abandonment.

He felt hurt by the distance she was putting between them. Last night was special. To them both. He
wanted to shout his love aloud . . . to the kids, to Aunt
Clara, to Jessie. He wanted to hold hands. To kiss under the mistletoe. To hug. And make plans.

But she was as skittish now as a cat on a hot tin roof.

"Candy canes! Oh, you dweeb!" Julio snorted to
Willie, pulling Luke back to the present. Julio was sitting on an easy chair with his feet propped on a has-
sock, basking in the glow of his benevolent charity,
albeit at Jessie's expense. "It's probably skin warming
oil, like they sell in porno shops," Julio explained.

"Porno shops?" Willie inquired.

Everyone turned to look in question, first at Jessie,
then him. Luckily, Aunt Clara was in the kitchen having a cup of tea.

Before he and Jessie had a chance to turn crimson with telling humiliation, Darlene piped in, "Julio, you are such a jerk. You think you're so hot. You think you know everything. You think—"

"Hah! I know a slut when I see one."

"Eff off!"

Julio flicked a middle finger at her.

"That's enough!" Luke roared. Really, someone needed to lay down the law with these kids. They all looked chastened as he continued to glare at them, hands on hips. Eventually they grumbled and went back to examining the Christmas gifts that Julio-Santa had brought them.

At least attention had been diverted away from him and Jessie.

That is, until Willie peered up from his tape once again and asked Luke, "Do you wear a jock strap when you practice karate?"

Luke couldn't speak. Only a gurgling sound came out.

"Gawd!" Henry said and left the room.

"I know what a jock strap is," Kajeeta exclaimed with glee in the middle of an amazing pirouette.

Even Darlene blushed.

"A blush from you, Dar-lene-ey," Julio teased. "Well, wonders never cease."

It was obvious to Luke, if not to anyone else, that Julio had a crush on Darlene. This continual baiting was his juvenile way of showing it.

Darlene was sputtering unintelligible words about cutting out Julio's tongue and sticking it someplace unmentionable.

Jessie fled to the kitchen, muttering something about

helping Aunt Clara with the breakfast dishes. The coward! They'd eaten fruitcake and leftover cheese steaks on paper plates.

Well, she wasn't going to escape from him this time. Perhaps he needed a little help, though.

"Oh, Wil-lie," Luke said in a sugary, coaxing voice. "How'd you like to do me a *big* favor."

Early that afternoon, the house had settled down to a peaceful hum, and Jessica retreated to the kitchen where she was singing "Silent Night" under her breath while puttering around with preparations for Christmas dinner. Julio, God bless him, had purchased an already prepared roasted turkey dinner for ten from a supermarket. It had cost him . . . *her* . . . a hundred bucks.

Jessica planned to take every dollar out of his hide, but not today.

A wonderful peacefulness enveloped Jessica. A feeling of family. Darlene was sitting under the tree playing some of her new CD's on a disc player "Santa" had brought. Henry was teaching Willie how to play a computer game. Kajeeta was watching *A Christmas Carol* on TV with Luke. Aunt Clara was upstairs taking a nap.

If only things could stay this way.

"Aunt Jessie," Willie said, padding into the kitchen barefooted, wearing his new white karate outfit. "Can I ask you something . . . um . . . personal?"

Uh-oh. Jessica looked at the red-haired imp and groaned inwardly. There was a suspicious twinkle in his eyes.

"Do girls like guys who do karate? I mean, does it turn them on?"

"Wh-what?" she stammered, backing away from him and looking around blindly for a quick exit or somewhere to hide.

"I know that girls like football players. And wrestlers. But what about karate guys?"

Oh, God! "Willie, why don't you go ask Julio, or Uncle Luke?" She made a couple of crablike sidesteps, hoping she could make it to the hallway leading to the front door before having to answer.

"Julio's the one that told me to start doing karate. Either that or get a tattoo."

"A . . . a tattoo?"

Willie shuffled around, inadvertently blocking her route to the hall. "And I asked Uncle Luke about this girls and karate and sex stuff, but he told me to come ask you."

"Oh, he did, did he?"

"Yep. How's a guy supposed to know what turns a girl's crank? I mean, really, Aunt Jessie, guys like just about anything, but girls are different. Aren't they? Huh? Aren't they?" He was pressing closer, gazing up at her with wide-eyed innocence. Still, there was that suspicious twinkle in his eyes, too.

How could she answer such questions? "Uh, I'm busy right now, Willie. Come back later. I'll tell you then," she promised. And, gutless wimp that she was, she dashed into the pantry.

To her shock, she heard the door close behind her and the lock click from the other side, followed by the sound of Willie's snickering. That shock was followed immediately by another as she discovered the rat who'd planted the cheese—Willie—in her path, diverting her toward this very spot.

Luke stood leaning against the window on the far wall of the narrow pantry. If this was intended to be a joke, he wasn't laughing.

"So tell me, Jessie, what does turn a girl's crank?"

Chapter Seven

"What's going on?" she said shrilly, twisting the knob unsuccessfully.

"You tell me, Jessie. What the hell's going on?"

"I . . . I don't know what you mean." She knew exactly what he meant. She'd been dodging him all morning, ever since she'd awakened, alone, in her bed.

Oh, she didn't blame him for leaving. He'd probably been concerned about her reputation with the kids and Aunt Clara. Still, his leaving had reminded her that he would leave eventually, and she couldn't allow herself to get too attached.

Last night had been wonderful. End of story.

Stepping away from the window, Luke moved closer to her. Bright sunlight reflected off his brown hair, giving it golden highlights. He wore a crisp, pure white T-shirt of Julio's tucked into faded jeans.

And already she felt warm and tingly. It was probably the aftereffects of the warming oil.

"You know, Jessie, when you look at me, your eyes give you away."

She lowered her lashes.

He laughed mirthlessly and tickled her under the chin.

Her head jerked up. How had he discovered that that tiny section of skin was a particularly sensitive spot on her body? *Hah! He knows that and a whole lot more about my body.*

He braced his arms on either side of her head. There was a touch of anger in his clenched jaw, as well as hurt in his hazel eyes, which glittered more gray than green today. Stormy.

"What gives, Jessie?" he gritted out. "Tell me what's going through that quirky mind of yours."

"Luke, let me go. Let's go outside. Then we'll talk." The pantry was very small, no bigger than a walk-in closet. Too intimate. She could smell a hint of coffee on his breath. She could feel the heat of his body. She could imagine a whole lot more.

"Why can't we talk here?" He cocked his head, then a slow grin spread across his face. "Do I make you nervous?"

"No, but . . . but I should keep an eye on the kids while Aunt Clara's sleeping."

"Liar."

She groaned in resignation. He wasn't going to let her escape until they'd cleared the air. "What do you want, Luke?"

"You."

She whimpered.

"Why are you fighting this? Is loving me such a bad thing?"

"Love is never a bad thing," she declared vehemently, angry herself now, "but it's just not in the cards for me."

"You're not going to mention that damn Christmas Curse again."

"No, I'm pretty sure the Christmas Curse is over. Last night just about wiped it out, I would think."

"Damn straight!"

"Oh, Luke, last night was wonderful, for both of us, but I don't want you to make it into something more than what it was."

"Which was?" he asked icily.

"People have a way of getting caught up in the magic of the Christmas season, but the glow rarely lasts beyond the tinsel and mistletoe. It's sort of like vacation romances where lovers forget each other once they go home."

"Bull!"

She winced at his harsh scorn.

"I love you, Jessie."

"You think you do," she corrected.

"Don't tell me what I think. I love you, and you love me, dammit. Deny it. Go ahead. Tell me you don't love me."

Tears welled in her eyes as she tried to tell him she didn't love him. The words stuck in her throat.

"Jessie, honey, have you ever told anyone you loved them?"

She shook her head mutely.

"Because they always left first, right?"

She nodded.

"Ah, sweetheart, don't you know . . . can't you trust that I'm not leaving?"

She shook her head again, but a soft sob escaped.

He bent his knees so he was at eye level with her and pressed his lips lightly against hers, shifting from side to side, as if trying to show her his sincerity. "I'm in this for the long haul, babe," he said in a choked voice. "I've waited too long to find love again. I'll prove to you that my love is for real. I will."

He was lowering his mouth for another kiss when footsteps clamored loudly on the other side of the door, followed by a rattling of the door knob.

"Uncle Luke, your phone is ringing like crazy, and there's a car coming up the driveway . . . a stretch limo."

Jessica canted her head at Luke in question. Giving her a quick peck, he looped an arm around her shoulder, firm notice that he wasn't going to let her bolt again.

Henry was speaking on Luke's cellular phone in the hallway when they emerged. His eyes seemed watery with unshed tears and his glasses were all fogged up.

Jessica's maternal instincts kicked in. "Henry, what's wrong? Is it bad news?" Henry was an orphan, but there might be some distant relative she didn't know about.

He ignored her with a wave of his hand. "Yes, sir. I will, sir. I promise," Henry said into the mouthpiece, a tone of awe in his voice. "A summer school for computer whiz kids? No, I never heard about that. A what? Oh, Gawd! A college scholarship, maybe, sometime down the road?" Tears streamed unrestrained down Henry's face now. "But, Mr. Gates, how did you hear about me? Oh. Yes, Lucas Carter is still here." Henry gave Luke a sideways glance of adoration.

"Bill Gates?" Jessica said, turning to Luke. "You called Bill Gates on Henry's behalf?"

"No big deal," he said dismissively.

"Yes, it is a very big deal," she asserted and hugged him tightly.

And a tiny grain of trust began to build between them. Well, actually, it was more like a rock.

He winked at her. "Hey, if a telephone call turns you on, I've got a really good dialing finger." He jiggled his eyebrows at her.

Lord, she loved it when he jiggled his eyebrows.

Not that she'd tell him that.

Not that he probably didn't know it already.

Oh, this was turning into the best Christmas ever. And it wasn't over yet.

Darlene and Kajeeta stood at the open front door, gaping at the limo which had just pulled to a stop. The two teenagers looked outside, then looked at each other, threw their hands up in the air, and squealed girlishly.

Jessica felt like screaming, too.

Janet Jackson walked in the door. For real.

"Shut your mouth, Jessie," Luke advised her with a chuckle. He squeezed her shoulder before releasing her and stepping forward to welcome his guest.

"Yo, Janet, glad you could come," Luke said, kissing the star on the cheek. Janet wore a skintight, red jumpsuit with a fuzzy white fake-fur jacket. A dozen tiny gold Christmas bells tinkled from her earrings as she moved.

"Which one of you is Kajeeta?" Janet asked, homing in on the astonished black girl. "You and I have a lot to talk about, girlfriend." Then turning to Darlene, she added, "You must be Darlene. Great makeup!"

The three headed into the living room where Willie stood like a frozen statue watching Janet Jackson approach. The expression on his face couldn't have been more delighted if he'd been handed a karate black belt on a silver platter. Jessica shuddered to think what questions he might ask the sexy rock singer/dancer. Julio put his hands in his pockets, striking a nonchalant pose, and Jessica was pretty sure he planned to hit on the celebrity.

That left her and Luke to follow dumbly after the crowd. Henry was still chattering away on the phone with Bill Gates.

Luke watched her watch Janet with a great deal of amusement.

"Glad you could make it," Luke said to Janet once he could get a word in edgewise.

"Hey, man, I wouldn't have missed this for anything. When you told me yesterday that you'd met your dream girl, I had to come take a look-see."

Luke draped a proprietary arm around Jessica's waist.

"Yeah, you done good, Luke-master," Janet said teasingly, giving Jessica a sweeping appraisal. "Maybe too good. Maybe I should introduce her to my chauffeur. He's studying to be an actor."

Luke stiffened beside her.

But Janet just hooted and tapped Luke on the chin with one of her very long fingernails. "Gotcha, good buddy!" She told Jessica then, "This guy of yours is the best bodyguard I ever hired. Did you know that Brad Pitt has been trying to convince him for years to take a job as his body double, but he refuses to move to the West Coast? Maybe you can talk some sense into him, honey."

Jessica was too flabbergasted by that news to respond.

"So where's this famous fruitcake?" Janet asked Luke.

Everyone started to laugh, but then a car horn blew outside.

What next? Jessica mouthed to Luke.

"Damned if I know," he replied, peering out the window. Immediately, he exclaimed, "Oh, my God!"

"What's the matter?" Jessica asked with concern.

He gave her a rueful glance. "It's my sister, Ellie. I told her to bring some Christmas presents."

"So?" He'd already told her of his fondness for his sister.

"And my mother, too."

Oooh, boy!

Early that evening, Luke sat on the floor before the fire with his arm wrapped around Jessie. Their backs were propped against the sofa where Aunt Clara knitted away on an afghan—a Christmas present for him. Luke had to chuckle when he saw her latest creation for the first time. Brown and speckled with red and orange and green, it resembled a big slice of fruitcake.

The kids sat around the room playing with their Christmas gifts. Although everyone was tired from the long day and the excitement, they were reluctant to go to bed and end what had been a perfect day for them all.

Janet had left soon after dinner, dog-tired from dancing with all the kids, stuffed from Julio's Christmas feast, and ears ringing with all the questions. She'd brought little nonsense gifts for the orphans, which they would, no doubt, cherish for a lifetime.

Before they'd gotten in the limo—the limo driver had joined them for Christmas dinner, too, and to Luke's annoyance he was way too good-looking—Luke had heard Willie ask Janet, "Do you think girls are attracted to karate guys?"

"Oooh, yes!" Janet cooed with a straight face. "I think Steven Seagal is the number-one stud in the nation. In fact, I'm thinking about using some karate moves in my next music video." That about made Willie's day.

And Julio had somehow managed an invitation from Janet to go to Hollywood for a job next summer. He probably had a strategy mapped out already for taking the town by storm . . . or just taking it.

A smiling Aunt Clara had made a gift of five fruit-cakes to Janet. She was struck speechless with gratitude.

Luke's mother and Ellie had approved heartily of Jessie. Well, why wouldn't they? She was wonderful, although she'd appeared half-paralyzed by their exuberance. Ellie, especially, came on like gangbusters sometimes. His mother had started to ask Jessie whether she could help with wedding plans, but backed off, luckily, when she'd seen the sheer panic in Jessie's eyes. He'd given his mom a silent signal that he'd talk to her later.

Now he sat in the afterglow of the best Christmas he'd ever had, with the woman he loved in his arms. Later, after everyone else sacked out for the night, he and Jessie would talk. Then wild sex again. Or should they have wild sex, and then talk?

"Why are you smirking?" Jessie tilted her head to gaze at him.

In the background, he heard his cellular phone going off. Probably his mother or Ellie. He'd told them to call when they arrived home safely.

"I was *not* smirking. I'm just happy. Aren't you?"

She nodded, and he could see that she was getting weepy-eyed again. She did that a lot when unable to express her emotions. He was a little weepy-eyed himself.

"Uncle Luke, it's for you," Henry called out. "Your secretary. She says it's an emergency."

Uh-oh.

Jessica sat on the floor waiting for Luke to return. Little by little, he'd peeled away the armor of her distrust today. She'd already admitted to herself that she loved him, but she was beginning to actually believe he could love her, too . . . that they had a future together.

When Luke came back a short time later, he'd already donned a jacket. With worry lining his voice, he said, "Come here, Jessie, I have to talk to you."

"What is it?" She jumped up in panic. "Has there been an accident? Your mother and sister?"

"No, no," he assured her quickly. "They're fine, but there has been an accident. One of my employees was shot. Dead." He swallowed with difficulty, then went on, "His partner's badly wounded. I have to get back to Philadelphia right away."

"Of course," she said, rushing to his side.

Luke said all his good-byes to Aunt Clara and the kids, telling them he'd return as soon as possible. Then, a short time later, Luke was kissing her at the side of his car.

"Wait here for me, Jessie," he ordered gruffly.

She nodded, unable to keep her cold hands from caressing his face and shoulders, memorizing him till he returned.

"I'll call you later tonight. I should be able to get back by tomorrow, but I'll know better once I see what the situation is with this job. Okay?" He was nuzzling her neck and giving her little nibbling kisses the whole time he talked.

Jessica tried to keep up a brave front. She was missing Luke before he even left.

"I have to go," he said finally, setting her away from him and opening the car door. "I love you, Jessie."

She started to say the words she knew he wanted to hear, but he put his fingertips over her lips to silence her. "No, I know that you love me. But I want you to say the words on your own, without the pressure of my leaving."

She nodded and watched through a screen of tears as Luke drove away.

Two days later, Jessica hadn't heard from Luke.

The night he'd left, there'd been no call, even though he'd promised. And all the following day, she'd waited in vain.

At first, his lack of communication had stunned her. There had to be an excuse.

Then reality had sunk in.

Despite Aunt Clara's admonitions to trust in her heart, Jessica accepted the truth. Luke wasn't coming back.

By the third day after Christmas, Jessica had her

shield of cynicism firmly in place again. And she began packing for her return to Chicago, with oaths of secrecy forced from Aunt Clara and the kids not to divulge her address or phone number if Luke should ever show up again. She suspected that a twinge of pity might strike Luke sometime in the future, if not for her, perhaps for the kids, and she didn't want his damn pity. Or anything else from him, for that matter.

So Jessica traveled back to Chicago alone, except for ten fruitcakes which she intended to dump at the first roadside rest stop, and memories of candy canes and a rogue Santa that would stay with her forever.

Some Christmas miracles weren't intended to last.

On New Year's Eve, Jessica stood in the kitchen of the Shangri-la Inn, arranging Roquefort-stuffed shrimp and crab canapes on an appetizer tray.

The loud rendition of the Jewish folk dance "Hava Nagila" being played by the orchestra at the wedding reception rocked the entire building, but did nothing for her low spirits. The band soon moved on to a fast-paced number, and the shrill announcer encouraged everyone to get up and dance the Chicken. *The Chicken?* She clucked her tongue woefully. What was it about weddings that made grown people behave like imbeciles?

She heard the whoosh of the swinging door from the dining room and grabbed for the meat tenderizing hammer in front of her. The lecherous bridegroom, Cecil Goldstein, had been making passes at her all afternoon, and she'd had about enough. As it was, she probably had bruises on her butt from all his pinches. Well, time to give the schnockered newlywed a lesson good and proper, where it really hurt.

"Put your hands up, lady. This is a stick-out," she heard behind her. And it wasn't the bridegroom's voice.

Oh, my God! Jessica turned abruptly and dropped her meat mallet to the floor with a clunk of surprise.

Santa Claus stood before her with a raised pistol. Madder than hell, if his flaring nostrils and steely eyes were any indication.

"What are you doing here?"

"I came for something that belongs to me. This is *not* a robbery," he emphasized, parroting some words she'd said once. "And get those hands back up, lady, or I'm gonna have to wipe you up."

A grin twitched the edges of her lips. She couldn't help herself. Was that how silly she'd sounded? And Luke looked so comical standing there with a gun pointed in her face. *A gun?* "You shouldn't aim a loaded gun at anyone. It is loaded, isn't it?"

"You betcha, babe," he said, and squirted her in the face.

Jessica laughed and wiped the moisture away while Luke pulled the beard and wig and hat off, dropping them to the floor. She saw immediately that his teasing words conflicted with the stone-cold fury stiffening his body, flattening his lips into a thin line.

"Why didn't you wait for me, Jessie? And why did you tell everyone to keep your whereabouts from me?" Luke was bristling with anger.

"Why didn't you call?"

"Because I had to go to London to take over for Jerry and Mike." His voice cracked at the end.

"Oh," she said, remembering the accident the night Luke had been called away. She wanted to reach out her arms in comfort, but Luke's stony expression daunted her. "How is he . . . I mean, the one employee, did he survive?"

"Jerry was buried three days ago, and Mike will recover," he said grimly.

Agitated, she brushed some stray curls off her forehead. "How did you find me?"

"Julio," he responded tersely.

She waited for him to say more. When he didn't, she took a deep breath and pressed forward. "Why?"

"He said he'd never met two old fogies as dumb as us," he informed her with a rueful shrug.

She tried to smile, but her facial muscles froze.

"You didn't answer my question, Jessie. Why didn't you wait?" He studied her so calmly and coldly that Jessica's heart began to splinter.

"When you didn't call, I figured that . . . well, you changed your mind. That you didn't really . . ."

". . . love you?" He shook his head sadly. "Dammit, Jessie, why couldn't you have trusted me?"

"But you didn't call," she accused.

"I did call, Jessie."

She waited for an explanation, puzzled.

"Did it ever occur to anyone to recharge the battery on the cellular phone, or plug the thing into a wall outlet?"

"Battery?" she squeaked out. Then, "You called?"

He nodded somberly.

Jessica understood then how foolish she'd been. And she understood something else, too. This was good-bye. Luke hadn't come to woo her back.

Without trust, a relationship was nothing. And she'd proven they had nothing . . . no foundation to build on, not even the love she'd failed to profess to him. But Luke was an ethical man, and he would have felt a responsibility to explain himself.

Could he possibly doubt her love?

Of course. Hadn't she doubted him, with even less reason?

"Good luck, Jessie. I hope someday you'll find what you want. I hope you'll let yourself," Luke said, about to turn and leave. "I really did love you."

Did? Jessica's heart was beating a mile a minute. She had to do something, but things were happening too fast.

"Since you've traveled all this way, wouldn't you like to go back to my place? We could . . ." At the disbelieving scowl on his face, her words trailed off.

"For what?" he scoffed.

"Fruitcake?" she proffered weakly. She was in such a panic she couldn't think clearly.

"No, thanks. I've had enough."

He'd had enough. Was there a double meaning there? Did he mean her, too?

He stared at her for one long, excruciating moment, then spun on his heels.

"I bought something for you," she blurted out to his back as he walked stiffly toward the door. Then she put a palm over her mouth to stop herself from saying more.

"You bought something for me?" He turned. "What?"

Heat suffused her face. "Some peppermint oil," she mumbled.

His eyes widened. "What did you say?"

She gulped. "I bought some damn peppermint warming oil. And, believe me, it took all my nerve to go into one of those places by myself. I was going to mail it to you with my address on the package. And then if you contacted me, I figured . . ." She had to stop because tears flowed down her face and she was blubbering.

"You figured what?" He came back to stand in front of her.

She closed her eyes for a minute to collect her nerve. "I figured it would mean that you might still love me then, like . . . like . . ." She couldn't go on.

"Say it, Jessie," he insisted. His hazel eyes locked with hers, no longer in anger or despair. There was hope there now.

". . . like I love you," she whispered.

Luke let out a loud sigh of relief and roughly pulled her into his arms, kissing her face and neck as if he couldn't get enough of her. "Geez, Jessie, I thought you were really going to let me go. You had me scared to death. I thought maybe I'd been wrong all along, that maybe you didn't love me."

"I love you, Luke," she said on a sob, framing his handsome face with two hands. He made her say it ten more times before he stopped grinning like a silly idiot.

When the bridegroom stomped into the kitchen demanding to know what the hell was going on, she shoved the appetizer tray in his hands and announced, "I quit, Cecil."

"You can't quit," Cecil sputtered.

"Wanna bet?" Luke stepped in.

"What am I supposed to do with all this food?" he whined.

"I'd suggest you serve it yourself. Unless you want me to tell your bride how you offended me," she threatened.

"How did he offend you?" Luke narrowed his eyes and began to advance on the cowering lech.

"Never mind," Jessica said and pulled on Luke's arm, dropping her apron to the floor. Nothing else mattered now that she had Luke back. Nothing.

"Don't forget to serve the almond creme wedding cake," she added. "It cost you five hundred dollars."

Cecil stammered incoherently. She wasn't sure if it was over his being forced to serve at his own wedding, or the price tag she'd just quoted.

Laughing, she and Luke emerged from the back exit of the restaurant moments later.

Stopping abruptly, Luke asked, "So, Jessie, where's this present of mine?"

"In the trunk of my car," she said, leaning her head into the crook of his neck and shoulder.

"I hope you bought a gallon," he growled.

"I did," she laughed. "And I also bought some in peach. How do you feel about peaches?"

He never answered.

But he showed her a short time later.

Noel Carter was born ninth months later, having been conceived on Christmas Eve.

Some might say that Lucas's faulty birth control had been a Christmas Curse. But Lucas and Jessica Carter believed they were blessed with a Christmas Miracle.

Christmas Unplugged

JOY NASH

*To Mary Lynne—don't forget to unplug
every once in a while!*

Chapter One

The computer screen went dark.

Casey blinked, head jerking up, brain blanking, her elbow smacking an almost-empty coffee mug. It disappeared over the edge of the desk with a crash.

"Looking for this?" a sweet voice asked.

"Damn it, Emma." Casey snatched up the mug, eyeing the dark splashes on the hardwood floor. "Look what you made me do."

"Me?" Emma laughed. "That mug was already hanging on the edge of the desk. I'm not even sure what law of gravity was keeping it upright."

Casey eyed the computer plug dangling from her sister's manicured fingertips. "Whatever. Just plug that thing back in, okay? I'm busy."

Emma swung the cord like a lasso. "Oh, really? Doing what?"

"Working."

Emma's brown eyes went wide with feigned surprise. "So you're a professional minesweeper now? I had no idea."

Casey blew a strand of hair out of her eyes. "Just. Plug. It. In."

"No. Not until we talk. I hate competing with your electronics."

A flicker of real hurt showed in Emma's eyes. Casey

felt a vague stab of guilt as she scrutinized Em more closely.

Her hair wasn't done, and she was wearing her old community college drama club sweatshirt. The one with "Chicago" on the front and a list of cast members on the back, Em's name near the top. The thing was so ratty, a homeless ragpicker would have rolled his shopping cart over it without so much as a first glance.

"Something's wrong." It wasn't a question. "You didn't get that audition you wanted so badly, did you? But so what? It's a Broadway production. You knew just getting in the door would be a long shot."

A very long shot. A minimum distance of about a dozen light years, in Casey's private opinion. Sure, Emma was a decent actress, with the looks of a beauty pageant contestant, but this was New York, for chrissakes, not Broward County. It was Broadway theater, not center stage at a South Florida community college.

There had to be a zillion aspiring actresses with Emma's looks and talent in the city. Most of them, including Emma, were waiting tables. But Casey's star-struck sister was ever hopeful. Casey tried hard to keep her skepticism at a low boil.

"No, I didn't get in," Emma sighed. "But then, I didn't really expect to. I don't know the right people yet."

"Then what's with the sweatshirt?"

Emma sank down on the chair next to Casey's desk, shoving a stack of tech magazines onto the floor. She dropped the computer's cord on top of them.

"Oh, Case, it's over. Me and Todd." She made an

angry sound in her throat, and Casey could almost see the steam coming out her ears. "I caught him with his tongue down Ashley's throat! Can you believe it? There I was, covering three of the jerk's tables, along with all of my own, while he was getting hot in the walk-in freezer!"

"Hope you told the maitre d'," Casey muttered, eyeing the plug, just inches away from the tapping toe of Emma's knock-off pink Prada sneakers.

"You bet I did," Emma shot back. "She was on Todd's balls in two seconds flat."

"Fired?"

"Yep. Ashley, too."

"Good. So forget the loser. You can do better."

"Oh, I know that."

Casey hid a smile. Her little sister was nothing if not confident. And not without reason. Emma was blonde and beautiful, with a Barbie-doll figure that caused men to drool and women to turn green. She was never single for long.

Casey leaned over and picked up the computer cord. She really needed to think about getting a backup power system.

"I suppose it's all for the best, really," Emma went on. "Now we can spend the holiday together. Honestly. I never should have booked that Adirondack Christmas weekend in the first place. What was I thinking? Why didn't you talk me out of it?"

The trouble was, Casey thought wryly, that Emma *didn't* think. Ever. She acted on impulse, and could rarely be talked out of anything. Emma's sudden Christmas plans had caught Casey by surprise, to say the least. She'd been a little hurt at first—this was their first Christmas in New York, after all, and Casey had assumed they'd spend it together. But after some thought, she'd decided she really didn't mind the prospect of skipping Christmas. She had a lot of work to do before New Year's Eve.

But now it looked like Christmas was back on. Casey, plug in hand, dropped to her knees and reached sideways into the dark space between her desk and the filing cabinet. The electrical outlet was back there. Somewhere.

"That's great," Casey said. "We can go uptown, maybe see the big Christmas tree at Rockefeller Center."

"Well, I suppose we could drive by the tree on our way out of the city."

Casey twisted her head to look at her sister. "What do you mean, on our way out of the city? What are you talking about?"

"The *Adirondacks*," Emma said with exaggerated patience. "Hello? Weren't we just talking about this?"

Casey sat back on her heels. "You mean you still want to go to the Adirondacks? With me instead of Todd? Oh, no. No way."

"Why not? It'll be fun."

"Fun?" Casey repeated. "Fun? Are you nuts? What it'll be is cold. Freezing. Forget it. Just cancel the hotel and get your money back."

"But I can't. It's a small family-run lodge, not a hotel. A special holiday deal, no refunds. And, Case, I really was looking forward to it. It'll be so pretty. Like Christmas in the movies. Do you realize there's already snow in Dutch Gorge? Probably more than either of us have ever seen in our lives."

"And that's way more than I ever want to see. I was perfectly fine with South Florida Christmases."

It hadn't been her idea, after all, to migrate north. It had been another of Emma's harebrained schemes—go to New York and become famous. Casey could hardly let her little sister launch herself on the New York theater scene without backup. Emma was barely twenty-two, without a penny in the bank, and with an erratic work history. She couldn't afford to rent a roach-infested broom closet in this city.

"Oh come on," Emma wheedled. "It's not like you're doing anything this weekend anyway."

Casey finally united cord and outlet. She pushed to her feet as the blessed squeal of the computer start-up began. "Not doing anything? Emma, are you insane? I've got to get an interactive billboard on Times Square linked up with three social networking websites by New Year's Eve."

"Oh, right. But Case, your boss can't possibly expect you to work over Christmas weekend!"

"Wanna bet?"

"That's criminal. What kind of Scrooge do you work for, anyway? You've been working night and day for weeks as it is! For heaven's sakes, you're not a machine. You need to unplug for a couple of days. And it'll be good for us to get away together. We hardly even see each other anymore."

That was true enough. Since they'd moved to New York last spring, Emma had spent every spare minute tracking down potential casting calls and networking with other wannabe actors, while Casey had worked about a zillion hours of overtime at her job as a computer programmer for a digital interactive marketing agency.

"We hardly need to go to the frozen back of beyond to spend time together," Casey said. "I can grab a few hours this weekend, and we can catch a play or something."

Emma grimaced. "Please. I need a break from the business. I need to get out of Manhattan for a few days. But I really don't want to go alone. Please say you'll come with me? *Please?*"

Casey's resolve wavered. "Geez, Emma, why couldn't you have bought Todd a trip to Jamaica?"

"Because it's Christmas! I want a winter wonderland. You know, like in the movies. Snow. Ice-skating. Chestnuts roasting on an open fire. Come on, Casey, say you'll come. It's only four days. Dutch Gorge is . . . well, it's kind of off the beaten trail. If I had to find it on my own . . ."

The thought of Emma lost in a rented car on some mountain back road sent a chill down Casey's spine. To put it mildly, her sister and road maps didn't mix. Even with a GPS, she couldn't find her way out of a cardboard box. Casey did some hasty mental calculating. She could probably spare the time to drive upstate.

"Oh, all right. My team's pretty much on schedule with the Times Square deadline. If Tony and George can cover for me, I should be able to take the weekend off. But you can forget about seeing me in ice skates. I'm bringing my laptop, and staying inside."

Emma blinked. "Your laptop? Um, Casey, do you really think you'll need it?"

"Yes. I really do. Don't argue with me on this one, Emma. I need to put in at least twenty hours between now and Sunday."

For a moment, Emma looked as if she would argue. Then she shrugged. "All right, then, bring your computer. I don't mind."

Chapter Two

Emma peered through the windshield. "The turnoff to Dutch Gorge is coming up. Soon, I think."

Casey sighed and kept driving. The narrow country road cut tight arcs through a forest of graceful white birch trees. The falling snow made things even more picturesque.

It was pretty, she supposed. Even if the rent-a-wreck subcompact car reeked of cigarette smoke. Even if Casey's phone had lost its GPS satellite linkup five miles of mountain road ago. Even if Casey had less than no experience driving on snow. Were you supposed to turn into a skid, or out of it? She could never remember.

Emma's blonde hair fell forward as she studied the tiny map on the Dutch Lodge brochure. "Actually, I think we might have already passed the turnoff."

The last thread of Casey's patience snapped. She hit the brakes . . . and felt her back tires slip to the left. She jerked the steering wheel in the same direction.

Thank God. She'd guessed right. Somehow, she managed to slide to a stop without pitching headlights-first into the drainage ditch that ran alongside the road.

She snatched the map from Emma's fingers. "Here. Let me see that thing. All I need is for it to get dark, and I'll never find the place. Geez. You might have told me Dutch Gorge was in the middle of nowhere! Any farther north, we'd be chasing down Canadian Mounties."

Emma sniffed. "But you have to admit, the snow is pretty."

"Yeah. Pretty dangerous."

Casey glared at the map. As she'd suspected, they'd gone too far. Shoving the brochure back at Emma, she executed a slippery three-point turn on the narrow road. The snow—the beautiful, dangerous snow—was coming down in big heavy flakes. Casey switched on the windshield wipers and prayed she was still on the pavement.

If they hadn't been so far from the state highway, she could have turned back. But the last town they'd passed had been miles and miles ago, and night wasn't far off. There was no way she'd make it back to civilization before dark. And they couldn't be more than a mile or two from Dutch Lodge.

"Finally."

The turnoff was barely paved, and all but unnoticeable. Frowning, Casey made the left, her muffler scraping ice as the rental car bounced in and out of a frozen rut.

"Lovely," she muttered.

From there, it was all downhill. Literally. Steeply. Apparently, the "Gorge" part of Dutch Gorge wasn't a fanciful marketing ploy.

She felt like she was descending into some kind of icy version of hell. At least the potholes provided some traction. And the series of hairpin switchbacks ensured she didn't fall asleep at the wheel.

"Oh. My. God," Emma breathed, one hand braced on the dashboard, the other clutching the side of Casey's headrest. "We're going to die."

"And to think," Casey groused, "we could have died in Jamaica. Lying on the beach. Drinking piña coladas."

Her knuckles had gone white. Her thumbs were numb. She would have turned around if the road had been wide enough. Or backed up if the road hadn't been so steep. As it was, she could do neither.

She rode the brake, inching forward as quickly as she dared through snow-dusted evergreens, the afternoon light fading far more quickly than she would have liked. She prayed the road leveled out before her nerves snapped completely.

"This had better be the right road. There had better be a lodge at the end of it. Because by the time we get to the bottom of this hellish ditch, it's going to be too dark to climb back out." She felt her blood pressure rising. "I swear, Emma, don't you have two brain cells to rub together? I should be shot for going along with this stupid idea."

"It wasn't stupid!"

"It was! It's another one of your half-baked schemes. Can't you ever think twice before dragging me into one of your fiascos?"

Emma stiffened. "Well. I'm sorry you feel like that about celebrating Christmas."

"You could have at least rented an SUV instead of this death trap."

"I was trying to save money! And anyway, there's no use complaining about it now. It's too late to go back up that mountain. We're committed."

"Oh, one of us should be committed," Casey said darkly. "I just don't know if it's you or me. How the hell did you find out about this place, anyway?"

"There was an ad in that free newspaper they give out all over the city."

"And just what, exactly, did it say?"

Emma half turned toward the passenger window. "Something like . . . Get away from it all. Enjoy a romantic old-fashioned Christmas."

"Lovely," Casey said again through gritted teeth. Her jaw was starting to ache.

The paved road ended abruptly. Casey's wheels skidded on gravel. The snow-dusted evergreen boughs seemed to part before her, as if revealing some long-held secret.

Some secret. A snow-slicked parking lot occupied by a battered pickup truck and five SUVs.

"There's no sign." Casey scanned the parking area and the old stone farmhouse on the other side.

"This is definitely the place," Emma replied on a breath of pure relief. She waved the brochure photo. "See?"

The rental car slid down the last few feet of road. Too fast. Casey hit the brakes. Too hard. The car went into a wide, taillight-first spin.

"Oh, shit!"

The back tires hit a mound of snow. Casey's head thumped against the headrest. She jerked on the steering wheel, but the front wheels kept sliding.

They hit the snow bank, Casey's right front fender kissing the back bumper of a massive black SUV with Massachusetts plates.

"Thank God," Emma breathed.

Cautiously, Casey turned the wheel to the left and eased her foot onto the accelerator. Her tires spun. She gunned the motor harder. The tires spun some more.

"That's it," she said. "The end of traction as we know it. This rotten excuse for a vehicle isn't traveling another inch. At least not tonight." She sighed and opened her door.

To a blast of frigid winter wind.

"Damn, it's cold." She hopped from one foot to the other as she fished her gloves out of her coat pockets.

On the other side of the car, Emma hiked her fur-lined hood up over her head. "But it's so beautiful."

It *was* pretty, Casey had to admit. Even—especially—in the falling snow. Like a Christmas card. The slate-roofed farmhouse stood framed against the steep-wooded hill behind, smoke curling from one of its three chimneys. A covered porch sheltered a large bay window, softly glowing. An old stone well adorned the front yard, while the huge old tree nearby, its leafless branches painted white with snow, spread its arms over the attic dormers. Casey could just identify the outline of a red barn behind the house.

"Look," Emma said suddenly, clutching Casey's arm.

"Emma. I've got to get the luggage—"

"Forget the luggage! Just *look*."

Casey looked. Two men had rounded a corner of the farmhouse, arms laden with firewood. Casey watched as they added the logs to a stack in a lean-to near the porch.

"Yeah?" she said. "So?"

"So? Ohmygod! Did you get a look at those guys?" Emma waved a hand. "Yoohoo! Hi!"

The men looked toward Emma, then back at each

other. Casey thought they exchanged a few words before dumping the rest of their firewood and starting
across the snow-covered yard.

"Oh. My. God," Emma breathed. "They're even better looking up close. That tall one is *gorgeous*."

He was. Tall, broad, and hatless, the bigger man was
blindingly handsome. Around thirty, Casey guessed,
with snowflakes gathering in his thick dark hair. His
legs were long, his faded jeans ending at battered tan
work boots. His bulky red sweater, and the old Army
surplus jacket he wore over it, were speckled with wood
chips. Casey had no trouble at all believing he'd
chopped every stick of firewood in the shed. The man
looked like every woman's lumberjack fantasy.

His eyes flicked past Casey, and settled on Emma.

Typical. Guys always noticed Emma first. Casey
was used to it. But for some reason—probably because
of the harrowing drive down the mountain—tonight
it *hurt*.

But it wasn't the lumberjack who returned Emma's
greeting. It was the other man—a bit shorter, a bit
thinner, a bit less handsome, but still way above aver-
age in the good-looks department—who grinned and
waved.

"Hello, ladies! Lost?"

"I don't think so," Emma said as the four of them
met on the path leading to the front porch. The walk
had been shoveled recently, but the new snow was
quickly recoating the flagstones. "This is Dutch Lodge,
isn't it?"

The men exchanged a look.

"Yeah," the shorter guy said. "It is."

"Then we're in the right place." Emma flashed him

a smile, then batted her eyelashes at the lumberjack. "We have reservations for Christmas weekend."

"Really?" Mr. Talkative asked. "Are you sure?"

"Well, of course we are! Do you think we would have driven all the way out here from Manhattan if we weren't?"

Amusement flashed in the lumberjack's blue eyes.

"And I have to say," Emma continued, "the lodge is beautiful. It looks just like the picture in the brochure. So romantic!"

"Well, then," the shorter man said, with an air of resignation. "Come on in, and Aunt Bea will sort everything out. I'm Jake, by the way. Jake Van der Staappen. And this is my brother, Matt."

"You two are brothers?" Emma exclaimed. "Why, we're sisters. I'm Emma. Emma Harbison. And this is Casey."

"Sisters, huh?" A wide grin blossomed on Jake's face. He elbowed his brother. "Well, hallelujah. I am damn happy to hear that. Aren't you, Matt?"

It was Matt's turn to look resigned. He snorted and shook his head.

"Now, let's get you inside before you freeze solid," Jake said.

"An excellent idea." Casey started up the flagstone path.

"Just watch your step." Jake took Emma's arm. "It's—"

Casey's heel hit a patch of ice. "Aaaah—!"

What happened next seemed to play out in slow motion. Her legs slid out from under her, sending her upper body lurching backward. Her arms circled wildly, as if she could catch her balance on the frozen air. No go. She felt herself fall . . .

The arms that caught her were solid, strong, and warm. She blinked up, into Matt's dancing blue eyes. For an instant, he held her frozen in a dramatic dip, in a pose straight out of *Dancing with the Stars.*

"—icy," Jake finished lamely.

And then the world turned right-side up again, and Casey's feet were once more planted firmly on the ground.

"Oh, God," Emma laughed. "I wish I'd caught that on video. Casey, you should have seen yourself. That was definitely one of your better moments."

Jake lifted an eyebrow. "Your sister falls down a lot?"

"More often it's other stuff hitting the ground," Emma said. "She's terribly clumsy. Want to hear something funny? In high school, they used to call her Klutzy Casey."

Heat rushed to Casey's face. She glared at Emma, sure her eyes were spitting sparks. Emma smirked and tossed her hair. It was obvious that little comment was payback for Casey's behind-the-wheel bitchiness.

Casey was going to kill her.

Jake's eyes cut from one sister to the other. "Ah, well," he said hastily. "Anyone could be a klutz in this weather. There's a wicked layer of ice under all this new snow." He caught Emma below the elbow. "Here, let me help you . . ."

Casey watched as the pair made their way to the farmhouse porch, Jake's arm sliding around Emma's waist. She fought an urge to roll her eyes. The Todd drama wasn't even forty-eight hours old, and Emma hadn't even started fishing for a replacement. And here she already had one on the hook.

Matt cleared his throat.

She looked up at him, her face going even hotter than before. She could practically feel the snow sizzling as it hit her skin.

"Think you can manage the path to the house alone?" he asked. "Or should I carry you, too?"

She nearly choked. "That won't be necessary." Though she was fairly certain he was strong enough to do it. That thought brought another rush of heat to her skin.

God. What a farce this Adirondack trip was turning out to be. She couldn't wait to get to her room. She might not even come out until Christmas was over and Emma was ready to drive back to the city.

Good thing she'd brought her computer.

"Twenty bucks, big brother." Jake's grin stretched from ear to ear. "Sisters. *Not* lesbians."

Matt eyed the two women standing under the flickering gaslight in the foyer, chatting with Aunt Bea. With a sigh, he extracted his wallet from his back pocket and pulled out a crisp Andrew Jackson.

"It was a logical assumption," he said as the money disappeared into his brother's pocket. "Those two look nothing alike. And this is supposed to be a couples weekend. Exclusively. I know for a fact Aunt Bea was not expecting three couples and a pair of sisters."

Jake shrugged. "Call it a gift from the heavens. A Christmas miracle. Jesus. What an angel."

He was talking about the blonde sister, of course.

Jake had a thing for blondes. This one was incredibly beautiful. And incredibly busty. Or maybe she just had an incredible plastic surgeon. She looked . . . plastic.

By contrast, the other sister looked . . . real. Dark smudges under her eyes, no makeup, her lips pressed into a frown. Her dark hair was a tangled mass of wild curls.

"Just let me remind you," he told Jake, "we're here to work. Not to hit on the guests."

"I'll be discreet," Jake said. "Hell, I'll be anything if it gets me close to Emma. Man, oh man, does she fill out that sweater. And those legs—"

But Matt had stopped listening to his brother.

". . . always wanted to act in the theater," Jake's blonde—Emma—was saying to Aunt Bea's interested nod. "On Broadway. So Casey and I, we moved to New York last spring. From Florida."

"You're a Broadway actress, dear? How lovely."

Aunt Bea glanced at Matt over her bifocals. Matt nearly groaned out loud. An aspiring actress? God Almighty, he should have known. She had the look.

"Well, not yet," Emma was saying, "but Broadway's been my dream forever! So far, though, I haven't had much luck getting into auditions. I just don't know the right people."

"Oh, Christ." Jake made a sound of disgust. "An actress. It just figures. If Emma finds out who you are, my chances with her are up in smoke."

"Your chances and my sanity," Matt grumbled.

"Jesus, Matt, then do something."

Matt cut him a glance. "Like what?"

"I don't know. Bribe Aunt Bea. Tell her I'll polish all

the silverware or something. Or chop another three cords of wood. Anything. Just make her keep quiet about you."

Not a bad idea, Matt thought as Aunt Bea opened her mouth to reply to Emma's comment. Just in time, he caught Bea's gaze, and made a cutting motion with his hand.

No, he mouthed. *Don't tell her . . .*

Aunt Bea pursed her lips and turned her attention back to Emma. "Acting is such a challenging career, dear. It's hard to get started. It does help to know the right people." Her eyes cut to Matt. "Or so I've been told."

Jake groaned. "That's it. Aunt Bea's gonna spill, and I'm gonna officially drop off the face of the planet as far as Emma's concerned. Though I suppose I might have a shot at the klutzy sister . . ."

"No." Matt was not in the mood to spend the next four days dodging the attentions of a wannabe actress. He reached the desk in two strides.

"Aunt Bea?" He slid a hand under her elbow. "Can I talk to you a moment?"

"Matthew! I was just telling Emma about your—"

"*Now*, Aunt Bea. Jake can take over the check-in."

A smiling Jake stepped up to the antique rolltop desk where Aunt Bea kept her reservations ledger. "It would be my pleasure, ladies."

Bea frowned as Matt guided her to the alcove under the stair. He lowered his voice. "Aunt Bea. Don't tell that woman anything. Please."

"But Matthew, why not? Emma's an aspiring actress, new to the city, and you're always looking for new talent."

"True enough, but I just don't want to get into it this weekend. I came upstate to help you and Uncle Fred, not to add to my call list. Just keep it quiet about the agency, okay?"

Aunt Bea was not pleased. "Emma's a guest, Matthew. And she seems like such a nice girl—"

"I'll have Jake get her number." Matt realized he must be truly desperate, to agree to that. He was one of the most sought-after casting directors in the city—only one rookie actress in a hundred made his Broadway call list. Though he could probably swing Emma a TV commercial easily enough. She had the looks for it.

"I'll call her in for an interview and screen test after the holidays," he promised. "But only if you promise not to say anything to her while she's here. And that goes for Uncle Fred, too."

The twin lines between his aunt's eyes deepened. "Well, all right, Matthew, if you insist. But I really don't underst—"

"Why are these sisters here, anyway? I thought only couples were booked for the Romance of Christmas weekend."

"Yes, well, that's true. But apparently Emma and her boyfriend stopped dating just a few days ago. So she brought her sister with her instead."

Maybe that explained why the wild-haired brunette looked less than thrilled. Probably, Casey hadn't wanted to come. Dutch Gorge in December wasn't everyone's idea of a vacation, least of all someone from Florida.

He guided Bea back to the sisters. His brother's head was bent over the reservation ledger.

"You ladies are in the Daisy room," Jake said.

"That's our nicest room," Aunt Bea said. "Almost a suite. It's a bit of a climb, of course, up to the third floor. But it does have a private bath."

"It sounds perfect," Emma said.

"Jake," Matt interjected, "why don't you take Emma to her room? Her sister can show me what luggage to bring up."

"Right," Jake said, springing into action. "Emma, right this way. Here, let me take your coat. Casey, careful out there on the path." He winked. "Wouldn't want Matt here to throw his back out . . ."

Emma laughed. Casey shot a glare at her sister, before turning to follow Matt back out to the porch. Full night had fallen. The muted light shining through the bay window cast a warm glow into the dark. Even in the yellow gaslight, Casey looked pale. And tired.

"Long drive up from the city?"

She snorted. "Only about five hours too long. And then it started snowing, and we missed the turn into the gorge, and the road got slippery, and we got into an argument . . . God. I can't believe I let my sister talk me into coming out here."

"Ah well, you made it safely."

"Barely. Who built that road, anyway? We're lucky we didn't go over the side of the freaking mountain! I'm telling you, if we survive the drive home, I am going to kill Emma. Slowly."

Her voice was trembling. More from fear than from anger, Matt thought. A delayed reaction to a drive that had truly frightened her.

"The road into the gorge can be dicey," he said.

"Especially in a snowfall. First northern winter, I take it?"

She shivered. "Yes."

"Driving on snow takes a bit of practice. But don't worry. You'll get used to it."

She made a sound of disdain. "I'd rather not, thank you."

Man, but she was prickly. With that frown and all that crazy hair, she looked like a disgruntled hedgehog. But even so . . . he scrutinized her more closely. Now that she wasn't standing next to her stunning sister, he realized she wasn't as plain as he'd first thought. She had a pleasant face, with good bone structure. Wide dark eyes—brown, maybe. It was hard to tell in the dark. She was probably very pretty when she smiled.

She wasn't smiling at the moment. She looked ready to strangle someone. Emma, probably. He swallowed a laugh.

Production title: Sidekick. Woman perpetually trapped in her sister's misadventures finally snaps, revealing a dangerous violent streak . . .

He shook the thought out of his head. Hadn't he just told Aunt Bea he didn't want to think about work? But the drive upstate apparently hadn't put the brakes on his obsessive habit of casting everyone around him into imaginary dramas.

The snow was coming down in a thick curtain now, the steady north wind blowing it at a stiff diagonal. A gust picked up a swirl of new-fallen snow from the front yard and threw it into their faces.

Casey gripped the lapels of her coat, savagely wrenching the fabric tight across her chest. Not that it was going to do her any good. The flimsy thing was designed for a city winter. Not a mountain one.

"God, it's cold." Her teeth were actually chattering.

"Actually, it's barely below twenty," Matt said, purely for the enjoyment of seeing her scowl deepen. "But it's supposed to drop to single digits tonight."

"Lovely," she muttered.

He took pity on her. "Listen, if you're that cold, just give me your key and tell me how many bags you've got. No need to come with me to your car."

"No." She hugged the coat tighter. "You won't be able to carry it all by yourself. Emma is not a light packer."

She stepped off the porch, tripped on the first step, and lunged down the rest. He barely managed to catch hold of her arm before she landed face-first in the snow.

"Wow. Your sister wasn't kidding, was she? About you making a habit of falling?"

She jerked her sleeve out of his grip. "I'm fine. It's just these boots. They're not the best on ice."

Matt extracted a small flashlight from his pocket. "Here. This might help."

"Thanks."

She plowed through the snow, following the thin beam of light, placing each step with care. "Damn it's dark out here," she said. "And quiet."

"That's the snow. It muffles everything."

They managed to reach her car without further mishap. "Nice parking job," he commented.

"Bite your tongue," she said.

He laughed. "Another inch and Jake's bumper would

have turned your fender into crumpled aluminum foil."

"I know." She climbed over the snow bank to open the trunk. The interior revealed a pair of pink suitcases and a worn navy blue duffle.

Matt handed Casey the flashlight and started collecting the bags, slinging the duffle over his shoulder and hefting the suitcases. Christ. The bigger pink one must be filled with bricks. He didn't have to ask which sister it belonged to.

"Your sister planning to stay the month?"

"Emma likes to be prepared," Casey answered, reaching into the trunk for one last bag.

"Might as well leave that one," he told her.

She glanced up at him. "What?"

"That's a computer, right?"

"Yes."

"Then why bring it in? You won't be able to use it."

She straightened, setting one hand on the open trunk door and trying to grip both her bag and his flashlight in the other. The beam bounced wildly.

"You mean because this God-forsaken crack in the Earth's crust is in a satellite blind spot? I already know that. My GPS lost its signal even before we started down the mountain. So I'm guessing there'll be no Internet, either. But that's okay. I can work without it."

He snorted. "Can you work without electricity?"

She froze in the act of slamming the trunk. Her eyes jerked to his, and even in the darkness, he could tell they were appalled.

"Without *electricity*? You can't be serious."

"Perfectly serious, honey. Dutch Lodge is off the grid."

Her head swiveled toward the house. "But . . . there are lights—"

"Gas light," he said. "And oil lamps. Don't tell me you didn't notice? It's usually the first thing that guests comment on."

"No." Her voice was barely more than a whisper. "I didn't notice. But . . . what about TV? Hot water?" She sucked in a breath. *"Heat?"*

"Sorry, no TV. But there's plenty of hot water, courtesy of a mountain spring Uncle Fred piped in years ago. A large propane tank out back takes care of the gaslights and water heaters. And there's a fireplace or wood-burning stove in every room. Don't worry, you'll get your hot baths, and you won't freeze."

"But—no electricity? How can anyone live without electricity?"

He laughed. "It's not so bad. I grew up here, you know, and managed to survive."

"But . . . but . . ."

The sounds of her sputtering shock made him wish for a stronger flashlight. "Didn't you know about the electricity? It's all in the brochure your sister was waving arou—" He cut off, and laughed outright.

"What's so funny?" she demanded.

"You didn't read that brochure, did you? And your sister didn't tell you."

Casey slammed the trunk. The crash echoed off the sides of the gorge like a gunshot.

"No," she ground out between clenched teeth. "She did not. But she is certainly going to answer for it now."

Still clutching her laptop case, she flung herself in the direction of the house, her footsteps hard and fast. Well, as hard and fast as footsteps could get in six inches of new snow.

"You know," he said, juggling the baggage as he fell into step beside her. "Most guests at Dutch Lodge consider the lack of electricity a good thing. In fact, it's the reason most people come here. To get away from civilization."

"Yes, well, I like civilization just fine. I don't want to get away from it. No electricity," she added under her breath. "This is insane. That brat is going to die. Painfully."

That repressed violent streak again, Matt thought, impressed.

"She's just lucky I've got some battery life. If I make it to tomorrow morning, I might let her live."

"Why?" Matt asked. "What happens tomorrow morning?"

She spun toward him, stumbling, then catching her balance. The flashlight beam glanced off the white ground. "What happens in the morning is that we're leaving. Whether Emma wants to or not."

Matt couldn't suppress a bark of laughter. "Leaving? Sorry to disappoint, but I really doubt that's gonna happen."

"Oh, it's going to happen, all right. The instant the sun comes up, I'm outta here."

The wind chose just that moment to kick up a wintery blast. "I'm curious," Matt shouted over the rising wind. "Did you happen to check the local weather report before driving into the gorge?"

They'd reached the house. Casey stomped up the

three steps to the porch before turning to glare down at him. "No."

He smiled.

Trepidation crept into her voice. "Why do you ask?"

"Because I was listening to the update on the short-wave just before you got here. This storm's turning nasty, and it's going to last all night. They're predicting two feet."

"Two *feet*?" Her mouth fell open. "Of *snow*?"

"Well, not of rose petals," he assured her. "So I'm pretty sure no one's going anywhere tomorrow. Least of all you."

Chapter Three

The farmhouse living room was cozy and welcoming, with flames snapping cheerfully in a fireplace hung with Christmas stockings and decorated with fresh-cut holly. The room's soft illumination was supplied by a brass gaslight chandelier. Glass-topped oil lanterns lit the corners. Casey couldn't believe she hadn't noticed the lack of lightbulbs on her first trip into the house.

The nonelectric illumination was, she supposed, enchanting. Muted, and a little mysterious. Though it did mean that the Christmas tree, decorated with intricate blown-glass ornaments, wasn't lit up like . . . well, like a Christmas tree.

An elaborate Nativity scene, complete with angels, shepherds, and kings, was arranged on a low table nestled close to the evergreen boughs. As for the rest of the room, it was a cozy collection of furnishings—some antique, others just old. The walls were hung with oil paintings of nature scenes, except for one large watercolor of a windmill. A spinet piano, its cherry finish polished to a deep luster, stood against one wall.

A low buzz of happy chatter circulated in the cinnamon-scented air. Casey's gaze flicked over a half dozen lodge guests, separated into three happy pairs.

One couple snuggled in a gold plush love seat, while another stood at the big bay window, arms entwined, watching the snow fall. Couple Number Three stood in front of the Christmas tree, exclaiming in low tones over the antique ornaments.

And then there was Couple Number Four. Emma and Jake. Casey's sister nestled in an overstuffed arm-chair near the fire, sipping a mug of something steaming. Jake sat on the chair's arm, leaning toward her, talking in animated tones. Even though there was a perfectly empty chair two feet to his left.

Casey adjusted her grip on her laptop case handle and stalked toward them.

Neither noticed her beeline approach. Jake gestured with his free hand, touching Emma's shoulder. Emma laughed, her low, throaty chuckle prompting Jake to lean even closer. He darted a subtle glance at Emma's cleavage. If the man was a dog, Casey thought unchar-itably, drool would be dripping from his open mouth.

She stepped into her sister's line of vision. "We need to talk, Emma. Now."

Emma smiled up at her, but the expression was be-lied by the frost in her eye. She was still angry.

But Emma was an actress, and right now, Jake was her audience. She smiled sweetly. "Casey! Isn't this room cozy? The tree is so beautiful. And the fire is so *delicious*."

The heat on Casey's back did feel good. Especially after that frigid trek to the parking lot and back. But she was damned if she was going to admit it. "That's neither here nor there," she said. "You've got some explaining—"

Jake jumped to his feet. "Um . . . Would you like

something hot to drink, Casey? Tea? Spiced cider? Hot chocolate?"

"Oh, let Jake get you some of the spiced cider," Emma said. "It's very good."

"Fine," Casey snapped. Anything to get rid of Emma's adoring puppy.

"Coming right up," Jake said.

Jake headed Matt off at the bottom of the stairs.

"I need a favor," he said.

"What, after taking my twenty dollars? You gotta be kidding."

"I'm dead serious. That Emma is a wet dream come true. And she just dumped some loser of a boyfriend. Which makes the timing even better."

Matt lowered Emma's rock-filled pink suitcase to the ground. "So? Have at it. What's stopping you?"

"Her sister. The woman is out of her mind. She's not a happy camper."

"That's because Emma didn't tell her about the electricity," Matt said. "You should have seen Casey's face when she found out."

Her expression had been priceless. If she'd walked into Matt's agency at that moment, he'd have immediately cast her into a TV commercial—maybe one for laundry detergent. As the housewife who discovers a pack of muddy dogs mauling her newly washed basket of whites.

But Casey wasn't hoping to be cast in a TV commercial. Or a print campaign, or a theater production. She wasn't an actress. She wasn't drop-dead gorgeous. She was just a normal woman. Matt chuckled. A normal woman with a hidden violent streak.

"Whatever," Jake said impatiently. "The thing is, she's getting Emma all uptight. The two of them are spitting like cats. Do you think you could distract Casey a bit tonight? You know, so Emma and I can have a little time alone? Please? A few private hours with that woman would really brighten up this drudge week for me."

Matt and Jake had been helping out with Dutch Lodge's Christmas weekend for five years now, so the middle-aged married couple their aunt and uncle employed could spend Christmas with their married daughter in Montreal. Jake came solely out of a sense of duty—he'd much rather spend Christmas in Boston. Matt, on the other hand, looked forward to the trip each year. To him, five days of mindless manual labor—chopping wood, shoveling snow, cooking and serving meals—was a perfect antidote to the pressures of his New York City life. Just the thought of spending a few days out of touch by e-mail, phone, and BlackBerry was heaven.

"Come on, Matt. Will you do it?" Jake said. "Keep Casey out of Emma's hair?"

And here was another chore Matt really didn't mind.

"Tell you what," he said, handing off the pink suitcases to Jake. "Haul Emma's bags up to the third floor, and I'll distract Casey for as long as you want."

"Isn't he cute?" Emma said, her eyes on Jake as he left the room. "And he really seems to like me."

"Big deal." Casey sank into the empty armchair opposite her sister. She put her computer case on the floor between her feet. "Every man likes you."

"Jake's brother doesn't."

"That's ridiculous."

"No, it's not. He's barely made eye contact with me. Every time I look at him, he grimaces and looks away."

"I really doubt that," Casey said. "But it hardly matters. Emma, this place doesn't have electricity! Why didn't you tell me?"

Emma's eyes slid away. "Because you never would have come if you'd known."

"Damn right, I wouldn't have come! I have a New Year's Eve deadline! I need to work. And now there's a freaking blizzard. We could be stuck here for days without so much as a single electrical outlet. I can't believe you'd do this to me."

"Well, I can't believe you can't handle a few days away from that stupid computer. Especially on Christmas. Casey, you work sixty hours a week as it is! Do you have to work on Christmas, too?"

"Someone has to pay our rent. Waitressing doesn't pay squat."

Emma's eyes turned frigid, and her next words dripped ice. "That was low, Case. And don't think I've forgiven you for what you said in the car. You can be such a bitch sometimes."

"The truth hurts, doesn't it?" Casey muttered, then immediately wished the words back when real hurt flared in Emma's eyes.

"You have no room to criticize me, Case. Just look at yourself. All you do is work, and surf the Internet, and play computer games. We've been in New York for nine months, and you haven't even tried to make a single real friend. Every time I invite you to a party, you turn me down."

Heat crept up Casey's neck. She tried to tell herself

it was because of the fireplace. "I went to some of your parties. I can't stand the type of people you're trying so hard to impress." *And I can't stand how dull I feel next to them.* "Actors. Models. Agents. Producers. There's not a single genuine person in a hundred of them."

"Well," a masculine voice said. "On that note, here you go." A solid set of jean-clad legs and a steaming mug appeared in front of Casey.

She looked up into a pair of dark blue eyes. Not Jake. Matt. He lifted a brow. Just great. He'd heard her whole rant. And now he probably thought she was a bitch. No—worse. A clumsy bitch.

"Um . . . thanks." She accepted her mug, sipping to cover her embarrassment.

"Where's Jake?" Emma asked.

"Taking your bags to your room," Matt said without looking over at her. "And after that we're both due in the kitchen. So if you ladies will excuse me . . . ?"

"Of course," Emma said.

Casey let out a long breath as he moved away.

"Way to go, Case," Emma said. "Let every man within a hundred miles know how stuck up you are." She turned to stare into the fire, sipping her cider.

Casey placed her own mug on the table next to her chair. Emma was right. Casey's temper and sharp tongue—not to mention her insecurities—tended to get her in trouble. Almost as often as her clumsiness produced bruises. Emma, on the other hand, was grace and graciousness personified. Not for the first time, Casey wondered if one of them had been switched at birth. It certainly would explain why they were as different as oil and water.

She zipped open her case and powered up her laptop. Just as she expected: her satellite Internet account status icon had a big fat red "X" over it. No service.

Mrs. Van der Staappen—or Aunt Bea, as she insisted everyone call her, invited her guests to dinner a few minutes later. Matt's aunt was a plump, pleasant woman with short gray hair and a ruffled apron. Her husband, Uncle Fred, sported a grizzled white beard trimmed in Dutch style, with no mustache. He looked like a friendly old lion in plaid shirt and suspenders.

The meal was served family style, and was already laid out on the long farmhouse table when Casey and Emma entered the dining room. Aunt Bea and Uncle Fred took places at either end, while their eight guests, and their two nephews, filled in the chairs on either side. Emma smiled as Jake slid into the empty seat beside her. Casey studied her flatware as Matt, coming in late from the kitchen, dropped into the only available seat, on Casey's left.

The fare was hearty and simple: pot roast, peas, and mashed potatoes, with apple pie for dessert. The dinner conversation centered, of course, on the weather. The storm was blowing with a vengeance now, whistling and rattling the windowpanes.

"Been a while since we had a good blizzard," Uncle Fred commented over coffee.

Privately, Casey didn't think the words "good" and "blizzard" belonged in the same sentence.

"Especially this early in the season," Fred continued. "It's shaping up to be a doozie. But don't you folks worry none—we're snug as bugs here in the valley."

"Will the road out of the gorge be cleared tomorrow?" Casey ventured.

"Oh, no, honey," Aunt Bea said with a soft laugh.

"I imagine it will take at least two days for the county snow plows to get to us. Maybe even three."

Tomorrow was Christmas Eve. So in other words, Casey was stuck here until at least the day after Christmas.

Matt gave her a subtle elbow in the ribs. Her head whipped around in time to see his lips curl. Casey could almost hear him thinking, *I told you so.*

"Oh, it sounds so romantic," one of the female guests sighed. She leaned into her husband. "Max and I have never been snowbound before."

"Me neither," Emma said, her eyes dancing. "It's going to be so much fun. Casey and I just moved to New York from Florida, you know. We've never so much as packed a single snowball before."

"Looks like I'll have a lot to teach you this weekend." Jake's seductive whisper, aimed for Emma, was loud enough for Casey—and Matt—to overhear.

Emma giggled.

Casey scowled.

Matt just chuckled.

Chapter Four

Casey was still camped out in the dining room.

Matt ducked back in the kitchen, wiping his hands on a dish towel. He'd been keeping an eye on her all evening, but so far he hadn't needed to haul her away from her sister. Just the opposite. Right after dinner, Casey had powered up her laptop at the dining room table. She'd ignored Emma all night. Matt was pretty sure Emma hadn't even noticed. She was too wrapped up with Jake.

Matt had washed and dried the dinner dishes, and prepped the kitchen for tomorrow's breakfast. All with minimal help from Jake, who'd disappeared with Emma more than an hour ago, right after Aunt Bea and Uncle Fred had finished delivering firewood and complimentary champagne to the guest rooms.

His work done, Matt propped one shoulder on the doorjamb between the kitchen and dining room, eyeing Dutch Lodge's most reluctant guest. It was well after eleven, and everyone else had gone to sleep—or at least, he amended, to bed.

But Casey was still tapping away at her computer, her wild curls sprouting from her scalp in every direction. Every few seconds, she'd drag a hand through the mop, making it worse.

Production: TV Commercial. Product: Curl control hair

gel. Harried career woman rushes through a typical day, losing precious minutes every time she pauses to tame her wild hair. Finally, a concerned friend offers to share her hair gel . . .

Matt shook himself out of his reverie. He wasn't quite sure why he found Casey so fascinating. She certainly had a sharp tongue. And she seemed much more interested in her laptop than in people.

What kind of work was so important she had to do it on Christmas vacation, anyway? He shoved off the doorjamb and peered over her shoulder at the screen.

Minesweeper.

He laughed. "I thought you had work do."

She hit another square on the screen, and didn't look up. "I do. But I'm too pissed at my sister to concentrate on it."

"What is it that you do? For a job, I mean."

"I'm a computer programmer. I work for an interactive agency."

"What's that, exactly?"

"We do viral marketing via mobile communications and social networking websites. Like, for example, the project I'm working on is a contest sponsored by Diva Diamonds. You know, the big jewelry chain? Starting at nine o'clock New Year's Eve contestants can upload pictures of the perfect romantic kiss via three social networking sites to a billboard in Times Square. Then people on-site and off will vote the kisses up or down via texts from their cell phones. The couple whose kiss is on the screen at midnight wins a diamond tiara and a trip to Paris."

"Wow. Interesting."

"Ha. A pain in the butt is what it's been."

She neutralized another section of the electronic mine field. He leaned forward just a little, his chest bumping the back of her head. She started, hit the wrong square, and blew up the works.

"Do you mind? You're crowding me."

She started a new game. He moved back a step, and kept watching.

"So how much juice you got left in that thing?" he said after a few minutes.

"Probably not much." She clicked the battery icon and grimaced. "In fact, hardly any at all."

She played a minute or so longer, then sighed when the low battery warning came on. Powering down the computer, she stowed it back in its case.

"Shoulda paced yourself," he commented. "You have at least two more days here."

She sat back in her chair, glancing up at him, and then away. "I know. I'll be bored out of my skull tomorrow. I'll probably be reduced to reading Emma's fashion magazines. By the way, have you seen her?"

"Not in a while." He crossed the room and glanced into the living room. "I'm pretty sure everyone's gone up to their rooms. The Romance of Christmas and all. You and I are the only ones left down here."

"Right." She stood, hefting the computer case in one hand. "Well, I guess I'll go up, too. Emma's probably waiting for me."

Matt really doubted it. He knew his brother only too well.

"Good night, then," Casey said.

He suppressed a grin. "Um . . . watch yourself going up the stairs. The gaslights are on the lowest setting."

He followed her into the foyer, then stood at the bottom of the stairs as her footsteps faded toward the third floor. The faraway rattle of a doorknob ensued. Then muted pounding. Then muffled voices.

Matt leaned against the newel post, waiting. The footsteps returned, descending, heavier and angrier than they had been on the way up. He gave in to a laugh.

Casey stomped down the last six steps from the landing, computer case in one hand, blue duffle in the other, her dark eyes flashing fire. With her wild curls sticking out from her head in every direction, she looked like Medusa.

"Something wrong?" he asked innocently.

"Yes, something's wrong. My sister's locked me out, and left my bag in the hall. I need another room." Her eyes narrowed. "You knew it, too, didn't you?"

"I had my suspicions," Matt said. "I saw Emma leading my impressionable little brother up the stairs about an hour ago."

"Impressionable? Jake? Oh, please—"

"And I might've gone up to the third floor a little while after that, and noticed your duffle outside the door."

She huffed. "You could have warned me."

"What, and miss out on the chance for a bit of entertainment? It's boring out here in the country. You have to take whatever amusement you can get."

"Yeah, well, you can stop being amused and find me another room. Emma's not going to open that door before morning."

His smile faded. "Are you sure she won't let up in an hour or so? I can't believe your sister would lock you out all night."

"Believe it. She's pissed as hell at me." She sighed. "It's partly my own fault, I suppose. First we fought in the car. Then I was so angry when I found out about the electricity, I said a few nasty things to her. This is her way of getting back at me."

"You and your sister fight a lot?"

"Like cats and dogs," Casey admitted. "We always have. But it never lasts. Believe it or not, we're actually very close. Emma will be all smiles by morning. But until then . . . just point me toward an empty room and I'll get out of your hair."

"Well," Matt said. "That's going to be a problem. Because there isn't one."

"It doesn't have to be anything fancy. I don't need a private bath—"

"Didn't you hear me? This isn't a huge house, and it's full. There is no empty bedroom. Bath or no bath."

Casey blinked. Then she sat down abruptly, on the second-to-last stair. "You're kidding me."

"No. Sorry. I'm not."

"Then where am I supposed to sleep? On one of the loveseats in the living room?"

"Wouldn't be my choice," Matt said. He paused. "Want me to go up and drag my brother's ass out of your room? I can do it easily enough. I outweigh him by twenty pounds, and I've got a master key."

"No," Casey shook her head, setting her curls dancing. "No way. You do *not* want to interrupt what's going on in there, believe me. Emma isn't a believer in slow courtship."

Matt laughed. "Neither is Jake."

"And I wouldn't want to brave Emma's wrath if you do throw Jake out." She sighed. "I guess it's a loveseat for me. Or maybe one of those big armchairs by the fireplace. They were pretty comfortable."

He hesitated. "Or . . . you could sleep where Jake was supposed to."

She blinked up at him through inky black eyelashes. "And where might that be?"

"With me."

I cannot believe I agreed to sleep with this guy.

Or, more accurately, sleep in his room.

Talk about embarrassing! But Casey hardly had a choice. There was no way she was going to confront Emma before morning. It would only lead to a shouting match. They'd wake up everyone in the lodge.

"This way," Matt said, leading the way, her duffle slung over one broad shoulder.

She clutched her dead computer and trailed after him, blinking when he stopped at the closet to get their coats. "Here," he said, handing her hers. "You'll need this."

She took it. "What for?"

"I don't sleep in the farmhouse," he said. "I stay in a cabin out back, in the woods behind the barn."

A cabin in the woods. Well, that was good, wasn't it? A cabin had to be bigger than a regular bedroom. It probably had multiple rooms. She followed Matt through the kitchen, where the massive iron woodstove supplied a lingering warmth, and the scent of baked apples still hung in the air. A small mudroom led to the back door. Matt opened it on a blast of wind of snow. The world beyond was white.

"Oh, my God."

Matt gripped her upper arm and pulled her into the

blizzard, slamming the door behind him. She hoped he knew where he was heading, because his flashlight barely made a dent in the night. But his stride was quick and sure. The wind abruptly died as they rounded the side of the barn and slipped into the bare winter wood. A minute later, she stumbled up two steps to a small porch. She huddled under the shelter of a meager over-hang while he shoved open the door.

God. She was frozen, and it wasn't much warmer inside the cabin than out. She rubbed her hands and stomped the snow off her boots while Matt struck a match. He lit the oil lantern standing on a small table by the door.

The room jumped to life. The single room. Which wasn't, she noted with some trepidation, all that much bigger than a bedroom.

The walls were rough logs, unadorned except for the deer head mounted over a small stone fireplace. Ugh. She could almost feel its glassy eyes staring. There was a kitchenette of sorts, consisting of two feet of counter, an old-fashioned icebox, and a small woodstove. A few dirty dishes were stacked in a stone sink.

Furnishings were few and simple. A tall wardrobe, an unmade double bed. A droopy leather couch faced the hearth, and the big square table sat in the center of the room under an oil lamp chandelier. The underside of the ceiling above was black with soot.

She wandered to a bookshelf crowded with animal skulls, birds' nests, rocks, trinkets, and, yes, even a few dusty novels. Out of the jumble, one item caught her eye. A wooden cube, fashioned from at least five different kinds of wood joined with flawless precision. The workmanship was beautiful.

"Try to open it."

She started, surprised to find Matt standing behind her.

"It's a box?" she asked, intrigued.

"Yeah." His blue eyes smiled down at her, and for a second, she forgot to breathe. "Go on. See if you can figure it out."

She ignored the funny jump in her stomach. And the way her skin suddenly seemed to be tingling all over. Concentrating on the box, she turned it over in her hands. There didn't seem to be a latch. Or any hinges. She ran her thumbs along the sides, trying to slide one of the panels. Nothing.

"You're not kidding me? This thing really opens?"

"Yes. It's a mystery box." The corners of his eyes crinkled. "Don't tell me a smart girl like you is giving up so quickly."

"Maybe not so smart after all," she mumbled.

He chuckled. "To open it . . . you have to press just . . . here." He touched one corner. "Then slide this side up, then twist here . . ."

She followed the complicated instructions. At the end of the sequence, one side of the box popped open. The compartment inside was empty.

"No mysteries revealed," she said.

"I guess the mystery is how I ever had the patience to make the thing in the first place," Matt said with a laugh.

She followed the sequence in reverse, marveling as the panels slid back into place. "You really made this?"

"When I was fifteen. Took an entire winter. But I had a lot of time on my hands back then."

"I guess so," she said, placing the box carefully back

on the shelf. "You had no TV, no stereo, no video games . . . I can't even imagine it."

"It's a wonder I survived, huh?"

"You still live here," Casey pointed out. "So it must be possible."

He hesitated. "I don't, actually."

"Don't what?"

"Live here. I dropped out of high school and left the gorge when I turned eighteen. I only come for visits now. Mostly in the summer, when there's more activity. My aunt and uncle run a campground from spring to fall, you know."

"No, I didn't know."

"It's all in that brochure your sister has."

She rolled her eyes. "The one I didn't read."

He set her duffle on a bench under the window. She stowed her computer on the floor beside it.

"Jake's been sleeping on the couch," he said. "But you can take my bed if you want." Amusement flashed in his eyes. "Aunt Bea likes her guests to be comfortable."

Sleep in his bed? The tangle of blankets and pillows on the couch looked a whole lot safer. "Um . . . no. I wouldn't want to put you out. Thanks. The couch is fine. It'll be warmer near the fire, anyway."

"True enough." Matt crossed to the hearth and began building up the fire, throwing on two logs from an iron basket. He jabbed at them with a poker. Sparks and flames leapt.

"I don't snore, by the way," he added, glancing back at her. "How 'bout you?"

He sounded like he might be teasing, but she couldn't be sure. "I don't think so." A sudden, panicked thought struck. "Please tell me there's a bathroom in this cabin."

"Over there." Matt jerked his chin at a narrow door half-hidden by the wardrobe.

"Oh, thank God."

Finished with the fire, he placed his hands on his thighs and rose. Casey was struck again by how tall he was. And broad. If he stretched his arm up, he could easily touch the bottom of the cabin's rafters. But it was his face that really made her nervous. It was just so . . . perfect. He'd fit right in with Emma's collection of beautiful acting friends.

"You can come over here by the fire," he said. "And take your coat off. I promise not to bite."

With some reluctance, she made her way to his side. The intimacy of this small cabin was disconcerting. She stared into the leaping flames, all too aware of his eyes on her.

"I think I'll keep my coat on for a while," she said. "It's not that warm in here yet."

"Not used to the cold, I take it?"

"No. Sometimes I can't believe I let Emma talk me into moving north. But she has this crazy idea she's going to land a role in a Broadway production."

"You don't think so."

"Seriously? I doubt she'll even get close. Don't get me wrong—Emma's a great actress, but Broadway? There's just so much competition. It's nuts."

"But you moved across the country anyway? Just to hold your sister's hand?"

"When Emma gets one of her big ideas, no force on Earth can talk her out of it. She was moving to New

York, come hell or high water. I couldn't let her go alone."

"Why not?"

She held out her hands to the fire. Her fingers were finally starting to thaw. "Because Emma and I . . . we're all the family we have. She's so young, and didn't know a soul in the city . . . I would've worried too much if she'd come to Manhattan alone. It was no big deal for me to move, really. A computer programmer can find work anywhere."

Heat was radiating from the fire in waves now, and she was starting to sweat inside her coat. She eased open the buttons, then reluctantly retreated from the warmth of the fire to unzip her duffel.

"Um, listen, don't feel like you have to entertain me. I'm beat from the long drive. I'm just going to listen to my iPod for a while."

"Until the battery runs out?"

"Yeah. And that bathroom—?"

He made a sweeping gesture. "All yours."

She rummaged through her bag and pulled out her toiletries, along with the gray sweatpants and over-sized T-shirt she slept in. She added a sweatshirt, too, for good measure—that fire wasn't going to last all night.

The bathroom was tiny. Basic masculine accoutrements—toothbrush, razor, comb—occupied a miniscule shelf. There was a sink with running water, and the smallest shower stall she'd ever seen. The toilet was some kind of environmental kind that didn't flush, but otherwise seemed surprisingly normal.

Her elbows banged against the walls as she dressed

for bed. She frowned at her reflection in the mirror, appalled at the sorry state of her hair. The dry, cold air didn't do her any favors—it looked like she'd stuck her finger in an electric socket. Brushing only made things worse. With a sigh, she pushed open the door.

And stopped dead.

In her absence, Matt had also readied himself for bed. But the man's tolerance for sleeping in the cold was, apparently, much, much greater than Casey's.

She sucked in a breath. He lay on top of his rumpled bed, turning the pages of one of his dusty novels by the light of the lantern. The only thing covering him was a pair of boxer shorts. Absorbed in his book, he didn't so much as look up when she emerged from the bathroom. Which was a good thing, because she couldn't stop staring.

He looked like a god.

And *she* looked like a witch.

She grabbed her iPod, dove under her blankets, and shut her eyes.

Too late.

The image of Matt's near-naked body was burned permanently onto the insides of her eyelids.

It was one of his favorite Agatha Christies, and any other time, Matt would've welcomed a few quiet hours to revisit the story. But right now he simply turned the pages, without reading a single word, all his attention given to his peripheral vision. Casey was a quirky, prickly woman. She put him in mind of a hedgehog. Especially with that hair. She was sarcastic and funny, but he suspected there was a vulnerable spot some-

where behind the façade. One she was trying her best
to hide.

Definitely not the kind of woman he dealt with at the
office. Models and actresses were a breed unto themselves. A woman didn't succeed in the business without
equal amounts of bravado, style, and ruthlessness. Matt
could spot the type a mile away. Casey's sister had the
attitude. In spades.

He imagined Jake worshipping at Emma's altar right
this very moment . . . and had to adjust the covers over
his burgeoning erection. But not because he wanted to
take his brother's place with beautiful Emma. Not by
a long shot. Oddly, it was prickly, wild-haired Casey
fueling his fantasy.

Matt was missing an important industry holiday
party in the city tonight. Rich food, beautiful people,
free-flowing booze, more BS than you could shovel
with a backhoe. If he'd been there, chances were he
wouldn't have left alone. There was always some woman
offering to warm his bed.

His reputation as one of New York's premier casting directors had soared in the last few years. His
company had handled casting for countless TV commercials, print ad campaigns, and a good number of
theater productions—four on Broadway in the past
year alone. He'd even, just for fun, cast an indie movie.
The money had been a pittance, but the film had done
well at Sundance, and the success had only added to
his cachet. In short, he was in demand. Both professionally and socially.

Easy sex was part of the bargain. He'd be lying if he
said it hadn't been fun at first. But after a while he'd

begun to notice that the less effort it took to get a woman into bed, the more dissatisfied he was the next morning. He was all too aware that his bed partners were hoping their association with him would further their careers. None of them cared about him as a man.

But the woman currently sacked out on his couch? She wasn't trying to land a spot in a magazine or on the stage. She didn't live from casting call to casting call. She was a normal woman, with a normal job, living a normal life.

And she'd walked right past his bed.

He glanced over the top of his book. Casey's eyes were closed, her breathing was deep and easy. White earbud wires snaked from her ears, disappearing under the covers. She'd fallen asleep with a slight scowl on her face.

She wasn't interested.

Perversely, that made him happy.

It also made him want her.

He almost laughed aloud at the absurdity of it all. Call it idiocy. Call it an experiment. But all he could think of was trying to change her mind.

Chapter Five

Casey woke to the aroma of frying bacon and perking coffee.

All in all, it wasn't a bad start to Christmas Eve morning. Her stomach recognized its good fortune a half second before her brain did, and let out a monster growl.

Mortified, she sat up. Matt stood in the cabin's kitchenette—fully dressed, thank God—tending an iron skillet. He wore plaid flannel and blue denim, and could have easily graced the cover of a hunting and fishing magazine. Casey had never had a thing for the outdoorsy look. Until just this very minute.

He glanced over at her. "Hungry?"

A hot flush rose up her neck and into her cheeks. She started to drag a hand through her hair, then stopped. She'd looked like a witch last night. How much worse did she look this morning?

"You're . . . making breakfast?" Inane, but it was the first thing she could think of to say.

"Bacon and eggs. Do you always sleep like the dead? You didn't so much as twitch when I banged this pan on the stove."

"Yes, well, I was exhausted." She fumbled around in the blankets for her earbuds and player. She thumbed the switch. Dead. Of course. She tossed it in the general direction of her duffel.

She rose, groaning a little when her muscles protested. The couch cushions sagged in all the wrong places. She felt indescribably ratty. Her teeth were fuzzy. She wouldn't be surprised if Matt could smell her morning breath over the bacon and coffee. Grabbing some clean jeans and a top, she fled into the bathroom.

She managed a quick shower under a low-pressure flow of not-all-that-hot water. She slicked some gel on her wet hair, and wished she'd packed some makeup. Which was ridiculous. As if some eye shadow and blush was going to transform her into someone like Emma.

She emerged from the bathroom, feeling more awkward than ever. Crescents of snow rested on the outside of the window panes. Frost painted the inside of the glass.

"Is the storm over?"

"Just about." Matt transferred several slices of bacon to a plate. "A few flurries now, that's all."

"Was it as bad as they predicted?"

"Hoping to escape the gorge, are you? Sorry, but not today. Or tomorrow. We got a good thirty inches."

She felt a spike of irrational panic. "Two and a half *feet*?"

"Of course, the drifts are a lot higher than that. Four or even five feet in some places."

Curious, she drifted to the window and rubbed a bit of frost off the glass. Holy cow. The aftermath of last night's blizzard was beyond her comprehension. Snow was everywhere, covering the trees, blown up against the back of the barn, piled high like mounds of confectioner's sugar.

"Oh, my God," she breathed. "It's freaking Little House on the Prairie."

"Except without the prairie," Matt said.

"We'll be stuck here eating turnips until spring!"

Chuckling, Matt broke an egg, one handed, into the skillet. "Not quite that long. The county's pretty good with the roads. The plows should make it down here by Sunday at the latest. That's only three days away. Coffee?"

"Um . . . sure."

He waved her into a seat and handed her a mug. A few minutes later, two loaded plates landed on the table, bearing fluffy cheese omelets, thick slices of bacon, fried potatoes, and hunks of homemade bread. Casey's mouth started to water.

Matt set an old-fashioned percolator coffee pot on a hot pad in the center of the table and folded his big body into the seat opposite her. Casey took a bite of omelet and washed it down with a sip of coffee.

"Delicious," she said.

He looked up. "Thanks."

The aura of morning-after intimacy, even though it was a morning after nothing, was beyond awkward. Casey cast about for small talk.

"Were you born here in Dutch Gorge?" she asked.

"No. Jake and I came to live with Aunt Bea and Uncle Fred when I was four, and he was two. Our sister Mary was an infant. Our parents died in a car crash."

"How sad."

"It was. My father was Uncle Fred's only brother. As for Jake, Mary, and I—we don't remember our parents. Our childhood was here, with Bea and Fred, until we each left for greener pastures."

"Don't you worry about your aunt and uncle now that they're getting older? Living in such an isolated place, I mean."

He put down his fork. "Yes. They refuse to move out. But they're not completely alone—there's a couple who live about a half mile up the valley who work here during the season. They're spending Christmas with their family in Canada right now. That's why Jake and I are here, to help out with the Romance of Christmas weekend. Aunt Bea won't give it up. She just loves to have the house full for the holiday. But as soon as the guests leave on Sunday, we'll close up the house until April."

"Really? Where will Bea and Fred go?"

"They'll drive with me to Boston, and spend the winter at my sister Mary's place. She's married, with three kids, and has a big house. Good thing, too. Neither Jake nor I have the room."

"Bea and Fred are lucky to have you," Casey said around a bite of omelet. "I'd hate to think of something happening to them in the winter, with the road closed and no one able to get to them. Are there a lot of storms like yesterday's?"

"It happens," Matt said. "We get a good bit of snow in the gorge. Some sort of lake effect thing. When I was a kid, it seemed the road was closed more often than it was open." He grinned. "Missed a ton of school."

"What happens if someone gets sick? Or hurt?"

"If it's a real emergency, we radio out and the hospital sends a helicopter." He cupped his mug in his palms. "But believe it or not, that only happened once in all my childhood. Jake ran a sled into a tree and broke his arm."

"Oh, my God! How old was he?"

"Seven."

"Wow. That must have been scary."

"Not for me. It was one of the most exciting days of my life. The only way it could have been better was if I'd been the one with the broken arm getting a ride on a helicopter. For years afterward, every time it snowed I tried to break an arm or leg. But I never quite managed it."

Casey laughed. Amazingly, she was starting to relax. Looking down at her plate, she realized she'd eaten almost everything on it, and her mug was empty, too.

"Your poor aunt," she said, reaching for the coffee pot. "It sounds like you and your brother—oh!"

Her fingers slipped on the handle. The pot tipped with a thud. Casey watched in horror as the battered aluminum top flew off, sending coffee pouring across the table and into Matt's lap.

"Ow!" He leapt to his feet, swatting at his pants with his napkin. "F—" He swallowed the curse. "*Damn*, that's hot."

"Oh, God! I'm so sorry. I'm such a klutz!"

Casey was on her feet, too, wishing the floor would open up and swallow her. She came around the table, thrusting her napkin in the general direction of Matt's groin. He grabbed her hand just before it landed on his crotch.

She jerked back, face flooding with heat. "I'm sorry," she repeated weakly.

"Wow," he said, shaking out his wet napkin. The front of his pants was soaked. "Your sister wasn't kidding. You *are* clumsy." He started to laugh. "A freaking disaster."

Casey flushed hotter than the coffee. Could she just shrivel up and die now? Please?

"My fingers slipped on the handle when I tried to pick it up," she said lamely.

"That'll be a lesson to me," he said. "Never let your cup go empty."

She covered her face with the napkin. "Oh, God, I—"

"Listen." He tugged the cloth away. His finger brushed her cheek.

Her eyes flew open.

"Don't worry about it," he said. "I'll live. But I've got to change. And then I need to gas up the snow blower and see about clearing a path to the house."

He crossed to the wardrobe and pulled out clean jeans, shirt, and underwear. Tossing the clothes on the bed, he bent to unlace his boots.

Then his hands went to his belt. "You might want to turn your back." He met her startled eyes and grinned. "Or maybe not?"

Casey quickly averted her eyes. "You're going to . . ." She nearly choked. ". . . change? Out here?"

"Bathroom's too small. I'm sure you noticed."

"Um . . . yeah. I guess it is." She spun around, fingers gripping the edge of the table. "Sure. No problem. Go ahead."

"Thanks."

She heard him unbuckle his belt. Listened as he shucked off his jeans. Shrugged out of his shirt. Stepped out of his underwear.

And she saw it all, too. In full frontal glory. Reflected in shiny window glass.

She sucked in a breath as Matt turned to grab his

clean clothes off the bed. he had an excellent butt. She knew she was acting like some kind of pervert, ogling his reflection. But she couldn't quite bring herself to look away.

Until he looked up, met her gaze in the window, and grinned.

"So how was your night with Emma?" Matt asked as he and Jake set up the brunch buffet. For the moment, they were alone. Aunt Bea was in the kitchen, mixing up her famous waffle batter. The guests had yet to drift in from the living room.

Jake cut Matt a swift glance. "Fine," he said with uncharacteristic reserve. "How was your night with Klutzy Casey?"

"Don't call her that," Matt said sharply. Then he remembered the way she'd nearly scalded his balls off. "Okay, so she is a bit clumsy. Otherwise, she's not so bad."

Jake positioned the bowls of syrup, nuts, and dried fruits, a smirk on his lips. "But not exactly your usual type."

"Maybe I'm tired of my usual type."

Matt stacked the plates and lit the gas under the trays of eggs and sausage. He could hear the lodge guests, chatting in the living room. Casey wasn't with them, he knew. With all this snow, the only path from the cabin was the one he'd cleared to the kitchen door. He'd have seen her if she'd come in that way.

He wondered if she'd even appear for brunch. She'd already eaten breakfast. But that was hours ago. Was she embarrassed about dousing him with hot coffee? Or irritated that he'd caught her eyeing him in the window reflection? He'd tried to flirt a little after that, warm her up, but she'd only snorted and given him the cold shoulder.

Maybe she really wasn't interested.

"Seriously," Jake eyed him. "You into Casey? I never would have thought it."

"Just tell me—will Casey be sharing a room with her sister tonight?" He found himself holding his breath, waiting for Jake's answer.

"Not unless she insists on it. Emma and I had a great time last night."

Matt's chest eased.

"And you know what else?" Jake continued. "Aunt Bea is right. You should call Emma in for a screen test. She's really something special."

"I told her I would. After the New Year. Get Emma's number for me, okay?"

"Will do."

Aunt Bea came bustling from the kitchen, carrying a large plastic pitcher of waffle batter. She handed it off to Jake. "Ready, boys?"

"You bet," said Jake. But his attention was on Emma, who had just entered the dining room. He thrust the batter at Matt. "Listen, do me a favor."

"Another one?"

"Yeah. Make the waffles."

"Sure thing," Matt said to his brother's back.

Aunt Bea smiled. "Jake is sure taken with that actress."

"I guess so." Matt just hoped his aunt hadn't caught

on to the revised sleeping arrangements. She wouldn't be pleased.

But Bea only wiped her hands on her apron and cast a critical eye over the buffet. "Perfect. I'll just tell the guests to come in."

An uncomfortable sensation rose in Matt's chest. As he kept the waffle iron sizzling, his gaze kept returning to Casey's sister. Emma was flirting with Jake, touching his arm and letting him feed her from his plate. Wasn't she thinking about her sister at all?

The meal was almost over by the time Casey finally appeared. Matt tried to catch her attention, but she wouldn't meet his gaze. Her eyes were fixed on her sister, her lips pressed into a straight, angry line.

Matt found himself wondering what Casey looked like with a smile on her face. Oh, not one of those tight little grimaces he'd managed to coax out of her so far. No, he'd really like to see a wide, unrestrained grin. And laughter, the kind she couldn't stop.

And he'd like to be the cause of it.

"Emma," Casey whispered the instant Jake left the table to clear the brunch dishes. She slid into the seat he'd reluctantly vacated. "What the hell did you think you were doing last night?"

Emma's gaze lingered on the doorway to the kitchen through which Jake had just disappeared. She sighed happily. "More than I ever did with Todd, that's for damn sure."

"Emma—"

"The man is a dream, Case. An absolute dream." Emma's smile was brilliant, and her eyes held no hint of their sisterly spats of the day before. Casey only wished she could forgive and forget as easily. But unfortunately, the night hadn't worked out quite so well for her as it had for Emma.

"He's so nice. And funny, too," Emma went on. "He's a musician, a keyboardist, did you know that?"

"Great. Sounds like a real stable job."

Emma ignored the jab. "He lives in Boston, and his band's called Shake It Up. They play clubs and parties all over New England." Her smiled widened. "And now I feel like I should thank you for being so nasty to me yesterday. I might never have hooked up with Jake otherwise."

"You never should have, anyway," Casey said in a furious whisper. "I still can't believe you locked me out of our room so you could sleep with Jake. For God's sake, Emma, you just met the man yesterday, and you just broke up with Todd two days before that. Would it kill you to take a week off between sex partners once in a while?"

Emma blinked, her smile fading. "Why should I? Just to make up for the *years* you take off between men? No, I don't think so."

"Now who's being nasty?" Casey said, her voice cracking a little. Her throat had gone suddenly raw. She blinked, hot tears pressing her eyelids.

Emma caught Casey's hand. "Oh, God, Case, I'm sorry. I never should have said that. I love you, you know that. But . . . you can't deny it's been ages since you've . . . well, you know."

"The trouble is, Emma, I just don't connect with men as easily as you do. I'm not pretty enough to catch a guy's attention, and I suck at flirting."

"Oh, Casey, that's nonsense. You are pretty, especially when you bother to put on a little makeup. And you have a great personality. You could catch a wonderful guy. What about Matt? He's hot. And Jake said you spent the night with him in some romantic cabin in the woods."

"Only because there was nowhere else he could put a paying guest who was locked out of her room by her own sister. Believe me. It's not like he wanted to spend the night with me."

"But still," Emma persisted, "a cabin in the snowy woods? A man and woman forced to spend the whole long, cold, wintery night together? Major romance potential, no matter how it got started. So tell me, how did it go?"

"How do you think it went? Horrible. My computer and iPod both died before midnight, and I spilled hot coffee all over him this morning."

"Oh, Casey," Emma said, laughing. "Leave it to you. You got a hot guy practically held captive, and first you ignore him, then you try to land him in the hospital."

"You don't have to spell it out for me," Casey muttered. "I was there, remember? And I looked a fright. It's a wonder I didn't scare him into the next county."

"From what I can tell, he's still interested, despite the danger. He can hardly take his eyes off you."

"Probably so he can be ready to duck if I get too close. And how do you know, anyway? You weren't looking at Matt. You were too busy with Jake."

"That's how I know. Jake said Matt's really into you."

"Oh, please," Casey said. "Guys who look like Matt Van der Staappen do not get hot for women who look like me."

"That's so not true. I'm telling you, Case, you can hook that man and reel him in. Tonight."

"Emma! He's not a fish."

Emma leaned back in her chair. "Maybe not, but Jake told me Matt wants another night with you. And I want another night with Jake. So don't bother bringing your duffel back to the room."

Casey gasped. "No way. You are *not* locking me out again tonight."

Emma smiled. "Just watch me."

Chapter Six

"Snowshoeing? In twenty degrees? I don't think so."

Matt ignored Casey's protest. "You'll need a warmer coat. But I'm sure Aunt Bea has something you can borrow. She keeps a few things on hand for city guests who don't know any better."

Casey settled herself more firmly in the overstuffed armchair, and shook her curls. "No. Forget it. I'm not leaving this room. Or this fire."

"It's a long time until dinner," Matt pointed out. "And everyone else is either ice-skating, building snowmen, or making love." He smiled as Casey's color rose. "And you're only pretending to read that magazine. Come on. Go snowshoeing with me. It'll be fun. I promise."

"I don't see how strapping oversized tennis rackets to your feet and wading though mounds of snow in the freezing cold can be any kind of fun."

"Don't knock it 'till you've tried it."

She glared up at him. "No."

He plucked the magazine from her fingers and tossed it on the floor. Grabbing her wrists, he pulled her bodily from the chair. She stumbled, falling against him, her breasts squashed against his chest. His body tensed as his hands ran up her back.

She found her balance and backed off a few inches.

"Please?"

He held out a hand and gave her his most winning smile, despite the voice in his head that urged him to give up. He had never in his life worked this hard for a woman's attention. Maybe that was part of the reason he just couldn't let go. "It's my job to entertain the guests."

"You can't really want to entertain me."

"Why not?"

"Because . . . because it's not necessary. I'm perfectly happy staying inside."

"You're perfectly bored out of your skull."

She eyed his outstretched hand. Then she sighed. "You're not going to take no for an answer, are you?"

"Nope."

"Oh, all right, then. I'll go. But if I die of hypothermia, it's all on you."

"I'll take my chances," he said.

Matt caught Casey's gaze and held it. "You have to open up your legs a bit wider, or you'll fall flat on your face."

He watched the crimson blush creep up from beneath Casey's borrowed scarf. Ducking her head, she looked down and shifted her snowshoes a couple inches farther apart.

"I don't know about this." Her curls peeked from the fur-lined hood of Aunt Bea's old parka.

Production Title: Inuit Nights. Florida girl gets lost in the wilds of Alaska. Lonely trapper offers to share his fire . . .

Jesus. He had to get a grip. Now he was casting himself into imaginary scripts. He'd never done that before.

She eyed the snow drifts on either side of the shoveled path behind the farmhouse. "You're really sure I won't sink if I try to climb that stuff?"

"Absolutely sure," he said.

He snagged her hand and tugged her up the snowy incline. The new snow squeaked under their snowshoes, but, as Matt had predicted, held their weight easily. As they reached the top of the drift, she took her hand out of his. He glanced over at her. She was looking down at her feet.

"Wow," she said, taking another step forward. "It really does work. Like walking on water."

"Which, I suppose, technically, it is," he said. "Let's go, then. Up the valley." He started walking north. After a brief hesitation, she followed.

"I just don't know why you asked me to do this with you," she said after a while.

"I wanted some exercise. And you were bored."

"We won't be out here very long, will we?"

He shot her a glance over his shoulder. "You know, you're always in such a hurry to get rid of me. I'm beginning to think you don't like me."

"Don't like—" She paused, then tucked her chin and resumed her hike. "You can't be serious. I . . . I like you just fine. It's just that . . . I'm Klutzy Casey, remember? You'll probably spend half the afternoon pulling me out of snowbanks."

"Hey," he said, catching her chin with one gloved finger. "I wouldn't mind."

Her eyes widened, then she ducked her head. "And I'm worried about Emma," she continued. "My sister falls into relationships so quickly. I don't think it's good for her."

Matt wasn't buying it. "Emma strikes me as the kind of woman who has no problem managing her love life."

A touch of defensiveness crept into her voice. "That doesn't mean I don't worry about her."

"I didn't mean to imply that you didn't."

He forged a trail through the new snow, following the edge of the forest, the mountain rising steeply to his left. In the slice of sky above the gorge, snow clouds were beginning to break up. Blue sky showed through the cracks.

"You're Emma's sister, not her mother," he said. "And she's a grown woman, not a girl."

Casey's next step kicked up some loose powder. "Maybe so, but I've been looking after Emma for so long. Our mother died when she was five."

"How old were you?"

"Twelve."

"Jesus."

"So after that, it was my job to take care of her. Dad was really no good at it."

"But you were only a kid yourself."

More snow sprayed into the air. "We didn't have any handy relatives to help out. And we couldn't afford a nanny. I didn't mind. In fact, I liked it. It made me feel important, and grown-up."

"So you still look after her. You're still the adult, and she's still the kid. You even moved from Florida to New York because you didn't think she could handle life on her own."

"She couldn't have! Not in New York. Her bank account would've been dry in a month."

Matt ducked between two evergreens, releasing a

shower of snow. Two displaced chickadees twittered and darted away. He held back a bough while Casey passed through.

"Who looks after you?" he asked.

"I take care of myself."

They hiked on in silence, and Matt's trail grew steadily steeper. He inhaled deeply, filling his lungs with air untainted by city smog. He really should find a way to spend more time upstate. His life in the city always seemed more hopeful after a visit home.

He darted a glance at Casey. He was beginning to have hope in that department, too. The hike was a good idea. She was definitely warming to him.

After about a half-hour climb, he reached his destination—a flat ledge where a break in the pines afforded a sweeping view of the valley. Casey halted behind him, pushing her hood back to reveal her wild black curls. Her cheeks were flushed pink with the effort of the climb. She was out of breath, and panting.

Project: Indie Film. Genre: Erotica. Title: Breathless . . .

He sucked in a breath of his own.

Just then, as if on cue from some unseen director, the sun broke from behind a cloud, flooding the valley with sparkling light.

"Wow." Casey's tone was filled with awe. "What a beautiful view."

"Worth the climb?" Matt asked with feigned casualness.

"Oh, yes. Definitely. Thank you. For insisting I come up here."

She turned and gave him a brilliant smile.

He took it full force in his chest.

Their eyes met and held. After a long moment, the

smile wavered, and the light in her eyes dimmed. She gave a self-conscious laugh and turned away.

Not good. In a fit of reflexive desperation, Matt scooped a handful of snow off a nearby bough and tossed it.

It exploded against the back of her head.

"Wha—? Ooh!"

She spun around, shaking her head, curls bouncing, white flakes flinging in every direction. A shudder wracked her body as some of the snow slipped down the back of her neck.

"Oooh! I can't believe you did that!"

Matt was already packing his second handful of snow. He gave her a slow smile as he tossed the snowball from hand to hand.

Her eyes widened. "You wouldn't dare."

"Just watch me." The missile burst against her upper chest, just under her chin.

She sputtered. "Why you—" Dropping into a crouch, she scrabbled to pack her own snowball. But not before he'd tossed a third one.

Her counterassault was two-fisted, and messy. It splattered his stomach and thigh. He retaliated with a quick feint to the left, followed by a well-aimed strike to her chest. She tried to jump backward, got her snow-shoes tangled, and fell on her butt. But she was laughing now, splashing armfuls of snow in his general direction. He bore the brunt of the attack stoically, looming over her as he packed a new ball of snow.

"See this?" he said. "It's going right down your neck."

"No!"

Somehow, even though she was lying on her back, she'd managed to form a decent snowball. With surprisingly good aim for a southern girl, she flung it directly at his nose.

He tried to dodge, but snowshoes weren't exactly designed for quick movement. It hit him square in the face. With a choked laugh, he lunged for her.

She screamed as he pounced. He tried to take the brunt of his weight on his outstretched arms, but the snow was soft and his hands, poised on either side of her head, sank through the surface. His body pressed Casey's into the cold, fluffy blanket of white.

He managed enough leverage to roll to one side, taking her with him. He flopped onto his back in the deep depression their bodies had made. Casey sprawled on top of him. Their legs tangled hopelessly, locked tight by their unwieldy snowshoes.

Her head was just below the rim of the snow. His arms were around her waist. She shoved against his chest, trying to lever herself up and off him. She didn't get far. She tried again, her hips shifting and wriggling against his. He felt himself go hard. His hands locked together against her lower back. When she tried a third time to get up, he didn't give her so much as an inch.

He watched her face, and saw the exact moment she realized he was pulling her down rather than helping her up. He waited, his breath barely moving in his lungs, frozen with anticipation. If she really didn't want him, now would be the time to let him know.

She held herself rigid for an instant, her gaze locked with his. He could drown, he thought, in the dark of her eyes. Her eyelashes were thick, and very long. They fluttered downward, and a breath of white-puff air escaped her lips.

She brought her hand up, and tentatively brushed her fingers over the stubble on his chin.

It was all the encouragement he needed.

His hands slid up her back, over her shoulder blades, to settle behind her head. Slowly, he urged her mouth down to his.

This is not the sort of thing that happens to me.

This was the kind of thing, Casey thought, that happened to Emma. Emma was the impulsive sister. The beautiful sister. The sister who inspired men to lust on a regular basis.

Casey was the practical one, the smart one, the industrious one. The sister men overlooked.

Matt wasn't overlooking her.

Not by a long shot. His lips were warm, brushed with cool snow. His body was hard and hot, pressing against her as his mouth worked magic. She shifted. He froze for a beat, as if he expected her to push him away. Instead she aligned her body more perfectly with his. His arms tightened.

A growl vibrated in his throat. His kiss turned urgent, his lips parting hers, his tongue stroking. And then, somehow, he'd unzipped her coat and was slipping his hands inside. What had happened to his gloves? He palmed her breast, his hand sliding over her sweater, his thumb teasing the peak of her nipple beneath the thin knit fabric. A jolt of electricity zinged through her body.

She felt her insides melting. She'd fallen with her

legs on either side of Matt's right thigh; she felt him flex, hard muscle pressing against the sweet spot between her legs. His erection ground against her lower belly, hard and insistent—even through layers of clothing.

"My God, Casey."

His fingers were doing something clever. She arched into the sensation. One of his hands stole around to cup her bottom. He pulled her down, against him, urging, coaxing. God, it felt good.

Too good? There was some reason, she thought, why this wasn't the greatest idea. But Casey's body, in soaking up the sensations flowing through it, had shoved the logical part of her into some dark corner of her brain. She couldn't quite remember the reason why she should stop.

He tugged up her sweater, insinuating warm fingers against her bare skin. They skated up, taking her sweater with them. Cold air brushed goose bumps across her abdomen. In the next instant, her bra went slack.

His mouth covered her nipple, suckling. Sensation curled, hot and aching, in her chest and belly. She cradled his head against her breast and closed her eyes. He fumbled at the snap on her jeans. His fingers slipped inside, touching her, and she gasped.

This wasn't real. It couldn't be. She felt as if she was outside herself, hovering about ten feet above her body, looking down at a man and woman about to make love in the snow.

How could that woman be her? Had the Casey she'd been all her life vanished so quickly? Or was she so desperate for male attention that she melted for the first hot guy to make a move? Was she so starved for sex she was willing to do it right here in the snow, with a guy she barely knew? A guy who was hitting on the only unattached female in a snowbound resort?

Her brain and her body abruptly reunited.

She jerked backward, shoving against Matt's chest. She must have caught him off guard, because she broke his grip easily. Cool air rushed between them. She felt the loss of contact like the twist of a knife in her gut; for an instant, she almost threw herself back on top of him. Their gazes met. His eyes showed his confusion. Hers, she was sure, revealed full-blown panic.

She tried to get off him, but only ended up falling sideways, widening the snow cave they'd created with their bodies. She kicked, trying to untangle their legs.

"Hey." He reached out and grabbed her arm.

"No. Let me go." She flailed at his arm with her fist.

"Whoa. Take it easy." He dropped his arms to his sides. "I'm not trying to do anything you don't want. If you don't want me to touch you, I won't."

She paused, panting. What was she doing? What was she afraid of? She hardly knew.

"I . . . I'm sorry," she said, finally freeing her legs. She flopped onto her side, panting from the effort. "I . . . know that. I just started thinking . . ."

His expression was inscrutable. "Maybe you think too much. Did you ever think of that?"

She was torn between laughter and acute embarrassment. "Or maybe I should have started thinking earlier, before we started this."

She crawled out of the hole and struggled to her feet. He followed her, saying nothing while she hooked her bra and zipped her borrowed coat up to her chin.

"I didn't mean to offend you," he said in a low voice. "I thought . . ." His color heightened. "I thought maybe you wouldn't mind if I kissed you."

"I didn't mind." Her voice was shaking. He must think she was an idiot. How could she explain? She didn't quite understand herself. "At first. But then, when you . . It's just that I'm not . . ."

"Used to men pawing you in the snow?"

She closed her eyes and sighed. "Used to men pawing me at all. I don't date much."

"Then the men you know must be idiots."

She opened her eyes and managed a half laugh. "Just the opposite, actually. The guys I know are brilliant computer geeks."

"Smart guys can be idiots, too."

"And they can be married. Which is what most of the men I work with are."

"You must know some single guys. Through Emma?"

"The actors, you mean? Please. Not my type."

His jaw tightened. "Not smart enough for you? Or is it just all the shallowness you object to?"

Her legs were cold. She busied herself with swatting the snow off her jeans.

"I know you heard me bad-mouthing Emma's friends before. But the truth is, I just don't click with the men she knows. They're all too good-looking, too confident, too extroverted. A guy like that wouldn't give me a second look."

"That's his loss, then. I'm way past giving you a second look. In fact, I think I've lost count."

"Yes, but that's only because of this place."

"What do you mean, this place?"

"This situation," she explained. "I'm the only available woman in the lodge, and you were all but forced to offer me the couch in your cabin."

"You can't possibly believe that. Did you see anyone holding a gun to my back when I asked you to go snowshoeing?"

"No," she conceded. "But be honest. If you passed me on the street, or met me at a party surrounded by twenty or so women as beautiful as Emma, would you even notice me?"

"Of course," he said. But not before he'd hesitated just a split second.

"No," Casey said. "You wouldn't."

He frowned down at her. "Then I'd be the idiot. Because you're a very attractive woman."

"No. Emma's the attractive one. She causes whip-lash every time she walks down the street."

He studied her, his expression intent. It felt as if he were looking under her skin. She wondered what he saw.

"Your sister is stunning, Casey. And yes, I won't lie to you, I noticed her first."

Why did his words hurt? They were only the truth.

"But that doesn't mean you're not pretty. Still, it feels that way to you, doesn't it? It must be hard, living in her shadow."

She rubbed her arms. The chill was seeping into her bones. She wanted to be back in the lodge, in her chair in front of the fire, with the magazine she didn't want to read. She wished she had never left.

"Emma's my sister. I love her."

"But you can't help being jealous."

"No. I'm not. I'm—"

"Of course you are. Sometimes. It's nothing to be

ashamed of. I love Jake, but that doesn't stop me from envying him."

She blinked. "You're jealous of Jake? But why?"

Now he was the one who seemed embarrassed. He rubbed the back of his neck. "It's hard to explain. Jake's always been . . . I don't know . . . more *real* than I am."

"That makes no sense."

"It does to me. With Jake, what you see is what you get. He doesn't have a self-conscious bone in his body. Me . . . I find it hard to show myself to the world. I always want a buffer. A mask." He exhaled. "Do you have any idea what I mean?"

"I . . . yes. Yes, I do."

An understatement. She knew exactly what he meant. She'd been hiding herself all her life.

"Tell me something, Casey. If you'd met *me* at a party, and found out that I dropped out of high school, would you have given me a second glance? Or would you have figured I was someone you didn't want to know?"

She didn't answer. After a moment, he cleared his throat. "I thought so." He paused. "Ready to head back?"

She touched his arm. "You're right. If I'd met you in New York, at one of Emma's parties, I wouldn't have talked to you. But not because you don't have a high school diploma. Because you're just too damn good-looking."

He shot her a look. "Usually, women like that."

She just shrugged and started walking.

Single file, they retraced their footsteps back to the valley floor. Matt didn't speak until they turned to follow the wider trail along the tree line.

"You know, when I dropped out of school, I went to New York. Just like Emma. I had this idea I was going to be an actor."

"You're kidding me."

"No. And I did score some jobs. Modeling, at first. Magazine ads, and then some television. I even managed to land a few off-Broadway roles before I quit. So I really would fit in quite well with your sister's friends." He paused. "The ones you don't like."

Her stomach gave a lurch. "Why did you give it up? The acting, I mean. It sounds like you were a lot more successful than Emma's been."

He shrugged. "Maybe. But acting's an insane way to make a living. I'm a perfectionist, and I just wasn't as good at it as I thought I should be. So after a few years, I gave up and . . . and moved on. But I've found that in a way, acting never gave me up. It's so much easier for me to see life . . . like a theater production, I suppose. It feels that way much of the time, anyway."

They'd reached the clearing behind the barn. Matt stopped, and caught Casey's gloved hand. "But last night, and today . . . I find I don't want to play a part. I know this is quick, Casey, and it doesn't seem like we're two people who would normally get together, but . . . it feels right, being with you. It feels real. And I have to tell you, I'm very, very glad your sister is going to lock you out of your room again tonight."

She looked up at him, her heart tripping, the bottom of her stomach falling, falling, falling.

"Just what are you asking, Matt?"

He dragged a hand through his hair. "I guess . . . whatever you want me to ask. Nothing more than that."

A breeze caught a curl and flung it into her eyes. He smiled, and tucked it behind her ear.

Leaning forward, he brushed a soft kiss on her lips. "I'll be waiting for your answer."

Chapter Seven

They returned to the lodge to find the rest of the guests relaxing with hot chocolate and spiked eggnog. Casey spotted Jake and Emma entwined under a ball of mistletoe.

Matt cleared his throat, prompting them to come up for air, to the general amusement of the other guests. Emma, eyes dancing, flashed Casey an unrepentant grin. Jake reached up and snapped a twig from the mistletoe ball. He dangled it over Casey's head.

"Your turn," he said. "Come on, Matt. Let's see what you've got. Or should I do the honors myself?"

"Don't you dare."

Before Casey quite knew what had happened, Matt had spun her around and dragged her against the hard wall of his chest. His lips covered hers, sending a sweet twist of desire down her body. For a moment, she clung to him, almost forgetting where she was, until a round of laughter and applause snapped her back to her senses.

She tore her lips away. Matt leaned in and whispered against her ear. "Lots more where that came from."

He straightened as Jake clapped him on the back and gave him some good-natured ribbing. Matt grinned and offered an insult in return. Soon after, when the brothers headed to the kitchen to prep for dinner,

Emma wasted no time in hauling Casey to a quiet spot near the Christmas tree.

"Soooo . . ." Her eyes danced. "Things are happening for you, too! Way to go, Case. I'm so glad. You'll be putting that romantic little cabin to good use tonight, I bet."

Casey touched a spun glass snowman ornament. "No, Emma, I won't be. It's way too soon."

"I think not. Did you catch that look Matt gave you on his way out? I seriously expected this tree to go up in flames. That man is deeply in lust. And if he's even half as good as his brother . . ." Emma rolled her eyes and exhaled a long, satisfied sigh. "You are in for one fantastic night."

"Emma, for God's sake, be quiet! Or at least, keep your voice down."

Casey's sister flicked a hand. "Oh, relax. No one's listening."

"They will be if you insist on broadcasting rave reviews of Jake's talents."

"Okay, then. Forget Jake's talents, many though they are. Let's hear about Matt. What's going on between you two?"

"Nothing."

Emma eyed her. "You're lying. I can always tell. Something happened on that little hike you took this afternoon, didn't it?"

"Oh, all right. Something did happen. But it was no big deal. He kissed me." *And then we did a bit more than kiss.* Heat crept up her neck and into her cheeks.

And damn it, Emma noticed. "You're blushing, Casey!" A smile tugged at her lips. "Just for a kiss? Must have been a good one."

"Em. It's none of your business."

"You know, I don't agree. You're my sister. Your business is my business."

"Forget it," Casey said flatly.

"Not likely! You're always so full of advice. Why shouldn't I be the one to give out a tip or two once in a while? And you have to admit, this is my area of expertise. So tell me, Case. Just how long has it been since you've had sex? Ages, right?"

"Emma! I don't ask details about your sex life."

"Just answer the question."

Casey sighed. "Okay. Three years, all right? With Doug. You remember him, right?"

"That long?" The horror in Emma's eyes was unfeigned. "And with that loser? Holy crap, Casey. No wonder you're so uptight. That settles it. You have to sleep with Matt. Tonight. Your mental health depends on it."

"If there's anything affecting my mental health," Casey retorted, "it's my sister. Not the fact that I don't want to jump into bed with a guy I barely know."

Liar, a little voice inside her skull taunted.

"But you like the guy," Emma persisted. "A lot. Admit it."

"So what if I do? That doesn't change the fact that I just met him yesterday."

"Who cares when you met him? Does he make your insides melt?"

Casey's shoulders slumped. "Yes."

"And are you an independent, adult woman?"

"That's neither here nor there. It would never work. Matt is just too . . . too hot."

Emma rolled her eyes. "Girl, there is no such thing."

"Honestly, Emma, look at him. Then look at me."

"You look fine," Emma said. "Or at least, you would if you believed in yourself. Attitude counts more than anything."

"That's easy for you to say," Casey muttered.

Emma huffed out a breath. "It's easy to say because it's true! Geez, Case, the guy already wants you. All you have to do is loosen up and give him a little encouragement." She nudged Casey in the ribs. "I know you want to. I can see it in your eyes."

A little shiver ran up Casey's spine. Emma was right. She did want to.

There. She'd admitted it. At least to herself.

She cleared her throat. "I'll think about it, okay?"

"Oh, Casey," Emma said, shaking her head. "For someone who's so smart, you really are dumb sometimes. Thinking is exactly what you shouldn't do. Promise me. When Matt asks, don't *think*. Go with your heart."

Matt, wearing a white chef's apron, carved a haunch of roast venison for Christmas Eve dinner. Jake emerged from the kitchen, a half-dozen platters of potatoes and vegetables balanced on his arms.

"Oh!" Emma jumped up. "Let me help before it all ends on the floor."

The platters were soon relayed down the table and the guests all seated. Aunt Bea carried in a tray of pastries while Uncle Fred lit a row of candles down the center of the table. Casey was all too aware of Matt sliding into his usual seat beside her.

Uncle Fred bowed his head and said the blessing.

"A fine Christmas Eve." Aunt Bea beamed down the table at her husband after his hearty "Amen." "With family and new friends."

Dinner and conversation began in earnest. Casey eyed the slices of venison on her plate.

"Never had it?" Matt guessed.

"No," Casey admitted. She tasted a tiny piece. "Why, it's not so bad."

Matt laughed. "Aunt Bea will be pleased to hear it. You know, Jake and I ate venison all the time when we were kids. Uncle Fred's a good shot, and Aunt Bea refused to let any meat he brought home go to waste. Broiled, stewed, dried . . . you name it, she's got a recipe."

After the dinner dishes were cleared, pots of tea were poured, and the tray of Dutch pastries was moved from the sideboard to the middle of the table.

"*Letterbanket*," Matt explained, placing a tubular pastry on Casey's plate. "Shaped like the letters of the alphabet. Here's a 'C' for you." He took an 'M' for himself.

Casey bit into hers. It was filled with almond paste. "Delicious."

After dessert, Matt and Jake swiftly cleared the table. As the guests finished their coffee and wandered back into the living room, Jake appeared at Emma's side.

"I need you," he declared.

She batted her eyelashes. "Oh, really?"

He grinned. "Not for that. At least, not yet."

He grabbed her hand and tugged her to the piano. Casey, left alone, watched her sister and her new lover bend their heads over a stack of sheet music. They made a handsome couple, Jake's brown hair brushing Emma's blonde head. Their body language was so in tune, and their laughter was genuine. It was as if they'd known each other for years, rather than just a day.

Aunt Bea and Uncle Fred began herding the guests toward the piano. "Time for carols," Aunt Bea explained. "You too, dear," she said when Casey hung back from the rest.

Reluctantly, Casey joined the outer fringe of the group. Everyone in the lodge was present, except Matt. Was he still in the kitchen, tackling the cleanup on his own?

Jake settled on the piano bench. Emma stood at his side, poised to turn pages.

"Sing loud," he told her with a wink.

He struck the opening chord to "Deck the Halls." Emma added her beautiful voice, and the other guests soon joined in. The farmhouse reverberated with song.

Jake's fingers flew over the keys. He really was a talented pianist, Casey mused. Maybe his musical career wasn't as frivolous a pursuit as she'd assumed. He kept song after song coming, with hardly a pause in between. But Casey found her attention straying. She couldn't get Matt—and the long night ahead—out of her mind. He'd put the ball firmly in her court. *I'll ask whatever you want me to ask,* he'd said.

The problem was, what was that?

Emma's advice spun circles in her head. Should she really throw caution to the wind? Go with her heart? Even if Casey wanted to, she was hardly sure what her heart was saying. The flapping butterfly wings in her stomach were drowning it out.

Jake struck the last plaintive chord to "God Rest Ye Merry Gentlemen." Then his touch softened on the opening bars of "What Child is This?" All other voices fell away as Emma's sweet soprano filled the air.

A rush of pride filled Casey's chest. Her sister was as talented as she was beautiful, and, despite her tendency to act first and think later, she had a good heart. And maybe, on occasion, she was wise, too. Emma had only met Jake yesterday, but he was already enthralled. Could Casey dare hope Matt felt the same way?

Emma held the final, lingering note until it evaporated into the air. A heartbeat of silence ensued, followed by hearty applause and enthusiastic praise.

"Beautiful," Uncle Fred declared. "Truly beautiful."

Aunt Bea smiled. "With talent like that, dear, I'm sure you'll find yourself on Broadway someday."

"I can only hope," Emma sighed.

Jake and Aunt Bea exchanged a glance. "Oh, I think you can do more than that," he said, shuffling the sheet music. "One last song." He sent Casey a pointed look. "And I want to hear everybody this time. That means you, Casey."

Casey laughed and dutifully joined her voice to a lively arrangement of "Santa Claus is Coming To Town." As the song drew to a close, a voice boomed from the foyer.

"*Vrolijk Kerstfeest!* Merry Christmas!"

The singing abruptly changed into a chorus of laughter. "Sinterklaas!" Uncle Fred called. "Welcome!"

A tall old-world Santa Claus, complete with long, curly beard, gold-trimmed red cape, and high bishop's hat, appeared in the archway under the mistletoe, a sack slung over his shoulder. Aunt Bea went up on her toes to buss his cheek. Santa's blue eyes caught Casey's gaze over the top of Bea's head.

Matt's lips curved into a rueful smile behind his fake beard.

Casey started to laugh.

"Oh, my God," said Emma, elbowing Casey in the ribs. "Matt is one sexy Santa."

He was, Casey had to admit.

"Vrolijk Kerstfeest!" Matt slung the pack from his shoulder. "Gather round, ladies. Sinterklaas has something for each one of you."

He presented Aunt Bea with her gift first—a beautiful embroidered shawl. "From your nephews," Sinterklaas told her.

"And now, from the Van der Staappens to their Christmas guests." Matt made a show of rummaging about in his sack, handing out gaily wrapped boxes to the female guests. When he came to Emma and Casey, he looked from one to the other and hesitated. "There's only one left."

"Because I wasn't supposed to be here," Casey said, hiding a twinge of disappointment. "You take it, Emma. It's your vacation."

"Are you sure?"

"Very."

Emma accepted the gift. The paper was gold, with silver stars. "It's heavy," she said, weighing it in her hands.

"Open it," Casey urged.

Emma set the box on the piano, tore open the wrapping, and lifted the lid. "Oh! How beautiful!"

The old-fashioned snow globe was real glass. Inside, flakes of white surrounded a tiny replica of Dutch

Lodge. The words *Romance of Christmas 2009* were inscribed on its polished wood base.

Emma inverted the globe and turned it upright again. Snow swirled all around the miniature farmhouse. A glance around the room told Casey the other women had received identical gifts. All were as charmed as she and Emma.

"Pretty, huh?" Jake said. "Uncle Fred found a local artisan who makes them by hand."

"It's lovely. I think I'll go thank Fred and Bea right now."

"Sure thing," Jake said. They stepped away, leaving Casey alone with Matt.

She smiled. "You know, you make a very nice Santa."

He tugged off his beard and placed it on a nearby table. His bishop's hat joined it. "Sinterklaas," he corrected. "The Dutch version of Santa Claus. Not as fat as the American one. And much more dignified. Normally Uncle Fred does the honors, but this year, I asked him to let me do it."

"Why?"

"Because I wanted Sinterklaas to give you this."

His hand disappeared into the folds of his cape. "It's not wrapped, though, so close your eyes."

A thrill of anticipation ran through Casey. Her lashes swept down. Matt caught her hand and pressed something smooth and cool into her palm.

Her eyes flew open. "Your mystery box! But . . . I couldn't possibly accept this. It's part of your childhood."

"I haven't opened it in ages, and it really seemed to intrigue you. I'd like you to have it."

She turned the box over, marveling again at the workmanship. "Thank you."

"You're welcome." He seemed uncertain for a moment, as if waiting for her to say or do something else. Finally, he drew a breath. "Do you remember how to open it?"

His voice had dropped to a near whisper. The intimacy sent a jolt of awareness through Casey's senses. "I . . . I think so." Her fingers searched for the hidden catch. "Let me see . . ."

She found a small, folded sheet of paper nestled inside.

"Open it," Matt said.

She extracted the paper, her fingers trembling slightly as she unfolded it. There was a single symbol on it. A question mark.

"What's this?"

"A question."

Her eyes collided with his. "What kind of question?"

"Your question. The one you want me to ask." He lifted his hand and cupped the side of her face, tracing the arch of her cheekbone with his thumb. "Do you know what it is yet?"

She closed her eyes and turned her head into his hand, brushing his palm with her lips. Heat gathered low in her belly. She couldn't capture a clear thought in her head—her emotions were too tangled. Desire, fear, anticipation, uncertainty, foreboding, excitement . . . She was so mixed up over this man she'd just met. And yet, in some strange, primal way, she was drawn to him. Could someone really fall in love that quickly? She didn't know.

His hand slid around to the back of her neck, urging her closer. She went, her eyes still closed. His heavy cape enfolded both of them, shutting the rest of the room out.

Emma had told her to go with her heart. That organ was pounding loudly now, and she knew exactly what it was saying.

She opened her eyes. And was immediately seared by the heat of his gaze. An answering fire flashed through her. Her knees went weak. She grasped the embroidered edge of his cape as his arm came around her, holding her steady.

"Yes." Her throat was dry. "I know the question I want you to ask."

"Consider it asked," he said. His lips touched hers. "And your answer?"

She felt her heart take a flying leap of faith.

"Yes," she said. "My answer is yes."

Chapter Eight

The walk from the kitchen door to the cabin in the woods passed in a blur. Casey was aware, on an intellectual level at least, that it was very cold outside. But the hunger in Matt's eyes left room for nothing but slow, dark heat.

His arm around her waist was solid and sure, and it seemed her boots barely skimmed the snow as he hustled her down the path to his cabin. The door swung closed behind them.

He toed off his boots, and left her briefly to light the lamp. Casey removed her own boots, then shrugged out of her coat and hung it on the hook by the door. She rubbed her arms at the sudden loss of warmth as Matt crossed the room to build up the fire, his long red cape swirling behind him. He tossed in two logs, then stood against a background shower of sparks.

Casey hadn't moved from her position by the door. He approached her slowly. "Second thoughts?"

"No." She swallowed hard. "Should there be?"

"I hope not." He caught her hand. "I'm praying there's not."

"I—" She cut off as a low, mournful wail, like a deep, rich foghorn, sounded in the darkness outside the cabin. "What's that?"

Matt smiled. "A Dutch *midwinterhoorn*. It's an ancient custom. Uncle Fred always blows it on Christmas Eve, over the old well in the front yard. It's supposed to chase away evil spirits."

The horn sounded again. "That's lovely." Casey toyed with one of the hand-tooled gold clasps on the front of his cape. "And what about this costume? Is it from Holland? It looks old."

"It is. It's a family heirloom. And yes, it's from Holland. My grandfather brought it with him when he emigrated."

"When was that?"

"1940. Just before Hitler invaded. Granda had a cousin in New York, and was able to get his wife and two young sons out just in time."

"That was your father and Uncle Fred? How old were they?"

"My father was about six, I think. Uncle Fred was an infant."

He unclasped the cape and swung it off his shoulders, draping it over the back of a chair with reverence. "I remember my father wearing this. Not on Christmas, though. On Saint Nicholas Day, the year before he died. It's one of my few memories of him."

He turned back to her, just Matt now, dressed in his usual jeans and sweater. The fire in the hearth leapt, throwing dancing shadows across his face. Out of the corner of her eye, his double bed loomed large. Casey tried to picture herself in it. With him. The image didn't quite appear.

Despite Emma's pep talk, it was still so hard to believe such a beautiful man really wanted her.

His warm palms descended on her shoulders. "Hey. Stop thinking. Relax."

"I'm not sure I can."

"Casey." His voice was sober as he guided her toward the fire. "I hope you know I'm not going to do anything you don't want me to. In fact, if you want to stop right now . . . If all you want to do is talk, or play cards, or . . . whatever, that's all right with me."

She inhaled, for courage. "No. It's not that. It's just that it's been kind of a long time for me, since . . ."

God. She could hardly say it. How was she going to *do* it?

A little smile played on his lips. His thumbs played on the bare skin at the neckline of her sweater. "How long?"

She gave a shaky laugh. "You would ask." She tried to look away, but he caught her chin and brought her gaze back to his.

"Three years," she admitted.

"Wow." His lips quirked. "Jesus. An eternity. You're practically a virgin."

She laughed. "Hardly."

His eyes turned serious. "Ever been in love?"

Yes. Since just this afternoon. "No. Not really." She paused. "What about you?"

He gave a half laugh, and looked away. "Me? Not even close."

The silence that ensued threatened to stretch into awkwardness. With a slight frown, Matt tugged her a few steps backward to the couch. He shoved the blankets she'd used the night before to one side and sat, drawing her down beside him.

He didn't speak. That was good, because as far as Casey was concerned, talking led to thinking, and thinking led to second guessing. *Go with your heart*, Emma had told her. Was that good advice? Casey's heart was reaching toward Matt, and telling her to let him in.

He exhaled a slow breath and leaned toward her, one arm stretched along the back of the sofa. With his free hand, he fluffed her curls around her face.

"Oh, stop," she laughed, catching his fingers. "I must look like a witch."

"A very sexy witch." His eyes were intent.

Desire unfurled in Casey's chest. The musk of his cologne teased her senses. In a sudden burst of boldness, she slipped her hands under his sweater and shirt and splayed her fingers on his bare skin. His heart thumped against her palms, beating almost as quickly as hers.

He grasped the hem of his sweater and, with one smooth motion, pulled both sweater and shirt over his head. God, but he was solid, his muscles taut under her fingers. His skin was hot, almost burning. Her hands skated up to tangle in the dusting of hair on his chest.

His lips came down on hers, hungry and demanding. She responded with a surging hunger of her own. Her hands slid up and around his neck, and he deepened the kiss, urging her lips apart. He rose over her, pressing her down into the cushions, his erection brushing her thigh. Instinctively, she shifted, opening her legs, cradling him. He froze for a split instant, then his lips slid from her mouth and pressed in an open-mouth kiss against her shoulder.

"God, Casey. I want to see all of you."

He lifted the hem of her sweater and eased it over her head, then went to work on the buttons of the blouse beneath. The shirt was soon gone, along with her bra, almost before she realized what had happened.

He drew back a fraction, his eyes sweeping down her body. She shivered, and fought an urge to cover herself. She was small up top, at least compared to Emma. But if Matt minded, he was hiding it admirably. Only the best actor could have feigned the hot burn of lust in his eyes.

He slid his hands up under her breasts, capturing her gaze and holding it as he brushed his thumbs over her nipples. The exquisite burst of pleasure dragged a moan from her throat.

"No. Don't close your eyes. Let me see you."

She obeyed, feeling even more vulnerable than before.

"You're beautiful," he whispered.

A protest leapt to the tip of her tongue. At the last moment, she swallowed it unsaid. *Attitude*, Emma had said. *Believe in yourself.* Maybe it was time to take her sister's advice to heart.

He bent his head to her breast. Her hips came off the couch when his teeth captured one peaked tip in a gentle nibble. His hands went to the waist of her pants, sliding the button from its hole and tugging down the zipper. They slid over her bottom, taking her panties with them. And all the while his mouth was worshipping one breast, then the other.

And then she was completely bare, his mouth trailing kisses between her breasts and down her belly. She gasped when he shifted his weight over the edge of the couch, dropping onto his knees before her. He hooked his arms under her thighs and pulled her to the edge of the couch, parting her legs wide at the same time. His chin brushed her mound. She felt his breath on her most tender skin.

Panic struck. "Oh God. No." She felt unbearably exposed. She'd never—"Matt. Wait. Don't—aaah!"

Her protests dissolved under the hot lash of Matt's tongue. She fisted her hands in his hair, intending to push him away. Then he licked a sweet, perfect stroke and she found herself clutching him closer. She heard a low chuckle, but by that time he'd added his fingers to his sweet torture and she was beyond caring.

She was so close to the edge. So close . . .

She gasped when he suddenly drew back. "What—?"

His answer was a tight smile. He half rose, hooking one arm under her knees and the other beneath her shoulder blades. He straightened, lifting her. Trembling, wanting, she wrapped her arms around his neck and pressed her cheek against his chest. His skin was damp. He smelled like sweat, lust, and wood smoke. She inhaled deeply as he covered the distance to his bed in three strides.

He tumbled her down on the rumpled sheets. His heat withdrew as he rummaged in the nightstand drawer. She drank in his profile, anticipation coiling in her belly. The mattress dipped. Matt tossed a wrapped condom down beside her.

Casey's breath left in a whoosh. She hadn't even thought of birth control. God, but her brain was completely scrambled. It was a good thing Matt's was still functioning.

He crawled over her on all fours, and the fire blazed

anew between them. She arched toward him, sliding her hands over his chest and stomach, and lower. Taking him in her hands, she stroked hot, velvety skin over hard muscle. Once, twice, three times . . .

He grabbed her hand, air sawing in and out of his lungs. "Watch it. Not yet."

His thigh sank between her legs. His eyes were closed, his expression almost one of pain. She could hardly believe she was lying in bed, naked, with a man like him. He was far more than she'd ever dreamed of—when she'd allowed herself to dream at all.

The thought made her resolve fade fast. Was she anything like the woman of Matt's dreams? Impossible. She was the woman who happened to be on hand.

Doubts started crowding in.

"Damn." Matt swore softly. Eyes open now, he dipped his head to nip at her jaw. "Don't leave me, Casey. Please. Whatever you're thinking—stop it."

His teeth snagged her neck and gently bit. Her misgivings wavered. His hands swept down her body. The doubts scattered further. His thigh rode up firmly between her legs, and her brain blanked completely.

And in that oblivion, a spark of confidence rekindled. Without stopping to think, Casey moved against Matt, matching his urgency. An instant later, she found the condom on the mattress beside them and tore it open. He supported himself on rigid arms above her as she covered him.

Both his legs were between hers now, holding her apart as his fingers played wickedly. She scraped her palms on either side of his jaw and drew him down for a kiss. He took her lips with a growl, the tip of his erection sliding into place and pulsing against her wet heat.

"Look at me, Casey."

She did. The expression in his eyes made her breath catch. Her need ratcheted up. Her hips tilted, inviting, pleading. He held her gaze as he entered her. Slowly. Her hands found the curve of his buttocks; she urged him closer. He flexed his hips and slid deeper. And deeper still.

She bit her lip as he started rocking inside her. Stunning waves of sensation rippled through her body. He was watching her face, his eyes too knowing. Her eyelids fluttered closed.

"No—don't," he whispered. He surged forward, then retreated. On the next stroke, he changed his angle subtly, and hit a spot that made her gasp. "I want to see it in your eyes when you come."

She wanted that, too.

She opened her eyes. Their gazes caught, and their souls seemed to link. Her inner muscles contracted; she felt Matt pulse, deep inside.

He groaned, and moved faster. "God, Casey. You feel . . . so good. So damn right."

"So do you." A slow smile curved her lips. "Sinterklaas."

His half laugh dissolved into a groan as his cadence quickened even more. "Good" dissolved into something much, much, better as his strokes came harder, and faster, and harder still. Casey clutched Matt's shoulders as the peak rushed her.

Then she was over the edge, gasping his name, flying free. Matt's arms wrapped firmly around her torso, drawing her flat against his damp skin. His lips pressed to the crook of her neck. His pleasure-roughened growl vibrated against her skin as his own orgasm hit.

Afterward, Casey floated down to earth without a single doubt.

Chapter Nine

Dawn came and went. It had to be the best Christmas Matt had had in years. He didn't even bother getting out of bed, except once, to build up the fire.

He slid back under the quilt as quickly as he could. Casey was curled up on her side, hugging an extra pillow. There were about a thousand snarls in her hair. He smiled. He'd put just about every one of them there.

He slid under the quilt and propped himself up on his elbow, facing her. She had a hickey on her neck. Looking at it got him hot all over again. The sex last night had been incredible. *Casey* had been incredible.

If he'd met her in the city, he wouldn't have given her a second look. Now he wondered what she saw in him. And all because he was a different man here in the gorge than he was in New York.

He'd always known there was a part of himself he'd abandoned when he'd left his childhood home to find his way in the world. What he hadn't known was that it had been here all that time, waiting for him to find his way back.

But he wasn't staying in this perfect world, was he? In a few days, he'd return to his life in the city, where he worked long hours, made difficult decisions, played complicated networking games. Where he wasn't a laid-back, simple-pleasures kind of guy. And the truth was, he liked his career and city life. His New York self was part of him, too. The bigger part now. He wasn't about to leave it all to return to his roots permanently.

His peaceful mood dimmed. He'd avoided telling Casey about his life outside Dutch Gorge. She'd made it clear what she thought about his world. Would she reconsider now that they'd slept together? Would she even like the man he was in the city?

Damn. His morning-after glow was shot to hell. And Aunt Bea would be needing him soon in the kitchen. Sliding carefully out of bed, he showered and dressed. He was lacing up his boots when Casey stirred and sat up, blinking sleep from her eyes.

"Matt?"

"Over here," he said. "Merry Christmas."

"Oh! It is Christmas, isn't it?" Her shy smile squeezed his insides. "Merry Christmas." Her gaze went to the window. "It's light out. What time is it?"

"Almost eight."

"And you're going out? Already?"

"Aunt Bea's expecting me in the kitchen." He hesitated. "I'll be busy today. You won't be seeing much of me before dinner. That's at three, by the way. But there'll be a cold breakfast spread in the dining room at ten. You can sleep until then."

"Or I could help you and Aunt Bea," She started to get out of the bed, then stopped abruptly, jerking the covers back over her nude body. "Um . . ."

Oh, man. Just one glimpse and he wanted to dive back into bed, and to hell with the city and the future. They were both here in the gorge now, weren't they? For a couple more days, anyway.

Unfortunately, he had work to do. He pulled on his

coat. "Don't even bother offering to help in the kitchen. You're a lodge guest. Aunt Bea wouldn't let you lift a finger."

"But—"

He leaned over the bed and gave her a quick kiss. "Do me a favor. Get a couple extra hours of sleep. Believe me, you're going to need it tonight."

"Why? What's tonight?"

He gave her a slow smile. "Tonight's when I get you back into that bed."

Casey passed the next two days in a happy haze. More than once, she wondered when she was going to wake up and find out it was all a dream.

Not that she wanted to wake up. No way. She was beginning to believe that Dutch Lodge was a little bit magical, like a wintery Shangri-la or something. She even found herself wishing for another blizzard. One that would keep the roads closed and her computer unplugged indefinitely.

Matt's Uncle Fred led a short prayer service before Christmas brunch, since the roads to the local churches were closed. Christmas afternoon, while Matt and Jake were occupied in the kitchen, Casey helped Emma and the rest of the lodge guests build a giant snowman in the front yard. Afterward, the whole group stomped back into the house, laughing and chatting, to roast chestnuts and drink hot cider.

Christmas dinner was an elaborate affair, featuring roast goose and *boterkoek*, or almond butter cake. After dinner, Uncle Fred told traditional Dutch stories by the hearth.

After Bea and Fred had said their good nights, and the fire had burned low, Jake tugged Emma up the stairs. Casey and Matt, arms entwined, made their way through the snow to the cabin. They made love half the night, and woke to the sun streaming through their windows.

The day after Christmas brought sled races, snow angels, and hot chocolate. Casey even let Matt talk her into a pair of ice skates. She clung to him, laughing, as he hauled her around the frozen lake. And she wished the weekend would never end.

But early Sunday morning, the outside world intruded, in the form of a pair of snowplows grinding down the road. The harsh reverberation of their engines shattered Casey's fairy-tale reverie.

Today was the day she and Emma returned to the city.

Breakfast came early; immediately after, Matt and Jake attacked the lodge parking lot with a snowblower and shovels. Casey returned to the cabin alone, to gather her things and shove them into her duffle.

She packed the mystery box last. Zipping the bag, she sat on the rumpled bed and hugged Matt's pillow. His scent lingered; she inhaled deeply. Then, with one last look around, she hefted her duffel and laptop and headed to the lodge.

Emma was sitting alone at the dining room table, sipping coffee. Casey poured a cup and joined her.

"Jake asked me to come up to Boston for New Year's," Casey's sister informed her. "What about you and Matt? Did you make plans?"

"No." Casey took more care than necessary spooning

sugar into her cup. Somehow, as if by silent agreement, she and Matt hadn't talked about what would happen between them after today. And what did that mean? She didn't want to face it. "Matt didn't say anything about New Year's Eve. And it doesn't matter. I'll be working anyway."

If she still had a job after dropping off the face of the planet for four days.

Emma made a face. "Working on New Year's Eve is downright inhuman. I hope they're paying you triple time. I guess you can see Matt afterward."

"I don't know," Casey said, trying to ignore an uneasy feeling in her gut. "Maybe, but then again . . . well, the thing is, Matt and I might not keep seeing each other. I mean, I'm not really into long distance relationships."

"What long distance? From the Village to the Upper West Side?"

Casey went still. "What are you talking about? Matt lives in Boston."

Emma looked at her oddly. "No, he doesn't. Jake and his sister live in Boston. Matt lives in Manhattan. He has a business there or something."

"No. That can't be. He said he lived—" She hesitated, considering. "No. Actually, he never said anything about where he lived. I just assumed he lived in Boston, because he talked about driving there today with his aunt and uncle. But he was talking about driving to his sister's house, wasn't he?"

Emma laughed. "I guess you two were so busy with other things, you forgot about exchanging addresses."

Casey frowned into her coffee. "I guess."

"Oh, don't worry. He'll call. I'd put money on it. Give him our number before we leave."

"Yeah," Casey said. "I will." But she wasn't at all sure Emma would win her bet.

Chapter Ten

The Diva Diamonds New Year's Eve deadline was breathing down Casey's neck like a rabid tiger. Her team had under twenty-four hours to get everything in place. Casey stared, bleary-eyed, at her computer. It was going to be one hell of a night. She took a fortifying swig of coffee. Ugh. Cold.

She dragged her sorry carcass to the kitchen to brew a fresh pot. She was lucky she still had her job. Her panicked colleagues had covered for her during her days off-line, wondering what had happened to her. They were immensely relieved when she'd returned. With a little added push, the project would come together tomorrow night at nine, right on schedule. And everything would be fine.

But everything didn't feel fine. It just felt . . . wrong. Her coffee . . . her apartment . . . her job . . .

Her life.

But that was ridiculous. Her life wasn't wrong. It was fine. At least, it had been fine two weeks ago. And nothing was really different now. Therefore, logically, her life was still fine.

Except that it wasn't.

Her life might be the same, but she wasn't. She was the one who had changed. Into an idiot. And all because of a man.

Pathetic.

She didn't want to think of Matt. But like that trick where you tried not to think of a pink elephant, every effort to banish the guy into some dark corner of her mind failed. He was onstage, front and center.

With a sigh, she filled the coffeemaker, eyeing the bottom drawer under the cabinet where odd bits and pieces of stuff always ended up. She'd shoved Matt's mystery box in there, with a rubber band ball, a couple of screwdrivers and the keys from her old apartment. The slip of paper with the question mark was still inside. She didn't want to look at it. She didn't even want to think about it. But she just didn't have the heart to throw it away.

She'd given Matt her phone number Sunday before leaving the gorge, just as Emma had suggested. It was only Wednesday now. Only three days later. Three days was nothing. And yet, it felt like a yawning chasm of time. In those same three days, Jake had called Emma at least a dozen times. And had texted her constantly in between. Well, of course he had. Men always called Emma.

Casey's little sister was currently holed up in the bathroom, humming as she put on her makeup. Jake had called from the train station a half hour ago; he'd be at the door any minute. He and Emma were going to a party tonight in the city, then heading back to Boston tomorrow for New Year's Eve. Jake's band was playing at some fancy hotel, and he'd insisted Emma join them as guest vocalist. Emma was thrilled.

Casey pressed a sudden throbbing pain between her eyes. Emma had, of course, interrogated Jake about Matt. Jake had returned only the vaguest answers.

Emma had made excuses for Matt, but as far as Casey was concerned, there was only one conclusion to draw. If Matt were interested, he would have called. He hadn't, so he wasn't.

She wandered back out to the living room. Her computer screen had timed out and gone blank. Slumping onto the couch, Casey faced facts. The days—and nights—she'd spent in Dutch Gorge hadn't been real. They'd been an aberration, a pleasant interlude. The problem was that she'd allowed herself to hope the gorge's magic would follow her back to the city. It hadn't.

Leaning sideways, she flicked off the floor lamp, plunging the room into silent darkness. Not Dutch Gorge dark, of course. Plenty of artificial light spilled through the venetian blinds. And it wasn't all that quiet, either. The closed window only blocked the worst of the street noise.

"Casey? You in here?"

She winced as Emma flipped on the overhead light. "There you are! I thought maybe you'd gone out. What are you doing sitting in the dark?"

"I have a headache."

"Poor baby! You're working too hard. Did you take something?"

"Yes," Casey lied.

"Well, what about some hot tea, or—" The street intercom buzzed, cutting Emma off. "Oh!" she said. "That'll be Jake."

Matt's brother arrived at the door half a minute later, flourishing a limp street vendor bouquet. Emma's face lit up as if she'd been presented with an armful of hot-house orchids. She disappeared into the kitchen to put the wilted daisies and carnations in water.

"Casey," Jake said, dropping an overnight bag on the floor. "Hi."

She stood. "Hi, Jake. Good to see you."

"Good to see you, too. Hey, listen. Emma said you'd have a few free days after your interactive New Year's Eve promo thing goes down, and I was thinking . . . Why don't you come up to Boston on New Year's Day?"

"You're kidding, right?"

"I'm not. You can stay at Mary's—she has tons of room. Aunt Bea and Uncle Fred are there, of course, and—"

"And Matt."

"Um, well, yeah."

"Does he know about this?"

Jake looked discomfited. "No. I just thought of it, actually, while I was riding in on the train. But I know he'll be glad to see you."

Casey snorted. "I don't. Thanks for the offer, but there's no way I'm going to Boston to inflict myself on Matt."

"Hey, now. I wouldn't call it—"

"Jake, come off it. Your brother hasn't called me since I left the gorge. It's obvious that he doesn't want to see me."

"I think you're wrong about that, Casey."

Casey didn't like the way his words caused a hopeful clench of her heart. "Then why hasn't he called? He's got my number. And even if he's lost it, *you've* got my number."

"It's . . . kind of complicated."

"No. It's not. It's very simple. One cell phone. Ten little numbers."

Jake shoved his hands into his pockets. "You're right, of course. Matt should've called you by now. And he should've called Emma, too."

"Emma?" Casey said just as her sister returned from the kitchen. "What does she have to do with it?"

Emma looked from Jake to Casey. "Did I hear my name? What are we talking about?"

Instead of answering, Jake pulled out his wallet and extracted a business card. "Here." He thrust the card into Emma's hand. "Matt was planning to call you next week, when he got back to the city. But you might as well know now."

"What—?" Emma looked at the card and blinked. "Oh. My. God. No. This can not be real."

Casey peered over her sister's shoulder. Emma's hand was trembling, making it hard to make out the printing on the card. She grabbed her sister's wrist and held it still.

Matthew Joseph, Matthew Joseph Casting. Theater, Film, Advertising.

"Jake," Emma breathed. "You can't mean this. Matt is Matthew *Joseph*?"

"Yep," Jake said. "He is."

Emma let out a squeal. "Ohmygod! I can't believe it!"

"Who's Matthew Joseph?" Casey asked.

Emma was gulping air in big breaths of air. "Only . . . one of . . . the hottest casting agents . . . in Manhattan!" She grabbed Jake's arm. "And he's really going to call me? Next *week*?"

"Yeah," Jake said, chuckling. "He really is. Matt's

got a few projects coming up he thinks you'll be interested in—Jesus, Emma!" He put a steadying hand on her shoulder. "Stop hyperventilating, for chrissakes. It's not instant stardom. A couple TV commercials. A citywide print campaign. And maybe, if you audition well, a small role in an off-Broadway production. It's only a start—"

"It doesn't matter! I'll take anything! *Anything.* Oh, my *God.* Matthew Joseph. And I didn't even know. Matt never said a word! I can't believe it."

"Wait a minute." Casey was lagging about three steps behind. "Matt's last name is Van der Staappen. Isn't it?"

"Well, yeah," Jake said. "But his middle name is Joseph. He goes by Matt Joseph professionally."

"And he's a casting director?"

"Yeah. A very successful one."

"But . . . why all the secrecy? Why didn't he just say something to Emma at Dutch Lodge?"

Jake rocked back on his heels. "Uh . . . well, I'm afraid that was kinda my fault. When I found out Emma was an actress, I asked Matt to keep quiet. I was afraid she wouldn't give me the time of day if she knew who Matt was. So I asked Matt to back off, and distract you a little, while I worked on getting Emma's full attention."

"Oh, Jake," Emma exclaimed, kissing his cheek. "That is just so sweet."

"And it certainly explains a few things," Casey muttered. Specifically, why Matt hadn't called. He'd hooked up with her as a favor to his brother. And once he got back to Manhattan, he was sure to be neck deep in actresses and models.

No wonder he hadn't called.

Sympathy flashed in Emma's eyes. "Oh, Casey . . ."

"Aren't the two of you late for your party?" Casey said abruptly. "It's after ten already. You'd better get going."

Emma sent her a worried look. "Um . . . we don't really have to go, do we Jake?"

"No," Jake said promptly. "Not at all. We could hang out here tonight if you want."

"No," Casey said. "I've got work to do. Please. Go."

"Well . . . okay," Emma said. "If you're sure you'll be all right here by yourself."

"I'll be fine," Casey said. "Just . . . fine."

Chapter Eleven

Matt felt like a goddamned stalker.

What was he doing, pacing up and down the sidewalk in front of Casey's apartment building? An hour to midnight on New Year's Eve, no less. He'd gotten her work number from Emma. He could have called her there, earlier in the day. But he knew she was working on a tight deadline. And besides that, the notion of talking to Casey on the phone just didn't appeal. He needed to see her, face to face.

Needle-sharp sleet spit from a charcoal sky. He should've brought an umbrella. Or a hat, at least. An icy wind gusted up the street. He turned up his collar and ducked into the meager shelter of the apartment doorway.

Production title: Idiot in Love. Pathetic loser lurks in a city doorway . . .

He located the buzzer for her apartment on the panel by the door. Taking a deep breath, he pressed it.

No answer. But she had to be there. He'd been on the phone with Jake not a half hour earlier. At the same time, Emma had been texting Casey, and Jake had assured Matt that Casey's company had met their nine p.m. deadline for the Times Square promo. At nine thirty, Casey had left the office and gone home. Alone.

He buzzed again. This time, a voice answered though the intercom.

"Yes?"

"Casey? It's Matt. Can I come up?"

Several beats of silence ensued.

"Matt Van der Staappen? Or Matthew Joseph?"

He sighed. "Please. Just let me in. It's cold out here."

He heard a soft snort. A couple seconds later, the door unlatched. He climbed four flights of stairs and knocked at the door.

She opened it. For a long moment, they just stared at each other. His heart gave a lurch. Casey looked adorable, with her messy hair and flushed cheeks. Her wrinkled jeans and comfortably rumpled sweater made him want to drag her right into bed.

Her gaze flicked over him, her expression inscrutable. He wondered what she was thinking. Casey might look just the same as she had in Dutch Gorge, but Matt, dressed in charcoal wool dress slacks and a black turtleneck, was a far cry from the denim-and-flannel guy she knew.

She leaned on the jamb, one hand on the doorknob, blocking his view into the apartment. "So," she said. "What do you want?"

He shoved his hands into the pockets of his overcoat. "Jake told you about me," he said. "I wanted to explain."

She shoved a curl out of her eyes. He fought the urge to tuck it behind her ear.

When she didn't answer, he continued, "He also said he told you why I didn't say anything about my casting agency."

Her lips twisted. "Yeah. Something about keeping me out of the way while he moved in on Emma."

"No! It wasn't like that at all." He shoved a hand through his hair. "Well, not exactly."

"And really," she continued, "it all worked out fine. Jake's a great guy. He and Emma hit it off. And you and I . . . well, we got a few nights of sex. So it's all good."

She started to close the door. He put a hand out to stop it from hitting him in the face. "Damn it Casey, that's not how it is between us, and you know it."

"No, Matt. I don't know it. I know nothing. I don't know why you worked so hard to get me into bed. I don't know why you bothered to take my number. And I don't know why you're here."

"Then let me in. Let me explain."

"That's not a good idea. I mean, what would be the point? You have your life, filled with actresses and models, and I have mine, filled with computer geeks. Believe me, I've been around enough of Emma's friends to know the two just don't mix well."

"I'm not going to discuss this in the hallway."

With a sigh, she stepped back. "Fine," she said. "Suit yourself."

He entered the apartment and closed the door firmly behind him. Turning, he found himself in a small, cluttered living room. A futon couch and matching chair flanked a coffee table in the center of the room. The potted palm by the window looked like it was in need of watering. A bookshelf crowded with computing titles half shielded a computer desk, where an oversized monitor fought for desk space with a collection of empty cola cans.

A flat-screen TV on the wall was tuned to coverage of New Year's Eve festivities in Times Square. Casey's laptop was open on the coffee table, nestled amid fashion magazines and empty coffee cups, flashing photo after photo of passionate kisses. Underneath, the vote tally for each couple rose.

"Your project?" he asked.

"Yes. It rolled out like clockwork."

"That's good."

She shrugged. Taking a seat on the futon, she punched the mute on the remote. "Okay, get on with it. Why are you here?"

Matt shrugged out of his coat and draped it on a clothes stand near the door. Dropping into the chair on Casey's right, he rested his forearms on his thighs and leaned forward. "You probably wondered why I didn't call."

Casey's eyes were on the computer screen. A photo of a couple kissing on a tropical beach faded into a picture of a couple kissing in front of a massive barbeque grill.

"The question might have crossed my mind," she said.

"I drove out to Boston from Dutch Gorge on Sunday. I just got back to Manhattan today."

"There are phones all over New England, I've heard."

"I thought about calling, but . . . I don't know. It didn't seem right. I didn't want to talk to you on a phone. I wanted to see you. But at the same time, I was afraid when I saw you it would be too . . . different. Awkward."

She didn't reply. He exhaled and continued. "Just

like it is now. I didn't know what you'd think of who I am here in the city. I'm not exactly the same man I pretended to be upstate."

"Why pretend at all?" She finally looked at him. "That's what I don't understand. Why didn't you just tell me who you were?"

"At first, I kept quiet for Jake. So he could get to know Emma without me and my agency as a distraction." He shrugged. "Sounds conceited, I know."

She snorted. "No. It sounds realistic. Jake was right. If Emma had known who you were, Jake would have become instantly invisible." Her gaze skittered away. "You must know hundreds of women as beautiful and as talented as Emma in your business."

"I suppose I do," he said with a shrug. "But truthfully? They all blur together after a while. Not one of them stands out. Not like you do."

"Oh, please."

"I'm serious, Casey. You got my attention that first moment in the parking lot, when you fell into my arms. And then later, when I was getting your luggage?" He chuckled. "Man, you were so pissed at Emma. I could practically see the smoke coming out of your ears."

She shot him a look of pure incredulity. "So you're trying to tell me we hooked up as a result of my clumsiness and bad temper?"

He gave a wry laugh. "Honestly? I think it was more the fact that you weren't trying to impress me. You have no idea how appealing that was. But then, the more time I spent with you, the more I liked you. I can't tell you how glad I was that Emma kept locking you out of your room."

"But . . . why didn't you tell me about your work

then? I wouldn't have told Emma until the weekend was over, if you'd asked me to keep quiet. But you never mentioned a word about being a casting director. You didn't even tell me you lived in Manhattan. Why not?"

"It's . . . hard to explain. In Dutch Gorge, the real world seems so far away, and I like it that way. I didn't feel like talking about my career, answering all the usual questions. And you didn't seem to have a very high opinion of the business anyway." He sighed. "Don't get me wrong, I love what I do. But last weekend, I just wanted a break from . . . everything. I found myself wanting to be the man I might have been if I hadn't left the gorge. Just for a few days, anyway." He rubbed a hand down his face. "Does that make any kind of sense?"

"A little, I suppose." She tucked her legs under her and looped her arms around her knees. "Dutch Gorge made me want to be someone different, too. Someone more . . . uninhibited, I guess. Like Emma."

"Once I got to Boston," he said slowly, "what we shared in the gorge . . . it seemed like a dream. Like it hadn't really happened."

"I felt the same way," Casey murmured. "Even when it was happening. At first, I couldn't believe you were sincere. I kept thinking it couldn't last. And then, when you didn't call . . ."

"I didn't call because I didn't know what to say," he confessed. "At least, not over the phone. I only knew what I wanted to tell you when I saw you again face to face."

"And what is that?"

"That maybe last weekend showed both of us who

we really are. And I wanted to ask if you thought we could find a way to keep some of that Dutch Gorge Christmas magic alive here in the city. All year long. Despite all the distractions and stress of the real world. What do you say, Casey?" He brushed a curl off her forehead. "Do you think we could work? Even with our lives plugged in?"

For a long moment, he thought she wasn't going to answer. Her expression was as serious as he'd ever seen it. She stared at the kissing couples on the laptop screen, twin furrows between her brows. He could almost hear the wheels turning in her head.

Then she drew a breath, looked at him, and her expression lightened. A smile played on her lips.

The tight knot in Matt's chest eased.

"I don't know if it will work," she said. "But I'd like to give it a try."

"Me, too." He grinned at her, then glanced up at the TV. "Only one minute to midnight."

Casey studied her computer. "The contest's down to the last three kisses—on a boat, on a mountaintop, and in midair, while skydiving. One of those couples is going to Paris." Then, to Matt's surprise, she powered down the laptop. It went dark just as the final ten-second countdown to midnight flashed on the muted television.

. . . *eight* . . . *seven* . . . *six* . . . *five* . . .

Reaching over the coffee table, Casey punched the TV remote, too. The screen went blank.

"Casey, what are you doing?" Except for a few strips of light shining though the blinds, the room was in total darkness. "You worked on this project for weeks! Don't you even want to know which kiss wins?"

Casey's outline was a dark blur in the unlit room. She rose from the couch. An instant later, her warm body slipped into his lap. His arms came around her as the peppershot sound of firecrackers started up in the street outside.

She nuzzled his cheek. "I don't need to watch. I already know who's going to win."

And when she kissed him, he knew, too.

JANA DELEON

"DeLeon is excellent at weaving comedy, suspense and spicy romance into one compelling story." —*RT Book Reviews*

Everyone in Mudbug, Louisiana, knows that when Helena Henry shows up, no good will come of it. Especially now that Helena is dead. And more meddlesome than ever.

Sabine LeVeche needs to locate a blood relative fast—her life depends on it. Her only ally is the smart-mouthed ghost of Helena Henry. Until Beau Villeneuve agrees to take the case. The super-sexy PI is a master at finding missing persons—and all the spots that make Sabine weak in the knees. But as they start to uncover the truth about the past, it becomes clear that someone out there wants to bury Sabine along with all her parents' secrets. And she realizes what they say is true: family really can be the death of you.

Mischief in Mudbug

A Ghost-in-Law Mystery Romance

ISBN 13: 978-0-505-52785-1

The *L.A. Informer* is Los Angeles's premier tabloid magazine, reporting on all the latest celebrity gossip, scandals and dirt. They're not above a little sensational exaggeration and have even been known, on occasion, to bend the law in pursuit of a hot story. Their ace reporter, Felix Dunn, has just been promoted to managing editor. Now, he's got his work cut out for him, keeping the magazine running smoothly while keeping his staff in line . . .

Scandal Sheet

Tina Bender is the *Informer's* gossip columnist extraordinaire. She knows everything about everyone who's anyone. And she's not afraid to print it. That is, until she receives a threatening note, promising, If you don't stop writing about me, you're dead. And when her home is broken into the next day, she realizes they're serious. Teaming with a built bodyguard, a bubbly blonde, and an alcoholic obituary writer, Tina sets out to uncover just which juicy piece of Hollywood gossip is worth killing over.

ISBN 13: 978-0-505-52805-6

"Craig's latest will DELIGHT . . . fans of
JANET EVANOVICH and HARLEY JANE KOZAK."
—*Booklist* on *Gotcha!*

Award-winning Author

Christie Craig

"Christie Craig will crack you up!"
—*New York Times* Bestselling Author Kerrelyn Sparks

Of the Divorced, Desperate and Delicious club, Kathy Callahan is the last surviving member. Oh, her two friends haven't died or anything. They just gave up their vows of chastity. They went for hot sex with hot cops and got happy second marriages—something Kathy can never consider, given her past. Yet there's always her plumber, Stan Bradley. He seems honest, hardworking, and skilled with a tool.

But Kathy's best-laid plans have hit a clog. The guy snaking her drain isn't what he seems. He's handier with a pistol than a pipe wrench, and she's about to see more action than Jason Statham. The next forty-eight hours promise hot pursuit, hotter passion and a super perky pug, and at the end of this wild escapade, Kathy and her very own undercover lawman will be flush with happiness—assuming they both survive.

Divorced, Desperate
and Deceived

ISBN 13: 978-0-505-52798-1

INTERACT WITH DORCHESTER ONLINE!

Want to learn more about your favorite books and authors?
Want to talk with other readers that like to read the same books as you?
Want to see up-to-the-minute Dorchester news?

VISIT DORCHESTER AT:
DorchesterPub.com
Twitter.com/DorchesterPub
Facebook.com (Search Pages)

DISCUSS DORCHESTER'S NOVELS AT:
Dorchester Forums at DorchesterPub.com
GoodReads.com
LibraryThing.com
Myspace.com/books
Shelfari.com
WeRead.com

☐ **YES!**

Sign me up for the Love Spell Book Club and send my
FREE BOOKS! If I choose to stay in the club, I will pay
only $8.50* each month, a savings of $6.48!

NAME: _____

ADDRESS: _____

TELEPHONE: _____

EMAIL: _____

       ☐ I want to pay by credit card.

☐ **VISA**   ☐ MasterCard.   ☐ DISCOVER

ACCOUNT #: _____

EXPIRATION DATE: _____

SIGNATURE: _____

Mail this page along with $2.00 shipping and handling to:
Love Spell Book Club
PO Box 6640
Wayne, PA 19087
Or fax (must include credit card information) to:
610-995-9274

You can also sign up online at **www.dorchesterpub.com**.
*Plus $2.00 for shipping. Offer open to residents of the U.S. and Canada only.
Canadian residents please call 1-800-481-9191 for pricing information.
If under 18, a parent or guardian must sign. Terms, prices and conditions subject to
change. Subscription subject to acceptance. Dorchester Publishing reserves the right
to reject any order or cancel any subscription.